The Reckless Secret
COMPLETE SERIES

ALEXA WILDER

The Reckless Secret, Complete Series

Copyright © 2015 by Alexa Wilder

All rights reserved.

No part of this book may be reproduced in any form or by any electronic or mechanical means including information storage and retrieval systems, without permission in writing from the author. The only exception is by a reviewer, who may quote short excerpts in a review.

This book is a work of fiction. Names, characters, places, and incidents either are products of the author's imagination or are used fictitiously. Any resemblance to actual persons, living or dead, events, or locales is entirely coincidental.

Find out more about the author and upcoming books online at **www.alexawilder.com**

Also by Alexa Wilder

Don't Miss Out on New Releases, Free Stories and More!!

Join Alexa's Readers Group!

AlexaWilder.com/readers-group/

Visit Alexa on Facebook:

Facebook.com/AuthorAlexaWilder

The Wedding Rescue

The Courtship Maneuver

The Stubborn Suitor

The Reckless Secret

The Temptation Trap

The Surprising Catch

With his player past, will she ever be able to trust him?

Maggie Emerson has had a crush on her brother's friend Declan for years. She knows he's not into girls like her - he's always surrounded by skinny model types. With her curvy body and a career choice that never made her wealthy family happy, Maggie is sure Declan will never fall for her. Except now that her job is in jeopardy, she has no one else to turn to...

Declan Archibald knows he wants no one else but Maggie. He wasn't ready for her before, but now he can't get her out of his mind. He tried wooing her a few months ago, and it didn't work - Maggie just thought he was using her. So how can he convince her that his feelings for her are real? When he discovers she's in trouble, Declan jumps to help. Will her crisis bring them closer together or push them apart?

Saving Maggie's job gets complicated, drawing dangerous secrets to the surface that threaten their already shaky bond. Maggie and Declan have plenty of chemistry, but can their growing love withstand so many obstacles?

CONTENTS

THE RECKLESS SECRET, BOOK ONE 1
CHAPTER ONE 3
CHAPTER TWO 14
CHAPTER THREE 33
CHAPTER FOUR 40
CHAPTER FIVE 47
CHAPTER SIX 57
CHAPTER SEVEN 66
CHAPTER EIGHT 75
CHAPTER NINE 90
CHAPTER TEN 102
CHAPTER ELEVEN 110
THE RECKLESS SECRET, BOOK TWO 115
CHAPTER ONE 117
CHAPTER TWO 125
CHAPTER THREE 132
CHAPTER FOUR 148
CHAPTER FIVE 158
CHAPTER SIX 164
CHAPTER SEVEN 178
CHAPTER EIGHT 189
CHAPTER NINE 196
CHAPTER TEN 203
THE RECKLESS SECRET, BOOK THREE 211

CHAPTER ONE	213
CHAPTER TWO	222
CHAPTER THREE	227
CHAPTER FOUR	240
CHAPTER FIVE	247
CHAPTER SIX	255
CHAPTER SEVEN	264
CHAPTER EIGHT	270
CHAPTER NINE	277
CHAPTER TEN	284
CHAPTER ELEVEN	295
SNEAK PEEK: THE STUBBORN SUITOR	309

the Reckless Secret

BOOK ONE

CHAPTER ONE
Maggie

Maggie couldn't really call this one of her better mornings.

Hot travel mug scorching her one hand and the purse sliding off her opposite shoulder, she dodged a group of elderly tourists checking out the monument on the corner and almost rushed head first into the path of a UPS truck.

"Oh sh—" Her heart leapt into her throat as she stumbled back up the curb, UPS truck honking its horn as it raced past, yanking the attention of all passersby directly to her.

Her face burned hotter than the palm wrapped around her hastily brewed coffee.

She took another step back to avoid any more near-death experiences and await a safe crossing, and brought her heel down on something that made a man shout, "Ow!" into her ear, like stepping on the press of a pedal trash can.

"God, sorry," she said, moving off the man's toe and

turning to face his livid death stare. "I'm so sorry."

Thick eyebrows hung low over his ice-cold eyes.

"Um," she said.

"*Go*," he snarled, looking behind her pointedly, and she turned back around to see everyone now crossing the street, traffic paused. She was very much blocking this angry man's way.

Which he rectified a split second later by barging past her and knocking the travel mug out of her hand. She watched, as if in slow motion, as the cup hit the ground on the edge of the street, burst open, and splattered all up the left leg of a passing nun.

After a full minute of flustered apologies and offers to dry-clean the nun's clothes, she finally made it across the street and halfway to work before her phone rang and had her fumbling in her overstuffed purse.

"Hey, can I call you back later?" she panted into the phone, contents of her purse threatening to spill out onto the filthy sidewalk as she attempted to close the zip. "I'm *so* late—"

"Just a quick thing," her brother said, and there was something odd in his voice. Something strained and cracked, not his usual rich tones. "I can't make Jen's wedding this weekend."

The words stopped her dead in her tracks, forcing several people to swerve around her, muttering their irritation. "Sorry," she mumbled vaguely to no one in particular, and then hurried over to an empty doorway, turning to face the wall to create some privacy. "What're you talking about?"

"I can't make it." Grant sounded entirely unapologetic, and that alone was enough to set her on edge. Her brother didn't let her down. Not him.

"But—you have to. You promised." Because he knew how difficult she found these things, attending events with her cousins and aunts and other relatives who didn't understand her, who judged her, who thought she needed to remember her place in the world—of country clubs and jewelry and brunch four times a week. Relatives who saw her chosen profession as an insult to the upbringing the family had given her. "We'll find you a medical charity to assist; I'm sure there's a board somewhere with a seat for you," they told her, back when she expressed her ambition of nursing. "At least become a *surgeon*."

Her father had been apoplectic. "I didn't pay to send you to all the best schools just so you could become a damn *nurse*!" he'd raged at her, for weeks on end, every time she saw him and watched that stain of disappointment blacken his eyes.

But her father's opinion didn't matter, not anymore—not since she was ten, and he turned her entire world upside down. Tore it apart with a savagery she would never forget.

Grant, her older brother, was the only man in her life who mattered to her from that point on, the only man she trusted. The one who promised to look after her, to protect her, to be everything her father couldn't.

And he spent the next fourteen years doing just that. Until recently, when hints of a different side of Grant started showing—a side of him she'd never seen before. A disheveled Grant, like the last time she'd seen him, showing up to her cousin Jen's rehearsal dinner with bloodshot eyes, messy hair, his T-shirt inside out, and a scruff on his face at least three days old. And he never came through with the money for his half of the wedding gift, always *next week, I promise,* and brief, cold texts about being busy.

"I don't have time to argue about it now, Mags," he told her abruptly, and while his tone wasn't unkind, he still sounded so very much like the opposite of her caring brother that it took her aback. "I gotta go. Sorry."

"Grant—wait—" But he'd already hung up.

Blinking stupidly at the grimy wall before her, Maggie took a moment to worry about her brother. A vague, abstract sort of worry, the kind without a defining cause she could focus on, think of ways to fix. But she had no time to analyze the change in him, not right now—she was already late for work, and there were a couple of people there who'd delight in her being reprimanded for tardiness. One person in particular.

And he didn't disappoint. Ronald Mitchell, Maggie's mistake of an ex-boyfriend, had a sneer the size of Texas on his face when she hurried in, breathless and apologetic.

"For someone so determined to have *independence*," he said, spitting the same word back at her that she'd yelled at him months ago, "you'd think you might figure out how to set an alarm."

"Family crisis," she snapped at him, half lying, as she yanked off her coat and stuffed it in her locker. "Don't you have work to do?"

He was always here in the staff room with her whenever she needed to use it, almost like he was stalking her, but for the sole purpose of chipping away at her, berating her, reminding her—daily—of why she'd split up with him.

"Unlike you, I've been here since dawn."

"And unlike *you*," she said, "I don't have my mom at home to wake me up every morning." The sass came out without any real bite, and she sighed as she slumped onto the bench, bending over to pull off her shoes. "I couldn't fall asleep."

He paused. And then, stiffly: "I told you to stop drinking coffee so late in the day."

"You also told me to quit my job and spend my life serving you." Work shoes slipped on, she smiled up at him as she stood. "So forgive me if I completely ignore you."

The icy smugness of his voice stopped her as she headed for the door. "Dr. Stevens is looking for you," he drawled, the unpleasantness of it creeping down her spine, "so I'd wipe that smirk off my face if I were you."

She swallowed and turned to face him, biting back her utter repulsion of his presence enough to ask, "Did he say what he wanted?"

He sniffed in a way that said he knew *exactly* what it was, but he wasn't going to tell her about it.

She huffed, rolled her eyes. "Fine, whatever," she said, leaving the room with what she hoped was a modicum of dignity, even as her heart hammered against her ribcage and her stomach churned with anxiety. Dr. Stevens hated her, and there was no way he wanted to see her for anything that would put a smile on her face.

But neither could she think of anything she might have done wrong, except her lateness this morning—and that wasn't enough for him to punish her in any way, was it? She was only late by a few minutes, and she still had twenty minutes before her first round.

She passed her friend Ashley at the nurses' station as she headed to Dr. Stevens' office, and they shared a troubled smile, making Maggie's stomach tense even more as she realized that Ashley knew, too. Whatever it was. Whatever had happened this morning that she'd missed, being a couple of damn minutes late. And Ashley wasn't the only one: three other people gave Maggie worried looks as she walked past, almost like she was heading down the green mile and at the end of it was her last meal…

There was a slight tremble to her hand as she knocked on Dr. Stevens' office door.

He called her in, and then didn't bother to look up at her as she entered the room, closed the door, and stood in front of his desk. He continued to write instead, scrawling on a large document, glasses perched on the edge of his bulbous nose and the silence in this room so thick and oppressive that the *scratch-scratch* of his messy writing was deafening to her, matching the amplification of her thunderous heartbeat in her ears.

"Ah, Ms. Emerson," he said eventually, his tone soft and sneering. He placed his pen back in its holder and folded his hands on the desktop. "Good of you to join us."

"I'm sorry, sir. I overslept, and traffic coming in this morning—"

"Traffic?" He raised a disdainful eyebrow. "I would've thought your driver might know how to avoid midtown rush hour…"

She blinked. "My driver?"

"Yes," he said, dragging the word out. "Your family makes use of an entire fleet of town cars, do they not?"

"I—yes?" This was new. Dr. Stevens wasn't exactly subtle about his dislike for her, but he'd never brought her family into it before. "I don't, though."

He tipped his head as if to say, "If you say so," his disbelief entirely evident, and she had half a mind to set him straight, if it wasn't for him catching her off guard with his next words.

"You know about the stealing, yes?"

It was like someone had very slowly, very delicately, dropped an ice cube into her gut. "No. I don't know anything about the stealing."

He observed her for a long moment. "Hmm," he said, and then, "Have a seat, Ms. Emerson."

When she sat, he rose from his chair, walked around the desk to perch on the end of it, and stared down at her. From this angle, he was relentlessly formidable.

"Where were you at four p.m. yesterday?"

She swallowed thickly. "I was here, sir. Working."

"Yes," he said conversationally, rubbing a thumb along his jawline. "And again on Monday afternoon, correct?"

"Yes…"

He let silence hang between them, staring at her while she tried not to squirm, not to panic, not to blurt out something wholly inappropriate and land herself in a world of trouble. She'd wait it out.

She didn't have to wait long, it turned out.

"Someone is stealing drugs from the nurses' store cupboard in your department, Ms. Emerson, and I'm sure it's no surprise for you to hear that right now it's all pointing to you."

The screech of her chair scraping back registered before she knew she was moving, and once on her feet, her pulse hammering in her ears, she found the voice she'd kept subdued since entering this office.

"Are you accusing me of *theft*, sir? What do you mean, it's no surprise to me? Are you suggesting—because let me tell you—"

"You'll tell me nothing," he said calmly, straightening a cuff. "The matter is under investigation, and for now you'll return to work until such a time as we have more substantial evidence."

"Evidence…" Her mouth ran dry, and she cast about wildly for the thread of her composure. "Evidence. What evidence?"

"That's confidential at the moment."

"I think I have a right to know!" she said, waving a hand in his general direction. "Considering I'm the one in the frame here."

"Are you?" he said, narrowing his eyes. "Would you put yourself in the frame?"

"Oh, for God's sake." She let out a billowing huff of a breath and shoved a hand into her hair. "This is insane. I've never stolen anything in my life!"

"Well, I'd hardly expect you to admit it, would I?" He sniffed again, then gave her a long, appraising look from her feet to her head. She felt naked all of a sudden, and she resisted the urge to hug her arms around herself. "Still, I wanted to give you the opportunity to come clean. Pity," he added delicately. "You can go now. We'll talk about this in due course."

She stared at him, entirely gobsmacked—watched him walk back around his desk and take a seat, pick up his pen and examine his document like he hadn't just tipped her on her ass.

"No."

He looked up at her, eyebrows raised. "No?"

"No." She folded her arms, making an attempt at hardening her expression. "I'm not leaving until you tell me why I—out of everyone in this hospital—am the one accused of stealing drugs."

"Like I said, Ms. Emerson, it's currently confidential infor—" The beeping of his pager cut him off and he looked at it, muttered under his breath, and then stood. "I don't have time for this now," he said to her, reminding her of her brother's abruptness not thirty minutes ago. As mornings went, this one wasn't her best.

She watched, entirely helplessly, as he swept past her, unable to stop him and demand more of his time when the pager was no doubt calling him out to perform some kind of life-saving procedure.

He paused in the doorway, framed by the hustle and bustle of the corridor behind him, his weathered face highlighted by unforgiving neon lighting. When he looked at her this time, he made no effort to mask quite how much the very existence of her displeased him.

"Call it a hunch," was all he said, the hint of a smirk on his face. And then he was gone, leaving her in a solitary panic.

Because it wasn't a hunch. He had evidence. And that meant everything she worked for, everything she'd put ahead of her family's wishes, all her years of hard work and dedication and her lifelong desire to help people—all of it, every last moment of it, was in danger.

And with Dr. Stevens refusing to tell her the evidence, to give her any information at all, the whole situation was completely out of her control.

Which was the most terrifying thing of all.

CHAPTER TWO
Maggie

It happened again. No one said so, but the vibe in the air was *knowing*. People whispered; the girls at reception eyed her strangely when she came off her rounds. At one point, Maggie thought she caught sight of a police officer slipping into Dr. Stevens' office. Her entire insides twisted with anxiety.

It wasn't her—of course, it wasn't. And yet, once again, it had happened on her shift. But she wasn't the only one who worked this shift. How could Dr. Stevens be so sure she was the culprit? How could so many of her colleagues give her such accusing glances?

The evidence must have been pretty clear, but... how? Even if there was a giant neon sign flashing MAGGIE'S THE THIEF, the fact remained she hadn't stolen the drugs. She just hadn't. That was all there was to it.

And she'd say that in court, if she had to. With full conviction.

Oh God, please don't let it go to court, she thought as she walked past a couple of whispering nurses, and then she stopped walking, and she straightened her back, and she turned and looked those gossiping nurses straight in the eye, stared them down until they both glanced away uncomfortably. Because she wasn't going to act guilty, not when she had nothing to feel guilty *about*.

* * *

"It's hard, though," she said to Ashley two days later, sounding to her own ears all downtrodden and pathetic. "Putting up with the stares and the whispers all day."

Ashley snorted and flipped shut the magazine she'd been perusing. Beside her on the bed, Cami finished detangling the silver chain she'd been fiddling with for the past twenty minutes and held it up to Maggie.

Both Ashley and Cami had shown up within an hour of each other this morning, sacrificing their Saturday to help Maggie get ready for her dreaded cousin's wedding—Cami swinging by after dropping off her daughter at a birthday party, and Ashley answering an "Oh my God, I don't know which dress to wear" SOS text from Maggie at stupid o'clock that morning. And, dress chosen, they'd apparently stuck around to listen to her moan, because she hadn't managed to stop since they'd arrived.

"No one *really* thinks you're the thief," Ashley said, and Cami nodded.

"Yeah, it's just hot gossip. The first bit of excitement that place has seen in months. Especially since your dad is on the board of trustees for the hospital."

Maggie gave her a flat stare, midway through attempting to clasp the necklace around her neck. "It's only a title, really. He never goes to the actual board meetings—he delegated that responsibility to his designated representative or something like that. In favor of golf, most likely. Plus, we deal with people who've been in car wrecks and gun fights," she said—which, while not quite as horror-movie-like as she'd made it sound, was the truth. The three of them were ER nurses, and life in the emergency department was hardly ever boring.

Cami waved a hand. "You know what I mean. We're not exactly *Grey's Anatomy*, are we?"

Ashley quirked an eyebrow at her. "As if you'd even notice."

"What's that supposed to mean?" asked Cami, her tone arched and indignant.

"You're too loved up to pay attention to anything these days."

Cami's face melted into one of dreamy happiness. "Yeah," she said with a floaty sigh, staring off into the middle distance.

Ashley and Maggie rolled their eyes good-naturedly at each other. It had been weeks since Cami and Drew confessed their mutual love, and still the honeymoon phase persevered.

Maybe it's not the honeymoon phase, Maggie thought, turning to look at herself in the mirror. *Maybe that's what people in love look like.* Not that she'd ever know—she couldn't imagine ever trusting a guy enough to let him into her heart the way Cami had invited Drew into hers. She'd seen first-hand how easily an untrustworthy man could destroy the woman who loved him, still remembered those long nights filled with nothing but the sounds of her mother's quiet but incessant crying. How her eyes never quite regained that spark she'd carried with her for so many years of blissful ignorance, married and raising her children and entirely unaware of her husband's second life of women and alcohol and debauchery.

They all found out in the end, learned the whole truth during one explosive evening that left them all reeling and scattered like shards of glass, a broken vase tipped carelessly onto the unforgiving ground by the hand of Duke Emerson. He didn't stay to pick up the pieces—didn't care enough to. There was an air of relief about him in the moment of truth, happy at last to stop faking this family life.

It was Grant who helped put Maggie and their mother back together, Grant who dealt with the transition of their father moving out, Grant who hugged Maggie and kissed the crown of her head and told her he would always look after her.

He'd been Maggie's rock ever since.

Which made today even worse. He was supposed to be doing this with her—weathering the nightmare that was a family function. Him letting her down like he had was so out of character that she still wasn't quite sure what had happened. He hadn't even given her a reason.

She smoothed her hands down her hips, flattening the material of her dress against her skin, looking for an awkwardly visible panty-line or marks on the pale-gold fabric.

"You look amazing," Ashley said. "Way better than that brown thing you were gonna wear."

"It was *sand*," Maggie said for what felt like the hundredth time.

She did look pretty good, she had to admit. The dress hugged her voluptuous curves in all the right ways, gave a soft and sensual roundness to her hips and breasts, cinched her in at the waist, the hem just grazing her mid-thigh. And the heels, a patent black she'd bought months ago and never got around to wearing, lifted her an inch—or four—and lengthened her newly bronzed legs like magic. Spending ninety percent of her life in a nurse's uniform, it wasn't often she felt glamorous and sexy. But seeing herself in this dress, with her hair teased into tumbled curls and her lips slick with matte red, she couldn't help but think, *Yep, you got it.*

"The point is, Mags," Cami said, picking up the thread of their earlier conversation, "you shouldn't worry about what everyone at work thinks. They all know you wouldn't do it—right now they're just getting swept along in the gossip. And you know these things always—oh my *god*, Grant, you scared the life out of me!"

Maggie swung around and there he was—her brother, standing in her bedroom doorway, pocketing the door key she'd given him the first day she moved into this apartment.

"What—I thought you were busy today." There was a flatness to her voice, even as her entire insides were melting with relief. Surely, this meant he would be accompanying her to the wedding, keeping her sane in the face of a hundred-strong throng of the upper-class.

He didn't answer her, too busy smiling and greeting Cami, who'd hopped off the bed to meet him and kiss his cheek, quickly followed by Ashley, the three of them devolving into a catch-up chat. It gave Maggie enough time to get a good look at him, and what she saw made her chest tight.

He didn't look good, not at all. Shadowed beneath bloodshot eyes, skin pale and stretched tight over bones that were definitely more prominent than the last time she'd seen him. He looked up at her then as if sensing her concern and offered her a smile that spoke of a kind of awkwardness they'd never had between them before.

"You look nice, sis."

"Thank you," she said, and then, "Wish I could say the same."

He gave a chipped laugh. "Yeah, I know," he said almost bashfully, rubbing a hand over his forehead. "This damn flu I couldn't shake."

"Flu?"

"You do look ashen," Cami said. She touched his cheek, a frown on her face. "Are you sure you should be out today?"

Gently, he lowered Cami's hand from his face and gave it a little squeeze. "I'm fine," he told her, and then he released her hand, pushing away from the doorway to approaching Maggie. "Couldn't let my baby sister down, could I?"

He stooped to kiss her cheek, and she returned it, confusion still clouding her mind. If he had the flu, why couldn't he have just said that on the phone, rather than get angry with her and shut her down?

He pulled back and looked her in the eye, a strained smile on his face that made uneasiness wash through her. She couldn't help but feel like she was missing something.

"We'll leave you to it, Mags," said Ashley, awkwardness in her tone and in the way she tugged on Cami's sleeve to get her moving too. Whatever atmosphere lingered in the air, it was enough for Ashley to feel like she needed to get out of the way.

"Yeah, we'll, uh—" stuttered Cami, catching on. "We'll see you at work."

They didn't stop to say goodbye—just swept out of the room and, a moment later, through the front door, shutting it softly behind themselves and leaving Grant and Maggie in a thick, deafening silence.

"That's a nice dress—"

"What's going on, Grant?" She crossed her arms and tried to fix a no-bullshit look on her face. It must've worked, because his own expression sobered.

"Honestly, I'm fine," he said, reaching out to give her shoulder a bracing squeeze. "I've just had a bad week with this flu—really knocked it out of me, you know? I'm sorry I was such an ass to you about it."

The earnestness in his voice—the sincerity—sounded exactly like the Grant she knew, the big brother who'd always been her rock, and she stepped forward to hug him. "I was really worried about you," she mumbled into his ear, and he offered a breathy laugh that sounded like relief. "Should've come to me if you were that bad. I could've helped."

"I know," he said on a sigh. "You know me, though. Never like to make a big deal out of things."

Always the strong one. Even after his horrible skiing accident last year, he'd still refused to admit that he needed any help. Grant Emerson looked after Maggie, not the other way around, no matter how much Maggie tried.

His ribs were sharper than normal, digging into her as she hugged him.

She squeezed him tighter.

* * *

"Maggie, dear, I've got a comb in my bag if you'd like to—" Aunt Gemma announced, rushing towards her down the center aisle, elbowing the wedding party out of the way as she went.

Maggie clenched her jaw. "I'm fine, thank you. It's supposed to look like this."

"I'm sorry?" said Aunt Gemma archly, coming to a stop in front of Maggie and Grant. She gave Maggie the once-over.

Maggie pointed at her hair. "I said it's supposed to look like this."

"Oh," said Aunt Gemma. She looked at Maggie's head like it'd grown a twin.

Grant cleared his throat. "She looks lovely, doesn't she?"

Aunt Gemma glanced at him sharply, then back to Maggie. "Yes. Oh yes. That's a very *brave* dress, isn't it? You haven't left yourself much room."

"Form fitting," Maggie said tightly, and then quickly, "If you'll excuse us."

"Breathe," Grant murmured to her as they walked away, sounding entirely too amused. "She's the easy one."

"Oh God, here it comes."

It was as if Grant had conjured her—no sooner had he finished his sentence, the much-less-appealing version of Aunt Gemma broke away from a crowd and made a beeline for them. Aunt Constance, the mother of the bride, and Maggie's biggest detractor.

"Ah, Maggie, dear, I'm glad you're here. I've got someone I want you to meet. Hello, Grant, lovely to see you. Goodness, you look ill. Now, Maggie—he's an investment banker, somewhat socially challenged but you're in no state to be choosy—"

She'd said it all without pausing, and as she spoke, the giant feather pinned into her hat waved around so dramatically that Maggie couldn't help but stare at it.

"Are you listening to me? Maggie." Aunt Constance snapped her fingers in Maggie's face. Beside her, Grant snorted.

"Yes, sorry. Investment banker." Then the words caught up with her, and she widened her eyes. "Oh God, no, sorry. I'm not interested."

Aunt Constance's eyebrows shot up like Maggie had cursed at her. "Not interested? Of course, you're interested. Don't be stupid."

"I'm not being stupid, I just—"

"Come on, Aunt Connie," said Grant, hitching that charming smile onto his face. The effect was somewhat lost among the graying of his skin and the dark circles beneath his eyes. "We're here to celebrate your daughter's wedding, aren't we? Maggie's love life should be the least of your priorities today."

"He's here at the wedding," Aunt Constance said firmly. "What other chance is she going to get? Now I've told him all about you, Maggie, dear, and he's willing to look past the whole…nurse thing"— she scrunched up her nose, perennially disgusted by Maggie's choices in life—"and he's eager to get to know you. I've told him you're free on Saturday."

"Saturday?" said Maggie, her voice sounding distant to her own ears.

"Yes. I assumed you wouldn't be busy. Lord knows your mother's made no effort to get you matched up. Now, come with me," she said, grabbing Maggie's wrist and tugging on it, "I'll introduce you—"

"She's busy on Saturday," Grant cut in.

Aunt Constance blinked at him. "What?"

"Yeah," said Grant, and it was painfully obvious how he was casting about for a believable explanation, his mind working a mile a minute. Apparently he immediately gave up, because he nudged Maggie and said, "Yeah, tell her, Mags. About the thing. On Saturday."

"The thing. Right." Her stomach tightened with panic, her mind going entirely blank. She widened her eyes at Grant in an attempt to scream *Help me!* but he wasn't looking at her. He was gazing across the room, and whatever had caught his eye, it made his expression light up.

"She's got a date," he said, nodding sort of vaguely, as if agreeing with his own thoughts. He turned back to Constance and hitched that charming smile back on his face—and this time, it looked far more authentic. "Sorry, Aunt Connie. She's already spoken for."

"She is?" Aunt Constance couldn't have sounded more shocked if she tried. She dropped Maggie's wrist.

"I am?" echoed Maggie, and at a sharp look from Grant, she added hurriedly, "I am! Yes. Sorry."

It took Aunt Constance a moment to find her voice again. "Well, who is he? What does he do?"

She was addressing Maggie, who swallowed thickly and said through her tight smile, "Grant, why don't you tell her. You're the one who set us up after all."

"He's a lawyer," Grant said without missing a beat. "But he's old money. Filthy rich. You'd love him."

Aunt Constance's tone when she responded was much more pleasant. "Oh, I see. From an old family, you say? I must know him then. Come on."

There seemed to be a long stretch of anticipation between Constance's prompt and Grant's answer, like time had stopped for a heartbeat or two. Then Grant said, "The Archibalds," and the floor dropped away beneath Maggie's feet. She grabbed Grant's arm, her insides twisting up with horror even as she tried to keep that passive smile on her face.

"The Archibalds?" said Aunt Constance, her face illuminating. "Lovely family. Just lovely. But—do you mean *Declan* Archibald?"

Of course, he meant Declan Archibald. There was no other male Archibald in her age range who hadn't already been married off.

Maggie clenched her teeth.

"But he's here, you know?" Aunt Constance continued. "I was speaking to him a few minutes ago—he didn't mention you, Maggie, dear." There was suspicion in her tone now, but Maggie could hardly focus on it.

Declan Archibald was here.

Declan.

And apparently, Maggie was dating him.

Never before had she so badly wished for a black hole to appear and suck her away.

"Well, it's early days," she said in a wobbly voice, trying to inject some coyness into it.

"But it looks promising," Grant interjected. Maggie wanted to slaughter him. "We better go say hello. Lovely to see you, Aunt Connie. Good luck with today." Then he leaned in to give her a swift kiss on the cheek and pulled Maggie away, leaving Aunt Constance affronted and wordless with the abrupt dismissal.

Maggie couldn't look up, focusing on her shoes as Grant pulled her towards the throng of people chatting along the aisle, waiting for the big event.

She couldn't look up, because she might see Declan, and she didn't trust her own reaction. What if her knees went weak and gave out beneath her, and she collapsed into a heap at Declan's feet? A distinct possibility, considering how much she'd lusted after him since…well, forever.

And she hated him for it. For how he'd led her on all those months ago and then discarded her like yesterday's trash. And how, despite it, thoughts of him still sent an electric tingle across her skin, settled warm and pulsing in her groin.

"You're welcome, by the way," Grant murmured to her, and right now she hated him almost as much as she did his old childhood friend.

"For what?" she snapped back at him. "Coming up with the most ludicrous—"

"Declan? Man, it's been too long, buddy," Grant said, coming to a stop and dropping Maggie's arm.

Oh God, she could smell him. That heady mix of far-too-expensive cologne and the pure masculinity of him. She swallowed thickly and looked up.

He wasn't looking at her.

"Hey, man," he said to Grant, smiling warmly as they shook hands. "How's it going?" His smile dimmed a little when he got a good look at Grant's face, but he said nothing.

Meanwhile, Maggie was praying for a hole to open and swallow her down. Again.

Maybe she could slip away, quietly and without notice, while these two old pals caught up…

"Not bad, yeah," Grant said. "Last time I saw you, we were at that Playmate party in the summer—"

"Yeah, well." Declan looked over his shoulder, and Maggie took the opportunity to creep away, one tiptoed step at a time. "The less said about that, the better. At least in this crowd." The two men laughed, and then Declan said, "And you, Maggie?" bringing her to a stop and making her wince.

She forced a polite smile onto her face and looked up at him. "Hello."

He stared at her a moment too long. "Always a pleasure." His voice was a smooth drawl, a rich tone he'd developed in his late teens and carried with him since, deepening as he aged and growing more confident with it. There was a grit to it these days, like caramel poured over gravel. The heat of it washed through her.

"Declan," she said tightly, her mouth running dry.

"Am I not getting a smile?"

"Do you deserve one?"

"Oh, by the way," said Grant, butting in like he couldn't sense the tension in the air, "if Constance asks, you and Maggie are dating. Just play along."

Declan tore his gaze away from Maggie and raised a brow at his friend. "We are?" There was a glimmer of something dangerous in his eye, something that made Maggie swallow thickly.

"Yeah, you know what she's like. Obsessing over Maggie's depressing love life—"

"*Grant*." Jesus Christ.

But something about what he'd said had caught Declan's attention, because he looked at Maggie with distinct interest. "What happened to that preppy doctor you were seeing a few months ago?"

She blinked, and all thoughts of creeping away disappeared beneath a wave of curiosity. And suspicion. "How do you know about that?"

He paused. "Word gets around," he said, swiping the tip of his tongue across his bottom lip.

Maggie's heart tripped over itself. "It didn't work out."

"I'm sorry," Declan said immediately, but there was that dangerous glint in his eye again, and her stomach lurched at the insincerity of his tone.

"No you're not."

"Not really," he said swiftly, and then turned to Grant, who'd been watching the exchange with a crease between his brows. "Did you know Maggie and I dated for a while?"

Grant's whole face spoke of shock.

"It was two dates," Maggie said quickly, and Declan smirked.

"She swapped me out for the doctor."

His words were joking, his expression relaxed, but his throat rolled with a dry swallow like the words didn't taste too nice. She'd never before considered the possibility that he might've thought she'd chosen Ronald over him. She hardly let herself imagine that he even thought of her at all. "I—no, I didn't."

"I last saw you on the Saturday," Declan said, talking entirely to her now, like the rest of the room had melted away, "and by the Wednesday you were with the doc."

"Were you having me followed or something?"

"I saw you," he said after a moment of hesitation, his voice quieting, growing intimate and honest.

She didn't know what to say. What she should even think.

"Hold on," Grant said, crashing into the moment with all the grace of a bodybuilder at a ballet recital. "You two were seeing each other?"

His interruption brought her back to earth, and all of a sudden it hit her again—why she'd spent all these months being so angry with Declan Archibald. "We went on two dates," she said. "And the second one we only made it halfway through before he bailed on me."

Declan didn't falter. "I had an emergency."

"Oh, yeah, it was one of those true emergencies. Of the leggy blonde variety." The words settled like ash on her tongue.

"Now who's following who?"

"Kinda hard to miss, with it splashed across the society pages."

"And the press never report anything but the absolute truth."

"Ladies and gentlemen," said Maggie's Uncle Lawrence from the front of the room, "if we could all take our seats…"

Maggie was breathless. She didn't know why, as nothing about this whole exchange should've affected her. It wasn't as if she still harbored a Texas-sized crush on the man.

And other lies she told herself at night…

She risked another glance at him, found his eyes pinned firmly on her, dark and intense, like he was trying to see past the words and to the meaning beneath. Like he was desperate for something.

"Maggie—" he started, his voice low and urgent, but Grant spoke simultaneously, much louder, and the moment shattered.

"We better head to our seats—"

Declan visibly shook himself free of whatever thought had him so captured. "Yeah," he said. "Yeah, it's nice to see you, man. Maybe we'll catch up at the reception," he added, glancing again at Maggie.

"Sure thing." Grant slapped Declan on the shoulder, added, "Enjoy the show," and then led Maggie away. She didn't look back. "You and I are gonna have a very long talk about this later."

"God, it was two dates," she hissed for what felt like the tenth time, pasting on an over-bright smile for all the guests nodding and greeting her as she passed them. "There's nothing to talk about."

"I just want to know how you—the girl who turned her back on this world—ended up with the richest one of all."

"I didn't *end up* with him. Jesus Christ." They found their seats—third row back, her view obstructed by the largest hat in the universe. "We had one dinner and one almost-dinner. I haven't seen him since."

"I didn't even know you were into him."

"I'm not."

"You must've been, at some point."

"Clearly I'd taken temporary leave of my senses."

"Clearly. The wedding's that way, by the way," he said, and she blushed all the way down to her chest as she realized she'd been staring across at Declan.

In her defense, it wasn't as if Declan didn't keep glancing in her direction, too.

The situation seemed to amuse Grant, judging by the twitching at the corners of his mouth.

"Oh, shut up," she muttered, sinking low in her seat. Grant snorted.

From across the room, Declan looked over his shoulder again and caught her eye.

CHAPTER THREE
Maggie

The wedding went off without a hitch, naturally. No event this expensive would ever suffer from lax service, not if the staff ever wanted to hear the end of it from Connie's acid tongue.

Jenna made a beautiful bride, and she looked genuinely happy as she exchanged vows with her husband-to-be, a stock broker she'd met only eight months previous.

Maggie couldn't help but give a watery smile as the newly married couple kissed for the first time.

Over at the reception now, with the party in full swing, Maggie was taking advantage of the free wine and canapes and enjoying the relatively isolated corner she and Grant had found themselves.

But the lull in action gave Maggie time to think again, and what she was thinking about now was the state of Grant's pallid face.

"But have you been to a doctor?" she yelled over

the band, watching white light pass over his sharp cheekbone.

"*Yes*, Maggie," he said, visibly sighing.

"And? What did he say?"

"It's the flu."

"Did he give you anything?"

"I—no." He shifted his weight, shoulders hunching forward as he leaned back against the wall. "Told me to sleep it off."

"Sleep it off? Which doctor was this? Not Dr. O'Malley."

"Uh, no. A new one. Closer to my condo."

"You shouldn't change doctors unless you really have to, you know. Dr. O'Malley knows your whole history—"

"Declan!" Grant said suddenly, his face lighting up as he lurched forward and grabbed hold of a passing Declan Archibald. "Buddy. Just the man. Maggie here was just saying how much she wanted to dance."

Oh my God. "What—*Grant*."

Declan raised an eyebrow. "Is that so?"

"Nope," Maggie said, shaking her head and stepping back, as if she could disappear into the wall and make this go away. "Not me."

Declan observed her for a long moment, his eyes glittering. Then he held out his hand. "May I?"

Maggie's stomach swooped. "I should just—" she said, staring at his proffered hand, panic welling up in her chest. Panic, and a hint of excitement. "The bride—" And she tried to leave, but her feet were quite clearly nailed to the floor.

"The bride is busy getting changed right now," Declan informed her, his voice maddeningly calm, his eyes dancing with amusement. "Are you gonna leave me hanging?"

Grant huffed out his exasperation. "Just dance with the man, will you?" he snapped, yanking Maggie's wine glass from her hand and shoving her forward, directly into Declan's space.

It happened too quickly. One moment she was muttering vague protestations, caught up in the whirlwind of it all; the next moment she was dancing, her hand softly held in his, the warmth of his other hand settled low on her back.

She caught her breath, and just for a moment, for one heart-stopping moment, she allowed herself to feel the heat and pleasure of his broad, strong, muscular body against her own—allowed herself to imagine, briefly but with startling clarity, how it would feel minus the clothes between them.

Then she shut down those thoughts and cleared her throat.

"So we're clear, this is just a dance."

"Of course, it is," he said immediately, his voice rumbling through his chest and into hers. This close, she could smell the richness of his cologne. Feel the sweetness of his breath on her face. She daren't look up at him.

"I mean it."

"I know." He was leading, of course—gliding them across the dance floor to a slow, sultry tune that had all the couples up and embracing. The confidence in his steps tripped her heart. "You look lovely, by the way."

"Thank you," she said, swallowing dryly. "You look…" She risked a glance up at his face, found him gazing down at her as if she was all he saw. She looked away quickly, blushing, and focused on the glint of his watch—a watch that was obviously worth more than her entire apartment. "Rich," she finished, and he chuckled, pulled her closer just a little. She didn't object.

"Something you find a complete turnoff, if I remember correctly."

"I don't hate society," she said. "I just want more from life."

"I always admired that about you."

She choked out a laugh. "Are you drunk?"

"Not yet," he said, "but it's on the agenda." And when she glanced up at him this time, he was wearing his bright, charming grin, the one he'd dazzled her with all her life.

They fell into a silence, and Maggie found herself lulled into a sense of calm by the rhythmic swaying of the dance, the moody tones of the music, the strength and warmth of Declan pressed into her, the steadiness of his heartbeat against her breast. Her stomach twisted dangerously, the same way it had back when she first developed her crush on him as a teenager. When every time she saw him, she'd felt like she was looking at perfection.

And when he'd flirted with her outrageously at the beach party all those months ago, then sent flowers to her apartment with a note asking her to meet him, and her heart had swelled with giddy anticipation…

And then he'd given her a date and a half and nothing else, no other contact, nothing but the cruelty of parading Ms. Leggy Blonde around in the newspapers and magazines.

As if following her train of thought, Declan suddenly drew in a breath and asked, "So…what did the doc have that I didn't?" There was an oddness to his voice, the words coming out rushed and stilted. She'd never heard that hitch of uncertainty in his tone before.

"What?"

"You traded me in pretty quickly."

"What was I supposed to do?" she asked, pulling back an inch or two, enough to look up at his face, "sit and wait for you to be done with your blonde?"

His jaw twitched. "She's not my blonde. She's my friend."

"Right," she said, injecting disbelief into the word.

His hand tightened on her back. "Were you jealous?"

"Were *you*?" she shot back at him.

"Extremely," he said without hesitation, the tightened hand on her lower back now forming a fist, catching the material of her dress and pushing her forward. Her breath stuttered in his throat.

"You didn't do anything about it, did you?"

"Didn't I?" he said quietly, and his gaze slipped down to her mouth. Maggie's head was spinning, and for just an instant, for one blindingly stupid instant, she felt the overwhelming urge to lean forward.

"Song's finished," Declan said, and the world rushed in on Maggie, lights and sound exploding back into her awareness. She blushed.

"Right," she said, pulling away from his hold. There was a hint of reluctance in the way he let her go, a lingering drag of his fingers across her back and hip. She straightened her dress and looked everywhere except his face. "Thank you for the dance."

"Pleasure."

Then she got away from him as quickly as this dress allowed her to move.

* * *

HE CAUGHT UP WITH HER again as she left the bathroom—she'd only gone in there to splash some water on her face, cool down, gather herself after the betrayal of her body. The way it reacted to Declan's proximity. The way she *ached* for him.

But he didn't let her; didn't allow her a reprieve.

He marched towards her down the empty corridor, fire in his eyes and deliberation in his step, staring directly at her as he drew closer and closer, as she lost her breath and slowed her pace and lit up with the anticipation of it—

Then he met her in the middle, and he took her waist, and he yanked her aside.

"What—"

"Shh," he said, tucking her firmly into an alcove, shadowed and separated from the world, the intimacy of it all as he swept in close, as he pressed his body to hers, as he settled one hand on the wall beside her head and the other on her hip… Then he dipped his face to hers, his breath teasing her lips, and murmured, "Can I?"

And in that moment, there was not one part of her that wanted to say anything other than the breathless, whispered word that tumbled from her mouth.

"Yes."

CHAPTER FOUR
Declan

Declan couldn't handle himself around Maggie Emerson. She lit him up like nothing else, burned through his blood and hammered into his heart, made him lose sense of himself and his composure, made him *desperate*.

He'd known she would be at this wedding, of course. It was her cousin's event. And it was because of that, he'd almost decided not to come himself. Nothing scared him; nothing intimidated him. But several months ago, this woman shattered his defenses and put a crack in his heart that he hadn't quite been able to forget. And he didn't know how he would react upon seeing her again.

He'd wanted her for years. Ever since that summer she came home from college and had discovered a confidence and self-assuredness she'd been missing as a teenager. When she showed up to her family's annual summer barbecue in a form-fitting sundress that showed off all of her delicious curves, allowed her wild hair to tumble down her back, barely a lick of makeup on her glowing face—and she was gorgeous. She was breathtaking.

Then she'd spoken to him—struck up a conversation about their studies, the differences between med and law school, what they both hoped to achieve in their careers, and the intelligence and passion that radiated from her had him captivated, had him wanting to hear more, listen to her speak for hours, ask her questions just to keep her going.

He kept his distance, romantically. Didn't pursue her. For years he watched her from afar, watched her develop into a bright, ambitious, stunning woman—the kind who could take on her family's expectations and crush them without fear, forge her own path in life. And while he didn't share her desire to turn her back on money, he respected her ability to make her own way, to be exactly who she wanted to be.

She was perfection, but still, he didn't pursue her. Because he wasn't ready, not in his life. He had the burden of a legacy on his shoulders, his father passing and leaving the centuries-old Archibald estate to him; and he had his career to develop, determined to make it in law on his own merit, not allow the many zeroes in his bank account to open any doors for him. He was too busy to devote any real time to a relationship, and Maggie Emerson deserved all the time in the world.

But then things changed. His life settled; he established himself in law. His family and his legacy continued ticking along and expanding like they always would, and he found himself with time to enjoy some finer things in life.

He captured her attention at the Emersons' beach party, and a few weeks later he asked her to dinner. He would not try to kiss her until the third date, he ordered himself, because he wasn't blind to his reputation—yes, he'd spent some years playing the field, living up to his playboy status. And yes, perhaps he was known for his philandering ways. But Maggie was no one-night stand, no bit of fun on the side. She was Maggie Emerson, and he would show her that he was serious.

She wasn't impressed by his wealth, of course, by the expensive restaurant or the luxury cars he drove. But she smiled at the sight of him, and her eyes glittered as they spoke over candlelit dinner, and maybe there was a chance she was impressed by *him*, at least. That perhaps she saw through all the public bullshit and found the man beneath.

He didn't kiss her on date number one, and he didn't plan to on date number two, either. Although there was something magical in the air on that second date, something that spoke of a connection, a pull between them.

He got called away before the second course, had no other choice, and he'd promised to call her the next day, see her very soon. He had no intention of leaving it too long before he could set eyes on that lovely face again.

She'd seemed fine about it, but hindsight was another story. He'd left her a voicemail the next day, and after spending the following evening at a charity event with his friend Trixie Lane, he'd tried calling her again. Nothing. For days, she ignored his calls, until eventually he grew worried enough to pay her a visit, desperately needing to see her in person and find out if they were still on the same page.

Only when he pulled up in her street, she wasn't alone. She was leaving her apartment building with another man—a man, Declan later discovered, who was a doctor at Maggie's hospital.

The doctor took her hand as they passed, and it wasn't until that moment that Declan realized quite how intensely he had developed feelings through these past few years of admiring Maggie Emerson from afar.

He spent that night with a bottle of scotch and a whole lot of bitterness. All that time he'd been worried about his own reputation as a playboy, and all the while it would be Maggie who was more inclined to play the field. And it wasn't as if he could even be angry at her. They'd had two dates—one of which ended early. She didn't owe him a thing.

And yet…it stung.

Seeing her today at this wedding only cemented

to him how much he needed her in his life, how he wanted to have a thousand conversations with her, look at her, *touch her*. How he *wanted* her, now more than ever. She was such a beautiful sight, such a radiant presence, that the moment he set eyes on her again, he didn't ever want to look away.

And now he was going to kiss her. *Finally*.

But first he had to be sure. Once and for all, he had to know that she wanted him as much as he wanted her.

He pressed into her space, breathed in the perfection of her, settled an unsteady hand on her hip and looked deep into her liquid-blue eyes. She was visibly breathless with it all, and he couldn't calm his racing heart.

"Can I?" he murmured, dipping in just slightly, tasting the scent of her in the air between them, allowing the muffled sounds of the party to disappear as every sense he possessed zeroed in on this woman his whole body was desperate for.

She licked her bottom lip, a tantalizingly brief swipe of a pink glistening tongue, and her eyes fluttered in the moments before she responded—an agonizingly long stretch of time that almost killed him in the anticipation. His hand tightened on her hip, fingertips pressing in, and he swallowed past a dry throat as she parted her lips and whispered, "Yes."

It wasn't a slow, gentle kiss—not after all this time. He kissed her hard and he licked into her mouth, and she gasped, and she whimpered, and she melted against him like she'd gone entirely boneless with it.

His blood rushed in his ears at the taste of her, his heart beating through his chest when he felt her press against him, his cock stirring ever so slightly and sending shockwaves of rich pleasure through his veins when her legs parted and allowed his thigh to slip between, and the heat of her brushed against him.

He buried a hand in her hair and tilted her head back a fraction, a better angle to kiss her deep, and she gave it back, all of it, gave as good as she got and fisted red-manicured hands in his jacket and pulled on him like she wanted to climb inside him, wanted to fuse them together.

He couldn't get enough of her, didn't want it to end, sliding a hand down the curve of her ass and bringing her closer, and it was that moment that she chose to pull away—all of a sudden and with a jolt, like she'd been electrocuted by regret.

Her cheeks were flushed red and her lips kiss-swollen and slick, and in that speck of time, she was the most desirable sight in the entire known universe. He drank her in, everything from her heaving breasts to her ravaged hairstyle, memorized the look of her in this moment because he got the horrible, bruising feeling that she would walk away now, and he'd never have it again.

It took her only a moment more to prove him right.

She sucked in a sudden breath, eyes going wide, and gasped, "I'm sorry," in the instant before she shoved at his chest and slipped past him.

CHAPTER FIVE
Maggie

She couldn't believe what had just happened. What she'd *allowed* to happen.

Oh God.

She'd kissed him. He'd kissed her. There had been a kiss, and it was the kind of kiss to split the earth beneath her feet. It was…*electric.*

And she couldn't cope with how it made her feel.

God, she wanted him. Wanted him so badly she could hardly think straight. Struggled to clear the lusty haze in her mind enough to figure out her next move.

Grant. And home. She needed to get away from here and *think*.

Because it didn't matter how much she wanted him—nothing changed the truth that he was still the man who'd pretty much ignored her for years, and then when he finally did decide to ask her out, abandoned her at the first opportunity. He had no real interest in her, not when he'd spent so many years working his way through a conveyor belt of thin, glamorous society girls, blonde heiresses, and bright starlets.

She was Maggie Emerson, the curvy, messy-haired woman who'd turned her back on money and society. She was the opposite of Declan. She didn't fit his lifestyle.

And she needed to protect herself here.

"Oh, Maggie, dear." Aunt Constance appeared out of nowhere as Maggie tried to locate her brother through the chaos on the dance floor. "Can you do me a favor?"

"Now?" Maggie asked, distracted. The last thing she needed right now was Aunt Constance's interference.

Her aunt narrowed her eyes—always a danger sign. "Yes, dear, now. I need you take all of these up to my room." And she gestured towards a pile of coats on a nearby chair. "We had them brought down but it seems your grandparents and the McKinleys have chosen to stay for the rest of the evening, and I can't find that helpful gentleman…"

Maggie blinked at her. "You want me to take the coats back upstairs."

"Yes. Are you deaf? What's the matter with you? The gentleman who brought them down has disappeared."

"But…the cloakroom…"

Aunt Constance stared at her. "You expect Sandra McKinley to leave a Prada mink-and-sable coat in a hotel cloakroom, do you?"

"Um—"

"I'll help you," a voice behind her murmured, a voice that simultaneously filled her with dread and set her heart racing with excitement.

She tried not to look at him. "I don't need help," she sniffed, and in a fit of stubbornness, hoisted all of the coats up into her arms while Aunt Constance simpered at Declan and then promptly lost interest and wandered off.

But Maggie had underestimated the sheer weight of extravagant outerwear. She let out a squeak in the staggering moment before she half collapsed to the side, back onto the chair, buried beneath the mound of fur. "Okay, fine," she muttered into it, burning hot and mortified, and heard a deep, sexy chuckle in punishment.

The majority of the burden was quickly lifted from her arms, letting the light back in, and Declan's smoothly amused face came into view.

Maggie looked away swiftly and stood, her share of the coats now hooked over one arm, and marched towards the doors with what remained of her dignity.

Then she stopped and grimaced in further embarrassment when she realized she'd forgotten—in her haste to appear as if she had her shit together—to get the room key from Aunt Constance.

She swallowed her pride and made to turn back, but the key appeared in front of her face.

"You might need this," Declan grinned, and Maggie glowered at him before snatching it from his hand and continuing her march onward.

Declan followed her mutely, no sound but the tapping of their shoes across the marble lobby floor; he stayed one pace behind her all the way through the lobby as if wanting to watch her, and she felt it, that pressure of a gaze on the side of her head, the weight of his stare boring into her, making her heart stutter.

It wasn't until they were waiting for the elevator that he spoke.

"So…that kiss."

His reflection glimmered back at her in the closed elevator doors, and her pulse thrummed in her ears, the back of her neck tingling and flushed through with heat.

"Can we not talk about it?"

"Why?"

"It was a mistake," she said at once, and then immediately regretted the harshness of her tone. She glanced sideways at him, but found him staring straight ahead as if entirely unaffected by her words… if it wasn't for the tightening of his jaw. "I mean…" Frustration gripped her as she cast about for the right words, and then she huffed. "Look, I'm not the girl who goes around making out with randoms at weddings, okay?"

He looked at her then, his brow quirked in gentle disbelief.

"I'm not a random," he said, and the elevator doors pinged and slid open.

They stepped inside and Declan pressed the button; then the doors swished shut, and all of a sudden they were alone in a very enclosed space, and Maggie half wanted to throw the coats on the floor and press this dangerously delicious man against the opposite wall.

Instead, what she did was mutter, "I don't really know you," and kept her gaze fixed firmly ahead.

"Maggie," he said, tone completely flat, as if she'd just spoken utter bullshit.

"Well, I don't! For years you were my brother's asshole friend—"

"Asshole?"

"Yes, asshole. You were a jerk when I was a teenager. Always teasing and saying horrible things…"

"You know that thing about boys pulling girls' hair?"

She looked at him, steadied her voice. "That doesn't make it okay."

His eyes, when he met her gaze, were sparking with fire. "No, it doesn't. I was dumb back then. But we're both different people now."

"Right," she said, feeling somehow validated and confused with it, her mind whirring with clashing thoughts and desires. The elevator came to a stop as she said, "And that means we don't really know each other. You're a random."

And then the doors opened, allowing her to flounce out before coming to a stop in the middle of the corridor, her mind too muddled for her to figure out which direction she should go.

"This way," Declan said quietly from beside her, briefly placing a hand on the small of her back to direct her and causing her stomach to flip over. "We dated," he added, picking up the conversation, his voice measured now, considered. Like reasoning with someone hysterical.

"Hardly. We had one date."

"Two."

"I seem to remember you abandoning me during the second, so I don't really count it."

They stopped outside of Aunt Constance's door and Declan put a hand on hers to still her as she swiped the key through the reader. He looked her straight in the eye and said quietly, with a soft kind of intimacy, "I didn't want to leave."

The lock clicked open, and Maggie swallowed the pressure swelling in her throat.

"Two days later, you were in the paper with Trixie Lane," she muttered, pulling her hand from beneath his, "so excuse me if I don't believe you." Then she pushed open the door and marched inside.

Declan followed her.

"Trixie and I have been friends for a long time,"

he said patiently. "We're both patrons of the same charity. It was an event we had to attend."

Maggie snorted, dumping the coats on the bed none too graciously. "It's not like she's the first."

"What?" Declan said, sounding genuinely confused as he copied her, tipping his own pile of coats on the bed and then standing straight, turning to face her.

"I've seen you for years parading yourself around with one skinny little thing after another."

"What does that have to do with anything?"

"Look at me!" she huffed, spreading her arms to give him a good view of her frame in this tight gold dress. "I'm not exactly your type, am I? I don't know why you asked me out in the first place." Suddenly, she felt awkward—not because she'd ever had a complex about her weight, but because she'd just opened herself up to scrutiny from a skinny-obsessed playboy and she didn't want to be found wanting. Folding her arms across her chest, she said grumpily, "Experiment, was it?"

"Experiment..." Confusion clouded his expression as he stared down at her body like he wasn't really seeing it, visibly trying to catch her thread. "What are you talking about?" And then it hit him, his eyes going wide and snapping to look at her with total disbelief. "You can't think—" he said, looking almost angry with it all, and then he added in a sort of aggressive, growly fashion: "Maggie, you're the most beautiful thing I've ever laid eyes on." He sounded entirely furious with her.

She couldn't lie—her panties melted a bit. But, more than that, she wasn't quite sure if she could believe what she heard.

"I—what?"

"You heard me," he stated, brooking no argument.

A weird, vaguely hysterical burst of laughter bubbled out of her. "You don't mean that. You've had too much to drink."

"I haven't touched a drop."

Now, that she could believe. Grant had thrown her at Declan so early into the wedding reception that she'd be surprised if Declan even had time to catch a breath, let alone get himself a drink.

Which meant he was stone-cold sober right now. Which meant...he knew exactly what he was saying.

She swallowed thickly, because while it skyrocketed her up to cloud nine to know that he desired her as much as she wanted him, it didn't change that not too long ago, when he had the chance to get close to her, he wasted no time in ditching her and then spending the following night with the leggy blonde.

The room had gone overwhelmingly silent in the moments she'd taken to wrap her mind around his statements, and he still looked at her now, unblinking, fiery-eyed, holding her gaze. She cleared her throat. "Then why...?"

"My mother isn't well," he said at once, as if he'd anticipated the question. "She doesn't want anyone to know, but... That night, our second date, she needed me. I couldn't say no. And Trixie—she really is just a friend. That was a charity event. I took her home and I called you."

"I don't understand."

"Don't understand what?"

She shook her head, frowning, her brain failing to believe what this all meant. "That's not..."

"It's not how you built it up in your head?" he asked wryly, eyebrow quirked. At her hesitant nod, the smile he gave her was almost shy. "I've been crazy about you for years now."

It hit her like a brick to the gut and it winded her, and the floor lurched beneath her feet, and had he just admitted to wanting her for the past several years? Because in no universe would she ever have been prepared for that revelation.

She half considered pinching herself to check she hadn't slipped into a sleep sometime during the wedding. Instead she blinked a few times, shook her head, failed entirely to make sense of whatever the hell was going on here.

For *years*?

"So you're saying..." she said, her tongue feeling too thick for her mouth, her fingers twitching with the adrenaline suddenly racing through her veins— the overpowering delirium of knowing she could have this breathtaking man right now if she wanted him… "You're saying you like me—"

"Jesus Christ, Maggie," he snapped, and then he closed the space between them and kissed her.

It was hot, and it was deep, and she let him sweep her away in it for the length of a swelling heartbeat.

But it was too much. She wasn't ready for this, didn't know how to deal with it—didn't even know what her own feelings were, not beyond the simplicity of base desires.

Because this sounded heavier than that. This sounded like it had weight, like it had history. Like it *meant something*.

That he wasn't just trying to sleep with her. *Hit it and quit it.*

It sounded like…well, it sounded like he had some kind of feelings for her. And that made it all too real.

Fantasizing about Declan Archibald from afar was one thing, but facing the very real possibility of perhaps letting him in, opening herself up to him, *trusting* him…

"No," she said, breaking away, catching the look of distress on his face as she wrenched herself out of his hold and stumbled towards the door. "No, I'm sorry. This isn't—no."

She left before she could change her mind, every ounce of her being screaming at her to turn back, to give in, to take what she so desperately, achingly wanted.

CHAPTER SIX
Maggie

Her hand shook as she fumbled her key card out of where she'd stuffed it in her bra that morning—had no idea what had happened to Aunt Constance's; had she dropped it on the bed with the coats? It didn't matter. Nothing mattered. Nothing except getting inside her own room and shutting out the world.

She couldn't breathe with the weight of how badly she wanted to go back and let Declan pull her apart in the most exquisite way.

"Maggie."

She nearly dropped the key card, pulse thundering through her veins, the sound of her rapid breathing deafening in this silent hallway.

"I'm gonna get changed and head home—*shit*." She'd dropped the card.

"Already? The night's young." Declan's voice was almost begging.

Bending to retrieve the card in the most undignified way possible—the dress not allowing ease of movement—she said, "I've had enough excitement for one day," and stood, and then went entirely still, suspended in anticipation.

She could feel him behind her, close but not quite touching—feel the warmth of him, the raw *need*.

"Maggie," he said, and she nearly whimpered. "*Maggie*. Look at me."

She swallowed and squeezed her fingers around the key card, coiling heat spreading through her pelvis. "I can't."

His voice, a breathy murmur, ghosted across the soft skin of her neck beneath her ear. "Why?" It wasn't really a question. It was a challenge.

"Because I've got no control around you," she admitted desperately, pleadingly, every ounce of her senses firing up for him.

"Tell me to leave," he murmured to her, and she felt it then—the shadow of a touch on the side of her neck, the very whisper of his tongue. "Tell me to walk away, and I'll never bother you again."

She nearly did—it was on the tip of her tongue. It would be so sensible…

But just for once, *please*, her body screamed at her—*please, screw sensible*.

Her heart threatening to burst out of her chest, she turned to him. The devastating agony of need on his face almost knocked her off her feet.

The breath punched out of her lungs as he suddenly pressed into her space, no warning, no word—nothing but the fire in his eyes that told her she was in trouble, and she was going to love it.

He said nothing, and she didn't blink; they looked at each other for a heartbeat or two, and then he took that final step, his wide, muscled chest knocking against her breasts, his face so close to hers now she could see every lash framing his fiery eyes.

She licked her bottom lip, and she whispered, "What are you—"

His next movement was so swift, it pushed a gasp out of her.

He grabbed her wrists, pushed her back against the door, lifted her hands above her head, and pinned them to the wood with one solid grip—and then he slid in close, his whole body from his hips to the arm above her head, pinning her down, and she couldn't breathe, couldn't think, couldn't remember why this was such a bad idea.

He smirked, and it was the sexiest damn thing she'd ever seen.

"Declan—"

"Shut up and kiss me," he said in a voice thick and heavy and so, so close, his breath brushing her lips and his eyes watching her mouth and the hand around her wrists flexing, like he couldn't help it, like he was barely in control.

And in that moment, her own control snapped like the thinnest gossamer strand of silk, a moan hitching in her throat as she gave in to her desires and he must've seen it, recognized the need in her, because he stuttered a breath and crashed his mouth to hers, kissing her deep like he wanted to suck the very air from her lungs.

He released her hands and grabbed her thighs, hitched her up and pressed between her legs, an awkward strain on her too-tight dress but she didn't care, not when his groin crushed against hers, his cock thickening and separated from her only by the fine panties she wore.

"Open the door."

"Yeah—let me just—oh God…"

She got the door open somehow, by some miracle, and they tumbled through it, Declan holding her up and Maggie slapping the wall in a blind attempt to find a light, unable to focus with how Declan was sucking on her neck and then devouring her mouth and God, *God*, she was gonna come undone.

Hand making contact, she managed to flood the room with light, and simultaneously kicked off her shoes and dropped the card as the door swung itself shut and Declan carried her across the room.

"Bed," he mumbled against her mouth.

"Couch," she responded, and he made a sound of agreement or arousal or *something*, something that shot straight to her clit and made her moan.

The world tipped up beneath her, and all of a sudden she found herself straddling Declan's lap; he'd found the couch and collapsed back on it, and now he had a handful of Maggie's ass and she was staring into his flushed face and staggeringly, so abruptly, she was knocked breathless by the pure perfection of him.

He must've taken her pause and whatever was on her face for something else entirely, because he said, "We don't have to—"

And she said, "Shut up," and pressed in to lick into his mouth, taste him, breathe the essence of him into her lungs. He kissed hard, but he touched her gently—hands roaming her back, the swell of her ass, creeping down her thighs to hook thumbs beneath the hem of her skirt. So clearly desperate to get under her clothes, and there was no part of her that wanted to deny him.

She arched her back, pressed her breasts against him, the angle allowing her to rub her crotch somewhere in the vicinity of his hardness, and he groaned into her mouth, put a hand at the base of her throat and pushed her away an inch.

His lips swollen and red, his eyes heavy-lidded, he kept her at bay with a hand on her throat and looked her in the eye, captured every ounce of her attention as his other hand traced a path between her legs, beneath her dress, and found the very edge of her wet panties and pulled them aside, exposing her aching pussy.

She stuttered in a breath, held it, and he slipped a finger through her swollen folds, directly over her clit. The whimper rushed out of her in the instant before he released her throat and pulled her in for a plundering kiss, pressed the pad of that finger to her entrance and rubbed his thumb over her clit, starting a rhythm that had her rocking into it, grinding against his hand, breathy moans escaping her as he went faster, harder. The kiss devolved into a press of open mouths and he didn't let up, relentless with it, rubbing her and pushing in and catching the tight bundle of nerves over and over again until she was fisting her hands in his shirt, her toes curling, and the noises coming out of her were primal, almost orgasmic—

"No," she gasped, reaching down to still his hand. "No, please—I want you inside me when I—"

"I don't have anything," he whispered, "Let me do this for you, God, I just want to touch—" and he didn't let up even as she tried to stop him, forcing her towards climax, working her clit like it was his one goal in life to tip her over the edge, swallowing her moans and tangling his other hand in her hair, but not like this—please—

"I do," she gasped desperately, almost manically. "I've got one." And he went suddenly, shockingly still.

"You do?" His chest was heaving, his cock visibly straining his expensive pants, and her words had obviously put him on the edge of *something* because the look in his eyes hit her like a dart of electricity to the groin.

"Yes," she said. "*God*, let me just—"

She leaned over him, fumbling down the side of the couch, found her purse and dug around inside it. Frustration had her groaning and then she was groaning for a whole other reason—his impatience and arousal had apparently won out, because he'd taken the opportunity to slip two fingers back inside her, swipe his thumb over her clit.

"*Please*, Declan, I can't…"

"You've got ten seconds, and then I'm making you come," he promised, and she could've cried with the beautiful agony of it.

Eventually, blessedly, she found the condom at the bottom of her purse, but by that point she was too far gone to make much use of it. Her eyes were fluttering shut with the waves of pleasure washing over her, her whole body sparking with electric heat, and even when he stopped, when he took a moment to fiddle with the condom, she couldn't stop the sensations flooding her system, and he said something that sounded like, "God, you're beautiful," in the instant before she felt it—the press of his cock against her entrance.

Somehow, while she'd been lost on the edge of climax, he'd managed to free his cock, sheath it, and lift her high enough to position himself ready to press into her.

But he didn't, not yet. He waited—waited for her to come back into herself enough to look at him, to meet his eye, to nod. And then he pushed into her in the same moment she pressed down on him, and they both released breathy moans of pure pleasure as they joined in the middle.

He gave her only a moment, long enough to pull her close and taste her tongue, for her to catch a breath or two and adjust to the size of him stretching her open. And then he gripped the curve of both her hips and guided her into motion above him.

It didn't take long for either of them. They jolted into a stuttered rhythm, Maggie grinding down on him as he rocked up into her, both of them wordless and breathy, panting through messy kisses and sliding their hands over sweat-slick skin. She wanted to touch more of him, feel the cut of his abs and the strength of his shoulders, but he still wore his suit and she had no coordination left in her to try to strip some of it away, so she hooked arms around his neck and fucked down on him harder and then she was cresting, and he was gritting his teeth, and her eyes rolled back in her head as she crashed over the edge.

Minutes later, slumped against him, she caught her breath enough to say, "That was…"

Crazy, was what it was. A snapshot of manic sexual energy colliding and making them both rut at each other like animals. She wanted to giggle.

He was busy tracing fingertips up and down her spine, his cock still inside her, soft now but so warm and big, still making her feel full. Satisfied.

"You still want me to leave?"

She tutted in exhausted amusement, sat up straight and looked at his sex-roughened face. Felt a surge of fondness rise in her chest, wrap around her heart. "I think I can put up with you for a while longer."

He ran a hand over the swell of her tummy and up to cup a generous handful of her breast, thumb brushing her hardened nipple through the material of her dress. "You're exquisite," he said, and she huffed a mildly embarrassed laugh.

"Shut up," she muttered back at him, and he kissed her.

CHAPTER SEVEN
Maggie

It took her a moment to figure out what was different as she drifted into consciousness the following morning. She blinked her eyes open, stretched out her back, groaning a little at the pleasure of it—and then it hit her. *Pleasure.* Declan. Sex. Last night.

Oh God. Instantly she was hit with the dual sensation of absolute satisfaction combined with a little bit of embarrassment. She wasn't ashamed of what had happened, but she did feel a little off about how easily she'd given in to her desire for the man. She was a make-'em-wait kind of girl, but it turned out that when it came to Declan, all of her preconceived notions went out the window. It almost made her want to laugh.

She stretched again, smiling, and rolled onto her side.

The bed was empty.

She sat up, holding the blanket to her chest, and glanced around for signs that he was in the bathroom or he'd popped down to get coffee. "Declan?" she called, her voice cracking with sleep. Silence met her.

Mildly unsure of the situation, she got up and began getting herself ready. None of his things were here. Surely he wouldn't have put his full suit back on to go down and get coffee?

Thirty minutes later, showered and dressed, she had to face the fact that he'd gone. He hadn't bothered waking her to say goodbye, hadn't left her a note, not even a message on her phone apologizing for slipping out so early. Nothing.

Ditched her. *Again*. Taken what he wanted and vanished.

The pit of her stomach went very hollow, and her heart thudded along dully as she left the room and headed towards the elevator.

She refused to feel badly about his disappearing act. Refused to give him the satisfaction of it. Because it turned out her instinct had been correct: Declan Archibald was not a man she should let in. He was looking for a bit of fun, and she'd been his toy. And that was the end of it. It wasn't worth one ounce of her time.

Her throat swelled thickly as she headed towards Grant's room. She spent minutes knocking and knocking at his door and getting no answer. The second man of the day to disappear on her. She was starting to sense a pattern here.

Several of the wedding party were loitering in the lobby when she made it downstairs, and if she cast a surreptitious gaze around for Declan, no one needed to know. He wasn't there.

All of a sudden, and for no explicable reason, Maggie so very deeply wished her mom was here. She was supposed to have been, of course, a big family wedding like this. But she'd very wisely chosen to take her latest boyfriend to Europe instead.

But Aunt Constance was here, holding court in the center of the lobby, loudly dictating the disposal of the wedding flowers.

Maggie ducked her head and hurried over to the desk.

"Excuse me," she muttered, trying to avoid drawing anyone's attention. *Especially* Aunt Constance's. The girl behind the desk smiled up at her blandly. "Did the guest in room 249 already check out?" Because it was either Grant had left her here at the hotel alone, or he'd gotten so black-out drunk last night that he was currently in a coma in his room, completely oblivious to her hammering on his door. Neither option was particularly pleasant.

The girl tapped at her keyboard. "Yes, ma'am."

"Thank you," Maggie said swiftly, and then tried to get the girl to move as quickly as possible through the check-out process. She could hear Aunt Constance's voice getting closer, and sooner or later, one of her cousins or a weird old uncle would spot her here, even as she half hid herself behind a large potted tree.

"Should I call a car for you?" said the girl, because of course there'd be a selection of town cars on retainer. No one from the Emerson family should ever be expected to make their own travel arrangements.

"No thank you, I'll get a cab," said Maggie, and booked it out of there.

The cab took her to the train station, and the hour-long train journey home was a battle in self-discipline. She point-blank refused to think about Declan Archibald or how terrible she now felt about the whole thing, but her overactive mind had different ideas. She fought against memories of his perfect face and toned muscles all the way home, and ended the journey with a headache and damp underwear.

She was full of bad mood as she slammed the building door behind herself, trudged up the stairs with irritation, feeling like a black cloud was hovering over her head and making her hate everything.

And then she froze.

Sitting on her doorstep, propped against the frame and brightening the gloomy hall like a burst of brilliant sunlight, was the largest bouquet of mixed flowers she'd seen in a long time. And in the middle of it, enclosed in a dainty silver envelope, was a note.

She knew instantly it was from Declan, her instinct firing up and filling her with annoying giddiness, and her stupidly romantic brain was already tumbling with possible messages:

...sorry I had to leave...had an early meeting...didn't want to wake you...

...hated leaving you...want to see you again...

...couldn't wake you...snoring...

The last one made her blush, because that could've been a very real possibility.

But the card didn't say anything like that—didn't express regret at leaving, didn't ask to see her again, didn't do a damned thing to dissipate her black cloud.

In a rushed, can't-be-bothered kind of scrawl, it simply said: *Thanks for the great time. -D*

Never in her life had she felt so soundly and instantly dismissed. And it left a wretched hole in her stomach that almost made her want to cry.

Which quickly and violently turned to anger.

How *dare* he use her like that—make her think his history of wanting her would lead to something more than a random hook-up at a wedding, so seedy and unfeeling and so very the opposite of how Maggie liked to conduct herself.

Who did he think he was? He might be Mr. Desirable Bachelor Number One in certain circles, but that kind of crap didn't wash with her. She didn't care that he was panty-meltingly attractive, that he oozed money and power, that he was dynamite in bed. The charm-offensive way he'd taken down her barriers had been little more than a tactic and it left a bitter taste in her mouth now, a sourness that smothered all appealing thoughts of him in ugly truth. He was a player, and she was no game.

She called her brother, needing to hear a friendly voice right now. Wanting to feel that old comfort of her brother's care.

What she got instead was a snappy tone that left her reeling.

"It's not a good time right now, sis."

"What? Why?" She was standing at her floor-to-ceiling window, staring out at the gloomy grey skyline like the world's most pathetic cliché. *And here we have our classic jilted heroine,* said a voice in her head that sounded suspiciously like Aunt Constance, *standing in misery and feeling sorry for herself.* She could almost hear the Adele soundtrack.

"I'm busy."

The words brought her out of her own ridiculous thoughts and back to reality. And not what he said—but how he sounded as he muttered them. Strained and scratchy and weak.

"You don't sound good," she said, frowning, already turning away from the window and searching out a pair of shoes. "Should I come over?"

"I'm fine. I'm just…tired. Don't fuss."

"I'm not fussing. I'm *worried*. This can't be the flu—you were okay last night."

"Speaking of last night—what happened to you?"

The abrupt change of subject worked—instantly she was flooded with embarrassment and anger again, drowning out her concern for her brother's wellbeing.

"Nothing."

"Mags," he said flatly. "You disappeared before the cake even came out."

She considered lying. A story about getting a headache and slipping off to bed was on the tip of her tongue. But there was a part of her, the part that still lived with the memories of her broken childhood, of her brother's strength in pulling her through it—that part of her desperately wanted to confide in Grant, just so he could make her feel better about it somehow. Like he always did.

She opened her mouth, closed it, swallowed dryly, and then took a sharp breath and said, "Declan."

"What about him?" Grant asked, and then almost immediately: "Oh my God, Maggie, tell me you didn't."

Her cheeks burned hot and she had to resist the urge to abruptly hang up. "You made me dance with him!"

"Yeah, *dance*. To give me a break from your nagging. I didn't want you to hook up with him, Jesus Christ."

Nagging. He didn't say it harshly, but it unsettled her all the same. Like she'd become a nuisance in his life, one he wanted to palm off to some other poor unfortunate soul.

She stored that thought away for another time and brought her mind back to the hideously mortifying topic at hand.

"I thought he was a good friend of yours."

"He is. You know we go way back. Which is why I know that this—you and him—is a terrible idea. It was bad enough hearing you'd been on a couple of dates with him, but *sleeping* with him?"

Rather than make her feel better in any way, the thinly veiled accusation in his tone put her hackles up. He was *judging* her. Never mind how dare Declan—how dare Grant!

"What's the big deal?" she bit out. God, she was so done with men today. "Girls can do the casual hookup thing, too, you know."

"Yeah, and as long as that's all it was, you'll be fine."

She scowled at her empty apartment. "What's that supposed to mean?"

Hesitantly, as if he could sense the danger zone he was currently tiptoeing through, he said, "The guy's not one for settling down, all right? He likes…fun."

"Fun."

That hollowness was slowly making a reappearance, making her wish she could end this conversation and go bury herself in bed for the rest of the day. When she'd hoped that Grant might make her feel better about all of this somehow, she never considered that he might instead confirm Declan's shitty behavior.

"Look, he's got a reputation," he continued. "He's known for this. I'm just saying—leave it at that, okay? Don't get involved. That's not who he is."

"You're saying he's a player."

"Of course, he's a player," Grant said, impatience in his tone, like she was an idiot for even having to question it. "He's Declan Archibald. The guy *every* pretty young thing wants. There's no way he's ready to give up the perks of that particular label."

Ten minutes later, Maggie took the flowers outside and down the street and chucked them in a dumpster behind a Chinese restaurant. She didn't even want the smell of them in her home.

CHAPTER EIGHT
Maggie

Maggie had barely taken three steps into the hospital when Dr. Stevens cornered her, as if he'd been loitering in the wings, ready to pounce.

"Ms. Emerson."

She jumped, coffee spilling and burning her fingers, her hair a total rat's nest from the strong winds they'd been hit with that morning.

Her stomach filled with dread at the badly concealed smugness on his face.

"What's going on?"

"Come to my office, please," he said, and then marched off, leaving her reeling.

Oh shit. This didn't feel good. This didn't feel anything *close* to good. Clearly, whatever was about to happen, it delighted him. That look on his face said he was going to enjoy every single moment of it. And considering how much he disliked her, that could only mean one thing: she was screwed.

Heart in her throat, she made her way up to his office. She was the only one working today, so she didn't even have Ashley or Cami to gather strength from. At least she didn't have to face Ronald—he was nowhere to be seen as she ambled through the ER ward, desperately trying to get her racing heart under control before she took whatever Dr. Stevens planned to throw at her.

When she entered his office, it wasn't the sight of *him* that filled her with overwhelming, ice-cold panic. Standing in front of the window, hands clasped behind his back, and framed by weak sunlight like something straight out of a made-for-TV crime movie, was a stocky gentleman wearing jeans and a leather jacket…with a police badge clipped on his belt.

Maggie swallowed past the rising tide of fear creeping up her throat, and said, "Is this about the—"

Dr. Stevens cleared his throat. "Please sit down," he instructed, doing a terrible job of hiding his glee at the situation.

She remained standing and looked at the policeman expectantly. He stepped forward. His voice was thin and reedy when he spoke, but not unkind.

"Ms. Emerson, I'm Detective Sanders." He paused, as if waiting for her to greet him in return, but she said nothing. After an awkward beat, he pulled a notebook from his pocket and flipped it open to a page somewhere in the middle. "Can you take a look at this list and tell me where you were at each of these times?"

With a shaking hand, she took the notebook from him and stared at his list. At first, she couldn't see anything, the panic making the letters run together like spilled ink, blurry and indistinct. But she needed to get a grip on herself, find some courage, because acting meek and tremulous would only make her appear guilty.

She blinked her vision clear and read the list.

And then fought the terror filling her entire body at the sensation of the walls closing in on her.

"Here."

"I'm sorry?"

"I was here," she said firmer, looking back up at him. There was no point lying. On this, at least, they had her over a barrel. "These were my shifts in the past month."

"All of them?" he asked, taking the notepad back from her. His question confused her a little. Or maybe the panic had removed her ability to make sense of simple statements.

"No, I mean—they're not all of my shifts, obviously. I've worked a lot more than it says there. But each of these have been during one of my shifts." She was snapping, she knew that, but she couldn't stop. Couldn't control anything about this, including her own reactions.

"I see."

"Well I don't. Am I being accused of something here?"

The detective pulled a pen out of his pocket this time, but he didn't use it. Just tapped it against his notepad and said, "Your DNA was found at the scene of the crime."

At her entirely dumbfounded reaction, Dr. Stevens leaned forward in his seat and added, ever so helpfully, "We found your DNA in the location of the missing drugs."

"That's ridiculous," she spluttered. "My DNA is all over that cabinet."

"Specifically, Ms. Emerson," Dr. Stevens said in his slick, greasy voice, "your hair was found directly after the drugs went missing again on Friday last week."

Was he actually trying to tell her that she was in the frame for a crime because they'd found her *hair*? Her panic gave way to utter disbelief, and for a brief moment, relief washed over her like a warm blanket.

"Sir. I'm sorry, but if that's all the evidence you have—"

And then Dr. Stevens said, "It's not," and the relief turned to a blanket of ice.

"Then what else is there?"

Dr. Stevens stared at her, his eyes glittering, but said nothing.

The detective coughed gently and stepped towards her, pen and pad outstretched.

"Ma'am, if I could just take your contact information—"

"My hair could've gotten in that cabinet at any time," Maggie said, her mind tumbling into a whirlwind of renewed panic, desperately trying to find the logic in all of this and the one thing that would prove, beyond all doubt, that she had nothing to do with it. "What about the other nurses with access to that cabinet? I bet you'd find their DNA, too."

"As I said, ma'am," the detective said, while Dr. Stevens leaned back and folded his arms over his chest, smirk firmly in place, looking for all the world like the cat that got the cream. "I need your contact information for further inquiries."

"Am I a suspect?" she asked, voice rising, refusing to take the pad from him. Backing down now would mean defeat, and she wasn't ready to accept that anyone, anywhere, could think she was a thief. Even Dr. Stevens. Disliking rich people did not give him the right ruin her goddamn life. "I deserve to know what other evidence you have!"

Dr. Stevens gave a careless sniff and straightened his tie. "Let's just say you might consider getting yourself a lawyer."

A lawyer. What evidence did they have that made Dr. Stevens so sure that she'd need a legal defender? *Oh God*, she thought as the detective once again held the pad out to her, *oh God, oh God. Please.*

"Phone number and address, ma'am, thank you."

Numbly, she took the pad and wrote down her details, hardly aware of her own actions. When she gave the pad back to him, she turned to face Dr. Stevens' hatefully smug face head on. "This is ridiculous."

He raised an eyebrow.

"I'll be in touch," the detective said, then tipped a nod at Dr. Stevens. "Doctor."

He waited for someone to answer him, but when no one did, he pulled a weary expression and left, leaving Maggie alone with Dr. Stevens, who immediately wiggled the mouse of his computer and stared at the screen like she wasn't even there.

"Sir—"

"Close the door on your way out."

"*Sir—*"

"If you don't mind, Ms. Emerson," he said, peering over at her, "I have work to do. And so should you. Unless you'd rather not...?"

He'd love that, wouldn't he? For her to imply that she didn't care about her job. Add more fuel to his fire. To his *vendetta*.

But it couldn't just be about his distaste of rich people. It wasn't just a personal vendetta. Because now the police had evidence, enough to keep her under suspicion, and Dr. Stevens aside, there seemed to be a very real case being built against her here.

She couldn't argue with Dr. Stevens, not when she had no idea what she was even arguing *against*.

She couldn't believe she was even thinking it, but Dr. Stevens was right: she needed a lawyer.

A sentiment she echoed to the girls that evening, after they'd both answered distress calls and met her at the bar.

"I can't believe I'm saying this, but I need a good lawyer."

"*What*?" Ashley and Cami said simultaneously, wearing matching, slack-jawed expressions of shock.

"There was a detective there and everything." Maggie let out a groan and flopped her head down into her hands. "I'm screwed," she said against the gross, sticky bar top.

"Don't be stupid," Ashley said from her right, giving her shoulder a squeeze. "There's got to be a rational explanation for all of this. What've they got on you?"

"They found a strand of my hair in the drugs cabinet."

"That's it?"

"And the drugs always go missing during my shift."

"That's—how the hell does that point the finger at you?"

"There's a lot they're not telling me," Maggie said, sitting upright with a sigh. "Either way, I'm a suspect. A *suspect*. The detective's gonna be in touch."

Ashley looked at her with fierce compassion, then said, "It'll be fine. It has to be. This is crazy."

"Dr. Stevens told me to hire a lawyer. I think this is gonna get ugly."

"The right lawyer will have this dismissed in no time."

From her other side, Cami made a noise of agreement. "If you're gonna get a lawyer, Mags, get the best. Your family probably knows them all."

Maggie snorted. "Doubt I could afford the best on my own." At a flat look from both of her best friends, she shook her head. "I'm not asking my family for money. They don't even need to know about this."

Ashley rolled her eyes, while Cami adopted a thoughtful look. Then her eyes went wide, and she gripped Maggie's forearm. "Luckily for you, my Drew and your brother Grant have a *fantastic* lawyer friend, and I'm sure he'll want to waive the fee." It was at this point that she obviously expected Maggie to know exactly who she was talking about, staring at her with anticipation, her face lit up. When Maggie failed to answer, Cami huffed and said, "Declan Archibald!"

Maggie's stomach jolted. "No."

"What? Why? You've known him for years! Of course, he'll want to help you. He really is the best, you know. There's a reason why he's so filthy rich." She winked at Maggie, as if this fact was a girl chat waiting to happen, then immediately conceded, "Okay, I know, family money. *But*, everyone knows he's made a fortune defending all those politicians and CEOs. He'll snap his fingers and get this cleared away like *that*." She snapped her own fingers to emphasize her point.

With her mouth running dry, Maggie croaked out, "I can't."

"Why not?"

Something must have shown on her face, because Ashley and Cami both suddenly leaned towards her and Ashley breathed, "Oh my God, Maggie, why not?"

Maggie squirmed. "Something may have…happened. At the wedding on Saturday."

"Oh no," Ashley whispered, before glancing around for the barman. "We're not prepared—hold on. Can we get more shots over here, please?" She turned back to Maggie, her eyes sparkling, and said firmly, "Tell us *everything*."

And so Maggie told them everything, from the dates all those months ago and onto Trixie Lane, accepting their chastising about how she'd not mentioned anything before ("I knew there was a reason why you jumped into the whole Ronald thing so quickly!" Ashley exclaimed), withholding such a juicy part of her life.

Then she filled them in on the wedding this past weekend, meeting Declan again, everything he said, all of his explanations…and then everything they did together, followed by his disappearing act the following morning, punctuated by the world's most dude-bro note ever.

"And he hasn't called you?" Cami asked.

Maggie downed another shot. "Nope," she croaked.

"It's only been two days, though."

"Yeah, and you know what guys are like," Ashley added. "He's probably waiting for you to text him or something."

"The note was pretty clear. It was just a fun one-off for him."

"Maggie—"

"It's *fine*," she lied, searching around for another full shot glass. "It's not like I'm into him or anything." Another lie, one big enough for her to choke on. "But now you get why I can't ask him for help."

"Of course, you can," Cami said. "You have to!"

Maggie dismissed her, waving a hand to brush her statement away, swaying on the stool as the rush of alcohol muddled her mind and her senses. She was starting to feel like she could float away from the whole thing, that maybe if she shut out all the noise of it, it wouldn't matter. But she knew that wasn't true—deep down, beneath the river of tequila taking control of her rationality right now, she knew exactly how screwed she was.

Not that bringing Declan Archibald into the situation would make her feel any better. He didn't *deserve* to fix her problems, make him feel good about himself. Make him feel *powerful*, having Maggie run to him for help—that woman who he slept with and then dumped.

She snorted. No way was she giving him *that* satisfaction.

And then Ashley spoke again, and her words shattered through Maggie's brain like a goddamn sledgehammer.

"What's more important to you, Mags—your pride, or your job?"

* * *

SHE WOULD BLAME IT ON the alcohol. She might even blame it on her libido. What she wouldn't do was pretend she was making any kind of good choice when she went home that night and called Declan.

He answered on the third ring, and his voice floated into her ear like the warm breath of a god.

"I was going by the three-day rule, but—"

She couldn't let him use that voice on her, the one he'd murmured to her during their night together. She couldn't listen to him and think about the agonizing pleasure of his touch. "I need your help."

"What?"

"I know you don't have any interest in…well," she said, squeezing her eyes shut and pressing knuckles against her forehead. "Whatever. But I need legal help now, and you're the best, so…"

He paused. And then, firmly: "What's happened?"

Taking a shuddery breath, she told him everything, barreling through all the details—what little she had—and barely pausing to consider her words. She was being entirely too emotional about it, heart on her sleeve, especially when she swallowed the hard lump in her throat towards the end of her speech and finished with a broken, "I can't lose my job, Declan. I just can't. This is…it's everything to me."

He'd let her speak, hadn't tried interrupting her. But it was his turn now, and she knew it was stupid of her, but she put everything she had on his response. She *needed* him to tell her, without doubt, that it'd be okay.

His voice was measured when he said, "They can't fire you without first proving it's definitely you stealing the drugs."

"It's not."

"I know that," he said gently. "Anyone who's known you for longer than thirty seconds would know that."

There was such certainty in his words that she let out a watery laugh, unaware until this moment that she'd started crying. He said a soothing, "It's okay," to her, sounding like he was right beside her in the room, and she sniffed a little, trying to regain a hint of composure.

"So you'll help me?"

"Of course, I will," he said at once. "Don't worry about anything, okay? How often do I lose a case?" he added in what was clearly meant to be a jokey manner, intended to put her at ease. Instead she groaned.

"Oh *God*, it's gonna be a case, isn't it? Like an actual public thing."

"No. It won't go that far—I'll make sure of it." He paused and she heard rustling from his side of the call, like papers or a book. "Can you meet me at the hospital tomorrow? I'd like to speak to your boss and then get some more details from you."

"I—okay." She blinked at the abrupt plan of action. Wouldn't a man like Declan Archibald be too busy to immediately jump onto this particular ball? She'd expected to have to speak to an assistant's assistant and make an appointment.

Unless…unless he was dropping everything for her. Making her a priority.

She bit her lip as her stomach swooped. "I'm there all morning."

"I'll swing by before lunch," he said decisively, and then, much softer, with a kind of intimacy that made her skin tingle, he added, "And, Maggie—I've got you. Okay?"

"Okay."

"Try to get some sleep."

She smiled, feeling inexplicably fond all of a sudden. "Sorry for calling you so late."

"I'm glad you did. Did you get my flowers?"

And then, almost as quickly, having the fondness snuffed out by the memory of what happened after.

—87—

"...yes."

He must've detected the bitterness in her tone, because he said, "What? Do you regret what happened?" There was a hesitance in his voice that suggested he wasn't quite sure if he wanted to know the answer.

But she was in no mood to protect his ego. "Kind of, yeah," she said bluntly. The alcohol made it easier to bare herself to him, made her tongue loose, letting her say the one thing her sober self would hate her for: "The last thing I wanted was a one-night stand with you."

It took him a moment to answer, and when he did, the words came out chipped and sharp.

"Is that what we're calling it? A one-night stand?"

"Wouldn't you?" she asked, the pleasurable memory of it rushing tainted through her mind. "It's what your cute little note implied."

"That's not what I meant," he said, almost darkly, and she couldn't do this. Not today.

"I can't think about this now," she said, unapologetic in her abruptness. "I've got something bigger to worry about."

The harshness of it appeared to strike him dumb. She wondered, briefly, if he'd ever had a woman brush him off before.

"Right," he said. She could tell he wanted to say more, but all he came out with was: "I'll see you tomorrow."

Then he hung up, and Maggie spent a few minutes agonizing about the state of her life before deciding the thing she needed right now was a soothing bath to help clear her thoughts. If she could get clean and relaxed, she would be in a better state to take stock of the situation. Make a plan. Tackle this like an adult.

She woke up four hours later trembling with cold and shriveled up like a prune, an entire construction crew hammering the inside of her skull.

CHAPTER NINE
Declan

Dr. Stevens refused to tell Declan anything, although what he *didn't* say was very telling. He couldn't have made it any more sneeringly obvious how distasteful he found the super wealthy, especially someone like Declan—and, therefore, Maggie Emerson, whose family was almost as wealthy as Declan's.

Could it be a personal attack? Was this little more than a sad, lonely man's fight against his own bitter judgements? With Stevens refusing to say anything without his lawyer present, Declan left his office without any real knowledge, but with the absolute certainty that this was a ludicrous situation. He'd have it cleared away before the dust even had a chance to settle.

"I know you," a voice pronounced as he made his way down the corridor towards the hospital meeting room.

He paused and turned to face the voice, and instantly his mood darkened. "No you don't," he said, but he knew this guy. The preppy doctor Maggie had traded him in for. Robert, was that his name? Declan had found it out several months back, but he hadn't retained the information. Didn't want to think about this man at all. Think about what he did with Maggie.

"Yes, I do," said the doctor, stepping into the florescent light and eyeing Declan coldly. "I see you in the papers all the time."

"That doesn't mean you know me, does it?"

The doctor scowled. "What're you doing back here?"

"I've just had a meeting with Dr. Stevens," Declan said, because he knew the truth was enough to shut this weasel up—and then, because he was feeling particularly spiteful, he added, "and now I'm due to meet Maggie."

The words obviously had the desired effect on the guy, but he was clearly trying to seem unconcerned. He sniffed and glanced at his bare wrist, as if looking at a watch. Declan felt sorry for him.

"What do you want with Maggie?"

"I don't really think that's your business."

The guy narrowed his eyes at that. "Maggie and I are involved," he said, and Declan was rocked by uncertainty for only a moment before he laughed.

"No you're not."

"We're on a break," the guy said imperiously, visibly affronted by Declan's dismissal of it. "We're sorting things out soon."

"Ah." Declan nodded, paused, then said, "Does she know that?"

"Our private matters are none of your concern."

"Right, okay." Declan checked his own watch—a real one, not a bare wrist—smirking as he did so, then added, "Well, until then, she's single. So if you'll excuse me—"

He got half a dozen steps away before the guy's slimy voice stopped him short.

"She'll never be interested, you know."

Declan turned to look at him, raised his eyebrows to invite the guy to continue. Despite himself, he was highly interested in hearing what reason this joke of a man would give.

Wearing a twisted grin, the guy said, "She hates the rich."

Declan gave him a second or two to feel victorious in his spite, and then he looked him up and down and sniffed a disdainful laugh. "I see her trying to date you, a resident, worked out so well for you."

Then he turned and walked away.

"We're on a break!"

"Whatever you say, Ross."

"*Ronald.*"

"Whatever," he said, and left the guy seething

in the corridor as he turned the corner and headed towards the elevator.

Five minutes later he was greeted with a sight too beautiful for this gloomy morning—Maggie Emerson waiting for him in a private room, wearing a pretty blue dress, her wild hair tumbling over her shoulders and the smile on her face shy and welcoming.

The only thing that tainted such a perfect sight was the storm of concern in her eyes, but he planned to get rid of that as soon as possible—he was almost certain the weedy Dr. Stevens had nothing concrete. Nothing he could make stick, anyway.

Declan closed the meeting room door behind himself and said, "I just met your charming ex," as he stepped closer to Maggie. "Apparently you guys are working things out soon?"

Seeing her now, after their time spent together in the hotel, brought so many delicious memories back into his mind that it was all he could do not to grab her and pull her close, kiss her breath away.

She buried a hand in her wild hair, grimacing. "Oh God, he said that?" She huffed out a laugh of mild embarrassment, looking up at Declan through her eyelashes. "That guy is the biggest mistake of my life."

Declan smirked. "But he seems like such a catch."

"It turned out that one of the conditions of a long-term relationship with him," she said with a dry tone, untangling her hand from her hair and propping it on her hip, "was that I give up work and play the happy housewife."

"Nice."

"Right?"

"You look beautiful," he said, and she blushed an instant pale pink. She was a truly breathtaking sight, every last inch of her.

"Shut up," she mumbled bashfully, "I'm hungover as hell."

He smiled fondly, reached up to press a knuckle beneath her chin, stroke his thumb along her jawline. "You wear it well," he said, but she didn't share in the joke. Her expression clouded over and she pulled his hand away, took a step back. He frowned. "What's the matter?"

"You're not here for that," she said—and yeah, okay. Maybe it wasn't the best time to be touching her. It wasn't as if they were in a relationship, where casual, intimate touches and gestures were normal behavior. Not yet, anyway.

"Of course," he said respectfully. "So tell me everything you know."

She leaned back against the conference table and sighed. "Like I said, it's not much. They found my DNA in the cabinet—a hair, they said. And I'm always on my shift when the thefts happen."

"That's it?"

"Apparently."

He almost laughed at the ridiculousness of it all.

"We'll have this put to bed in no time."

"No, there's more," she said heavily. "That—that *asshole* Dr. Stevens is keeping it close to his chest, but he couldn't make it clearer than he's got enough to nail me to the cross."

Declan doubted that, but there was no denying that the Stevens guy was being exceptionally shady about the whole thing. He definitely had something up his sleeve, and Declan was determined to figure it out—whatever it took.

"He wouldn't answer my questions," he confessed, "not without his own lawyer present."

Distress passed over Maggie's face. "What am I going to do? This job, it's—it's everything I've worked for. It's who I *am*." She made to shove her hands in her hair again but he grabbed them, held them, rubbed his thumbs over the backs of her knuckles.

"They need solid proof before they can take this any further," he explained, adopting the most soothing voice he could manage. Her eyes were glistening, and the sight of it made him want to take on the world just to see her smiling and carefree again. "Do you know the name of the detective dealing with it?"

She nodded shakily. "Sanders."

Sanders. Declan knew of him, which made this a little easier. He had some sway there. "I'll pull some strings, see what I can find out. But for now, don't even think about it. It's nothing."

She blinked up at him with vulnerable, Bambi-like

eyes, making his chest clench tight. "You think so?"

"I promise you, Maggie, on my reputation," he told her fiercely, squeezing her hands and pulling her closer, just a little, "I'll get this cleared away for you."

"God, thank you," she breathed, and then she yanked her hands from his grip and flung her arms around him.

He was so shocked by it that it took him a moment to pull himself together and hug her back, felt her bury her face in his neck and slide in close. He breathed in the coconut scent of her hair, curled his arms tightly around her waist, and froze in the next moment, sensing the change—the spark in the air as she suddenly went stiff in his arms, but not unpleasantly so, and very briefly pressed soft lips to the skin of his neck. Then she leaned back a little and he hadn't meant to kiss her, had every intention of respecting the distance she needed at this difficult time, but she turned her head his way as he dipped his towards her, and they paused, inches from each other, eyes locked.

An eternity ticked by in that one moment, and then she had a visible but very brief war with herself—the conflict clear in her eyes—before she leaned in that extra inch and kissed him.

It was a natural instinct to kiss her back, to softly lick into her mouth, to gather a handful of dress material at the base of her spine and pull her in.

Then she pushed at him, and disappointment flooded him. Even as he stepped back, as he took his hands off her, as he put all that space between them, the very core of him was screaming out to pull her close again.

She gave him an indecipherable look and then walked around him. She was leaving, walking away, because she didn't want him. She wanted his help—and he'd give it to her, gladly, whatever she needed—but she didn't want *him*.

He closed his eyes against the pain of it and waited for her to go.

But she didn't go. Instead, the sound of the lock clicking into place filled the room, and his eyes shot open.

She walked back to stand in front of him once again, her eyes soft, her cheeks flushed.

"You're saving my life," she said, and he shook his head.

"You don't owe me anything."

"I know that." She stepped closer, reached out a hand to thumb open the top button of his shirt. "But it makes it easier to take what I want."

He crashed into her with the force of a man finding water in the desert, pushed a gasp out of her before he plunged his tongue into her mouth and hiked her up by the swell of her ass, shifted her onto the edge of the conference table behind her.

She whimpered as he slotted himself between her thighs, and he said, "You're making me crazy," against her mouth before he left a lingering bite to her lower lip and pulled back. He placed a hand square in the center of her feverish chest and pushed her back until she lay flat on the tabletop, legs dangling over the edge, breasts heaving with panting breaths and her eyes dazzlingly bright with want.

"Stay like that," he instructed, pressing her hands above her head. "Don't move." He didn't wait for her response—lowered the zip running down the middle of her dress and revealed the generous mounds of her silk-covered breasts. She might not live off her family's fortune anymore, but she still had expensive taste in lingerie.

She held her breath as he brushed his fingers over the swell of one breast and it was almost like he could feel her rapid heartbeat beneath, see the fluttering of it in her throat. He leaned down to kiss that flutter and lower, pulling the cup of her bra away and taking a dusky, pebbled nipple into his mouth.

She moaned, and he let her settle into the feel of it, of the soft teasing of his tongue around her sensitive nipple—then he pulled off with a scrape of his teeth and fell to his knees between her thighs.

This time she groaned, long and deep, and he said, "Been wanting a taste of you for years," while simultaneously bunching her dress up around her waist and perching her feet on his shoulders. He took a moment to appreciate the fact she wasn't wearing heels and then buried his face against her soaking wet panties.

Her hips jolted as she sucked in a breath, thighs clamping around his head as if on instinct. He made a soothing noise and parted them again, and then pulled her underwear aside.

The sight of her glistening pussy made his head spin and his mouth water, his cock pulsing and straining against his zipper. The scent of her washed over him, her glistening lower lips twitching with her arousal, and he must've spent too much time admiring her because she released a breathy, "Declan, please," and jolted him into motion.

Using the hand not holding her panties aside, he traced a finger down the middle of her swollen folds and parted her, exposing her clit and entrance, releasing more of her delicious scent and making him lightheaded.

He leaned in and licked a stripe up the length of her, the sweet taste of her exploding across his tongue, before sealing his lips around her clit and flicking the tip of his tongue over it, pressing two fingers straight into her and feeling her throb around him.

He knew they didn't have much time, not here in a hospital, and he wanted to make her come before he had to leave. As much as he wanted to take his time, lap up the taste of her and bring her to the edge over and over again until she was a begging, tormented mess—that would have to wait for another time. And there *would* be another time. He wasn't letting her go again.

For now, his only goal was to make her come, and come quickly—and so the rapid, relentless flick of his tongue over her clit and the long, deep slide of his fingers inside her was a sudden attack of pleasure she hadn't been expecting.

Her thighs clamped around his head again and a hand fisted in his hair, and she gasped words that sounded like, "*God*," and "*Please*," and maybe even his name, but sounded more like incoherent desperation. He didn't pause, didn't stop to catch a breath, continued to thrust his fingers in and out of her and suck on her clit and fill the room with obscene sounds and the scent of her pleasure. And then he moaned against her, the sensation of it all overwhelming him, and the vibration caused her to cry out and flood his mouth with sweet taste, pulling on his hair to hold him still and grind against his face.

She was still shaking and gasping as he stood and wrenched his cock free from his pants, bunched her dress up even higher to reveal the soft skin of her belly and stroked his cock over it, once, twice—groaning from deep in his chest as he spilled over her skin, painting the soft tan of her belly a milky white.

Then he collapsed forward on her, uncaring of the mess of his own come between them, and pushed her hair off her sweaty forehead, pressed his cheek to hers, flushed and hot—listened to the sound of her panting through the aftershocks of her orgasm and murmured, "Come home with me," into her ear.

It took her a moment to answer, and when she did, her voice was thick with deep, lingering pleasure. "Okay."

CHAPTER TEN
Maggie

Maggie awoke to a minty-fresh kiss to the corner of her mouth and fingers tracing the hairline beside her ear. She smiled and rolled onto her back, stretching away the night's kinks and aches, and opened her eyes to find Declan standing over her, his expression soft and fond, as he buttoned a crisp white shirt over his bronzed, toned chest.

"Morning," she said bashfully, glaringly aware of how she must look right now, while he had obviously already been in the shower and made himself presentable.

She also couldn't help but focus on how naked she was underneath the silk sheet draped across her. She tugged the sheet up to just below her chin and blinked up at him.

"Morning," he replied, fastening his cuffs now. "I didn't want to wake you, but I figured I might be in trouble for making you late for work."

"Work…" She glanced about for a clock, attempting to wake her mind up enough to figure out her schedule, and then it hit her: "I'm not working today. It's not my shift."

"Oh." He paused mid-cufflink and stared at her.

"But I'll go home, it's okay—" she said hastily, a blush creeping up her neck. "If you can just give me a few minutes…"

She was in the process of wrapping the sheet around herself so she could maintain her dignity as she rose, when his hand landed on her bare shoulder and she startled.

"I don't want you to leave," he said, amusement lacing his tone. "Relax," he added, lifting his hand from her shoulder to trace a fingertip along her jaw. "I'll be right back."

Then, with a lingering touch and a warm smile that lit up his eyes, he left the room.

Maggie slumped back against the pillows and took stock of her situation.

She'd spent the night with Declan. She hadn't intended to—hadn't meant to get involved with him at all, not after her brother's warning, but Declan's reassurance and gallantry over this theft bullshit had weakened her resolve, reminded her of just how gigantic her crush on him was. How badly she wanted him, body and mind. He was brilliant, and he was also mind-blowingly attractive, and those two qualities mixed together had created a chemical reaction deep in her gut that made it impossible to resist him.

And it didn't feel wrong. It felt terrifying, but not wrong.

Last night had been…*God*. She didn't even have words. He'd brought them back here, to his penthouse in the sky, ordered take-out and put on some soft music and *didn't* try to tempt her straight into bed—and that made all the difference to her. How he was able to sit and talk with her as if there was more between them than just sex, how he appeared genuinely interested in everything she said—how he was so attentive, so open, so warm and charming and welcoming, that even the coolness of his glass-and-marble home felt cozy and embracing.

In the end, she'd been the one to initiate intimacy. When it grew late and the time came to either move things along or go home, and she found she didn't want to go home, not at all. She wanted to stay with him, and she wanted him to want her.

And when she plucked up the courage to kiss him again, he swept her away with his desire for her. He took her to bed and brought her to orgasm three times, before tucking her close and soothing her to sleep with fingertips tracing up and down her naked spine.

She didn't trust men. She didn't believe in the happily-ever-after. But right now, in the intimate bubble of this opulent apartment, she wanted this man.

But a darker, louder part of her knew that this man had a certain reputation, that her own brother had warned her of it, and it was that loud voice that almost had her up and getting dressed and leaving before he could give her the patented player brush-off. She had far too much self-respect to outstay her welcome and plan for anything other than what this was.

"Thanks for the great time. –D" That had been his response the last time they hooked up. She couldn't deal with that again.

It was in that moment of doubt that the door opened again, and Declan strolled through it. He had his cell in his hand and a bright smile on his face.

"Made a few calls," he said, settling on the edge of the bed beside her, "managed to move some things around. How does spending the day together sound?"

She blinked at him, her heart performing a somersault behind her ribs. "What?"

"There's a nice antiques market downtown I've been meaning to check out." He brushed a stray curl behind her ear, his expression so open and endearing. "And I know a great place for lunch."

When she said nothing, a crease formed between his brows and he pulled his hand back, mumbling, "Sorry, you've probably got plans. Maybe another time."

"No," she said quickly. "No, I just—I'm surprised, is all." She tried for a wry grin as she murmured,

"Didn't think hotshots like you got days off."

His face softened with relief. "Just don't tell my clients."

Feeling a little like she'd slipped out of reality, Maggie went along with it, giddiness flooding her stomach as she realized that he really meant it—he wasn't brushing her off.

That maybe he'd been honest all those months ago, and she'd discarded him. Traded him in for *Ronald,* of all people.

He drove her home first so that she could change and freshen up with her own things, and then took her to breakfast at a cute little café that served pancakes with syrup and hot chocolate with marshmallows—everything bad for her but oh so delicious.

The market was quaint, a long line of individual stalls with bright canopies and colorful salespeople, trading in old art and coins and tapestry, furniture with history chipped into it and books dogeared a hundred years ago. He didn't seem inclined to buy anything but he spent his time perusing all the same, holding Maggie's hand or the small of her back or slinging an arm round her shoulders when he wanted to pull her near and kiss her temple.

Maggie spent the morning in a bit of a daze, overwhelmed by the romance of an antiques market in fall weather, bronze and orange and fading green littering the walkway, the sun bright and the air cool and the man beside her, so very handsome, keeping her close and holding her like he never wanted to let her go.

It wasn't the weather for ice cream, but a vendor had set up shop anyway from a cart at the end of the parade, sold them both vanilla scoops with a berry sauce that she managed to make a mess of on her lips; Declan swept it away with his thumb and sucked the thumb into his mouth, eyes glittering as he looked at her, and she couldn't help but beam her most honest smile.

Lunch was late and light, salads on the waterfront, their bellies too full of pancakes and ice cream to manage much else, but it was perfect, conversation flowing over a glass of wine or two, arguing *Breaking Bad* vs. *Mad Men* and their favorite decades for music, the old classics and the horror of modern pop.

They took a stroll through the park, and he kissed her by the fountain, a drizzle of rain patting their faces before they took cover beneath the bandstand. A busker played the sax nearby and Declan asked her to dance and she laughed at him, at the corniness of it, and he shut her up with a bruising kiss that left her breathless.

They went home, back to Declan's, Maggie's mind too full of lustful thoughts after that kiss to consider the wisdom of spending another night with him—her heart thumping with the romanticism of the day and the intimacy of walking hand in hand with the man she liked, the man who made it so clear how much he liked *her*.

She couldn't stop laughing, the story he told her on the drive back not all that funny, but she was lighter than air and everything was a delight and she giggled her way into the elevator until he pushed her against the mirror lining the back wall and kissed her, slipped his hand beneath the hem of her skirt and teased the soft skin of her thigh.

Her phone rang as they exited the elevator into his apartment, and the voice on the other end brought her back down to earth with such a crash that it almost winded her.

"Ms. Emerson, it's Dr. Stevens. I'm calling to inform you that you've been suspended from work for a week, so you shouldn't come in for your shift tomorrow."

The living room of this splendid apartment spun around her, the walls closing in, and she couldn't breathe, could barely see through the narrowed vision of her panic. Declan tried to kiss her jaw, his hands settling on her hips, because he had no idea what was going on in this phone call—had no knowledge of anything but that kiss in the elevator, the one that said they would be in for a good time once they reached a bed.

But not anymore.

She brushed him off and turned her back on him.

"What—why?" she choked out to Dr. Stevens. "You can't do that." Her voice wobbled and cracked on the last note, and Declan appeared in front of her, his expression now full of concern.

"I'm afraid it's out of my hands now," Dr. Stevens said, entirely unapologetic. "The police will be in touch." And then the line went dead, and Maggie's world threatened to crumble around her.

"They've suspended me," she said hollowly, staring at nothing just past Declan's shoulder.

"On what grounds?"

"He wouldn't say." She slipped the phone back into her purse and met his hard gaze, the sensation of the floor swooping beneath her as the reality of the situation hit her with the power of a wrecking ball to the solar plexus. "He just told me not to come in for a week and the police will be in touch." Then she shoved both hands into her hair and said, "Oh *God*," with total, complete despair.

"Stay here," Declan said, moving about. Maggie had no idea what he was doing. She had no idea about anything right now. "I'll go see what's going on. It's okay," he added, stopping in front of her again. Then he grabbed her shoulders and stooped to look her deep in the eyes, and he said, "I'm not gonna let this happen to you." And then he pressed a bruising kiss to her temple and disappeared.

Maggie collapsed onto his Italian leather couch and tried to remember how to breathe.

CHAPTER ELEVEN
Declan

Declan didn't bother waiting for anyone to approach him. He tapped his knuckles on the desk and caught the attention of the lanky, pimple-faced hotshot in uniform nearby.

"Detective Sanders, please."

Several people in the surrounding area went quiet, and Lanky looked up from his phone and raised an eyebrow at him. "He's in a meeting."

"Then," said Declan, removing a business card from his pocket and sliding it across the desk, "get him *out* of the meeting."

Lanky took one look at his name on the card and swallowed thickly. "Take a seat, please, sir."

"I'll stand."

With a nod, Lanky hurried off to do what he was told.

Declan didn't really like throwing his weight around, making people feel intimidated or threatened. But this Maggie thing had already gone too far and he was going to get it sorted out now, today. Put an end to such bullshit accusations.

And if he had to trade on his name for that, remind certain people of how *helpful* he'd been in the past, then he'd do it. He'd do anything to end Maggie's pain right now, squash the thing that had taken out the sparkle in her eye this afternoon. Maggie was so vibrant, so full of light, and right now this hospital business was smothering her into the shadows. Declan wasn't going to let that happen.

Detective Sanders appeared from a door to the right and beckoned Declan over.

"Mr. Archibald. I hear you're looking for me."

"I'm here representing Maggie Emerson," Declan said, offering his hand. Sanders shook it. "D'you want to fill me in on what's going on?"

"Come with me," said Sanders after considering him for a moment. He held the door open to allow Declan into the dimly lit corridor beyond. "Is she a friend of yours?"

Friend? Right now, she's the only thing I care about.
"She's my client."

Sanders said nothing to that, just silently led Declan down the corridor and into the room at the end. An interview room, with nothing in it but a table and a large mirror. He gestured for Declan to take a seat and then sat opposite, clasping his hands before him on the desk.

With a hitched breath, he said flatly, "She's guilty. There's nothing more to be said about it."

Declan couldn't deny that the words knocked the sails out of him. He'd expected to beat around the bush a bit, coax the information out of the detective.

What he hadn't expected was for Sanders to sound so unequivocally certain.

"What's the evidence?"

"Her DNA."

"Not enough."

Sanders tipped his head, conceding, then added, "She's the only nurse on the floor when the drugs go missing."

"Doesn't have to be a nurse."

"The cabinet is secured by a keypad and the staff all have their own codes," Sanders said, with the air of a man who had his target by the balls, and he knew it. "It's her code every time."

Shit.

The assumption that Declan would be able to clear this away with a bit of hard questioning flew out of the window, and hot, sharp *worry* filled his chest. Maggie had just gone from a woman caught in the middle of some bullshit vendetta, to a fully-fledged defendant desperately in need of the best legal representation.

How was he going to break the news to her that this was serious—that he wouldn't be able to sweep it away like he'd promised?

Sanders was looking at him with a knowing glint in his eye, and all Declan could think of was gathering all the information necessary to go home and build a solid defensive case. He doubted he would even sleep, not until he was absolutely certain he could clear Maggie's name.

"What's the drug?" he asked, reaching into his inside pocket for a pen.

"Ah, I've never been able to pronounce these things," Sanders said, digging in his own pocket now. From within it he pulled a page from a notebook, flattened it on the table and pushed it towards Declan. "Here—"

Declan's blood ran cold, his heart plummeting down to his gut. The word staring back at him from that scrap of coffee-stained paper put one person squarely in the frame, one person who had the means to make Maggie look guilty of a crime she'd never commit.

The last person who Maggie would ever want to take the fall for this, and the one who'd tear her heart open the most upon learning the truth.

Grant Emerson.

the Reckless Secret

BOOK TWO

CHAPTER ONE
Maggie

The marinara sauce bubbled cheerfully in the pan, and the scent of blueberry pie wafted from the oven, the two combining to create a pleasant mix of smells in this sharp, expensive kitchen. Maggie was pretty sure that, until these past couple of days, this oven had never been used for anything resembling home cooking. And it wouldn't have even had that introduction now, either—except she had nothing else to do with her days. Because the rest of the world worked; the rest of the world had *purpose*. Not Maggie, though. She didn't have a job anymore. She didn't have anything.

It's just a suspension, she told herself, but the thought drifted vague and indistinct through the gloom of her mind. It didn't feel like just a short suspension. It felt like the end. And she was hopeless with it.

She couldn't *believe* it had come to this. That this

was her life now—suspected of stealing drugs from the hospital she worked in as a nurse, tossed out on her ass, *accused*.

It had taken everything she had not to break down in tears these past few days. But she was determined to stay strong. She refused to let them win. Let *Dr. Stevens* win.

Strong arms snaked around her waist and hugged her in warmth, and a smile hitched onto her face as she stirred the sauce.

Declan was the one thing going right in her life, and she still got the giddy feeling coiling in her gut every time he touched her, gazed at her—when that smile lit up his eyes, or he looked at her with the now-familiar fiery intensity that made her panties wet.

"Hmm," he murmured, tucking his face into her neck and tightening his arms around her, pulling her back against his chest. "Smells good." He punctuated the words with a nip at her neck, and she squirmed, electric heat shooting down her spine.

"It'll be ruined if you keep distracting me…"

"I could get used to this," he said against her hair, rocking her slightly, "coming home to you in an apron, cooking me up a nice hot meal every night…" At her sharp look over her shoulder, he grinned and added, "Kidding."

She tutted, smiling despite herself, and went back to stirring the sauce while he nuzzled her hair for a brief moment and hummed under his breath.

"I said I'd cook tonight."

She sighed, mostly to herself, and said with a voice laced in misery, "You're doing enough. And I'm...useless." She wasn't lying. Declan had been working to dig her out of this mess, and she'd spent the same amount of time holed up in this glittering penthouse, entirely hopeless.

"You're not useless," he told her sternly. "You've just hit a bump. Just because you're not working right this second, it doesn't mean you're no longer a nurse. An incredible nurse," he added, giving her a bracing squeeze around the middle.

She huffed and, apologetically, pulled his arms away and stepped out of his hold, reaching for plates as she muttered, "Doesn't feel that way."

He didn't speak for a long moment, and she tensed with uncertainty. They'd been "together"—or whatever this was—for no longer than a week, and she'd filled almost all of that time with her relentless misery. These early weeks should've been all about the first flush of romance, of getting to know each other intimately, of breathless, giddy excitement.

And it *was* like that. It really was. She'd spent every night here since *that* night, the one that rocked the foundations of her world, and while it hadn't exactly been a happy time, there was no denying that what she had here, now, with Declan, was the most thrilling experience of her life. The intensity of it, the *pleasure*, the all-consuming passion... She could hardly find a moment to calm her heartbeat.

But still, the black cloud lingered. Of course, it did. At any given moment, her new-romance excitement would abruptly and overwhelmingly make way for a rush of panic and fear.

She was at risk of losing her career. But, worse than that, she was very close to having her entire reputation and good standing dragged through the mud. She could rearrange her career ambition—somehow, some way, carve out a new road for herself that still included helping people, if not as an ER nurse. But what she couldn't cope with, not after all her hard work to prove herself, was knowing that people she respected would think of her as an untrustworthy, immoral, unethical *thief*.

She had to swallow away a newly formed lump in her throat as she started dishing up the pasta onto the plates, and nearly jumped out of her skin when warm, large hands settled on her shoulders.

"I'm doing everything I can to put an end to this," Declan said, very quietly, talking close to her ear and with a tone that said he understood, that he could read every depressing thought traveling through her mind.

She reached up to grip his hand for a moment. "I know." She was so grateful for everything he was doing, even if she didn't yet know if it would come to anything. But what she did know was that there was no way she could've afforded a lawyer of his caliber on her own, and she certainly wouldn't have gone to her parents for help.

Her father would've made her feel like the worst disappointment in the history of black-sheep children of the world, and her mother—bless her—wouldn't have been able to hide her true feelings on the matter. Supportive, sure, but still that part of her that would be deeply embarrassed to have *her* child caught up in such a scandal. *What would they think at the club?*

If it hadn't have been for Declan, Maggie would've had no choice but to just roll over and take it. Declan, right now, was her lifeline.

"Just trust me, okay?" he said, kissing her temple before pulling away. "You'll be back to work in no time."

She turned to face him, watched him retrieve a couple of wine glasses and set them on the counter. "Can I help with anything? I feel so useless just sitting around here."

"To be honest, there's not much you can do. I don't plan on letting this get that far—it's just a case of finding that one weak spot in their armor, and it's done."

Nibbling her lower lip, she waited for him to uncork a sauvignon blanc, the muscles in his forearms flexing pleasingly, and asked, "Do you really think you can put a stop to all of this?"

"I know I can." He glanced at her as he said it, his gaze full of sexy confidence.

Sometimes, she forgot how much of a high-powered lawyer he was. That he wasn't *just* a lawyer. He was Declan Archibald—the benchmark to which other lawyers were compared. He was a phenomenon in his field, a powerhouse, highly esteemed and downright frightening in his talent. He was, for want of a better phrase, the Alpha Lawyer in town, and he had the political elite, the troublemaking celebrities, and the business heavyweights sitting pretty in the palm of his hand.

It was a side of him she knew, but one which he kept separate from their time together—mostly. A hint of it slipped out, when he told her to *don't move* and *don't come yet* and, during last night's memorable intimacy, *gonna make you beg for it*. Her knees went weak at the thought of it, a tingle shooting through her groin.

He made her feel good in ways she didn't know possible, and added to that, like he wasn't already blowing her mind, he'd also decided to save her life—figuratively speaking—as if he even had the time to spare.

"I don't know what I did to deserve everything you're doing for me," she told him, feeling as if she was repeating a sentiment she'd muttered to him a dozen times before. But she'd keep saying it—never wanted him to think she was taking his generosity for granted. "I wish you'd let me pay for your time."

"You know I'd never accept it," he said at once,

and then, wine poured, he put the bottle down and approached her. "Besides," he muttered, a soft smile on his face, reaching up to trace the edge of her jaw with his fingertips, "there's no price you can put on helping someone you care about."

Her heart rate hitched at the words. Did he know what he was saying? Did he *mean* what he was saying, or was it just a figure of speech? She couldn't ask. Now was not the time, and it was *definitely* too early to be having any sort of talk about feelings.

For all she knew, this was little more than a bit of fun to Declan.

"Thanks for the great time. –D" The memory of that message, scrawled hurriedly onto a card within a bouquet after their first night together, filtered unbidden into her mind.

She sobered, heartbeat slowing, and smiled back at him—gently, but a little strained.

"Well, I can provide pasta, at least," she said, pulling away from him to continue serving up dinner.

"And…is that blueberry I can smell?"

"Yep."

"That was always my favorite."

"I know; I remember." She felt a little foolish now, making him his favorite dessert from his younger years. She remembered it vividly, how happy he seemed every time it was served at dinner whenever he came over to hang out with Grant. She'd even started to suspect that the kitchen staff made it on purpose, aware of his delight for it. Hers, now, wouldn't taste nearly as nice, but she'd wanted to make it anyway, a token thank-you he'd be happy to accept. Except it seemed massively insignificant now, when the time came to present it to him. *Thanks for all you're doing to save my whole world—here's a pie.*

To top it off, she couldn't even stick around to share it with him. "You'll have to eat it on your own, though," she said, apology in her voice. "I'm meeting the girls soon. Just got enough time to have dinner."

He paused. And then: "Should I pick you up after, or…?"

"No, I'll get a cab. But thank you."

Facing the counter, cleaning up the mess she'd made slopping the marinara sauce onto the pasta, she thought he'd left the room. It made her startle, therefore, when he suddenly murmured directly into her ear, "As long as you get that cab right back here," his voice full of sinful promise.

Her whole body flooded with heat. "You're gonna get sick of me soon."

"Trust me," he said, hand snaking over her hip, lips whispering against her neck, "I won't." And then, as her eyes fluttered shut, as his hand slipped around to her front and lower, *warmer,* he pressed a kiss to her throat and said, "I'll go set the table," before backing away and disappearing.

She let out a breath and made a mental note to change her underwear before she left.

CHAPTER TWO
Maggie

"How're you coping?" Ashley asked her mid-hug, giving her a tight squeeze. She pulled back, hands on Maggie's shoulders, looking her in the eye and adding, "You staying strong?"

"I'm okay," Maggie said, pulling away so she could hug Cami in turn. "Declan's been great."

Cami smirked. "I bet he has."

"Stop it."

"I can imagine he's *very* attentive," Ashley said, voice dripping in innuendo.

"Ashley!" Maggie couldn't help the laugh that bubbled out of her, a rush of joy twisting her stomach. It felt so good to laugh, after everything. She took her seat at the table and gave the girls a smirk of her own. "He is." And then blushed all the way up to her hairline. Ashley cackled.

Cami, meanwhile, had decided the joke was no

longer funny. She slumped into her seat, grumpy frown taking up residence on her face. "Can we not talk about our amazing sex lives right now?"

At Maggie's questioning look, Ashley supplied, "Drew's gone away on business." To Cami, she huffed, "It's only a week, girl."

Cami pouted. "It's the first time we've been apart." She received twin eye-rolls and sat straighter, lifting her hands. "I'm adjusting," she said, and Maggie bumped her shoulder, smiling softly.

"Hey, at least you've got a man coming home to you," Ashley said. "I'm so depressingly single."

"Well, now Maggie's all loved up, you're next."

"I'm not loved up," said Maggie. The girls both gave her a flat look. "I'm not! I don't even know if we're, you know…a thing."

Cami blinked. "Haven't you stayed at his penthouse every night this week?"

"That doesn't mean anything."

"Drew says word's getting round that Declan's canceling on all his clients this week. He's putting *everything* into making sure you'll be okay." She looked down to brush invisible lint off her blouse, adding casually, but with obvious veiled meaning, "Doesn't sound like a no-strings hook-up to me."

The words set Maggie's heart racing. Hearing it from a third party—that Declan cared about her, and was making her a priority—made it all seem so startlingly real. And she couldn't deny that it thrilled her.

But almost immediately, that same ice-cold blast of reality hit her square in the chest, and her heart thudded back down to her gut.

"He's wasting his time," she said morosely. "He hasn't said it, but I know it's hopeless. He's so guarded about it, like he knows I'm screwed but doesn't want to tell me."

"Well that's definitely not true," Ashley said bracingly, while Cami shook her head. "Sounds to me like he's just focused. You're all he cares about right now."

"Stop saying things like that." She couldn't cope with the roller coaster of emotions—hearing how much Declan cared about her, and in the next instant remembering the mess of her life right now. It was too much emotional whiplash.

Ten minutes later, after they'd received their drinks and chatted about other things—an attempt, Maggie knew, to take her mind off this horrendous situation—Ashley suddenly leaned forward, her sizable breasts squishing against the tabletop, and said out of nowhere, "Look, it's not you stealing the drugs."

Maggie didn't try steering her off-track. It gave her some comfort, somehow, knowing that her friends were so certain of her innocence. She didn't know how she could go on if they doubted her, too.

She took a sip of her gin. "Nope."

"So all we need to do is figure out who *is*," Ashley added, with the tone of someone who'd decided it was time for action. Rallying the troops. Problem was, Maggie's hands were completely tied.

"Right," she said, snorting, "let me just get out my detective badge—"

Ashley ignored the sarcasm. "Who would want to frame you?"

"No one, I hope!" Maggie said, coughing, caught mid-swallow. "God."

"But someone has. So you need to start seriously thinking about who has it in for you."

Maggie was hardly even on speaking terms with most people at the hospital. Not in a bad way, not at all—she was easy to get along with, or at least she hoped she was! But she was always so focused on her job that she hadn't really connected with many of the other nurses or doctors, at least not beyond polite hellos and exchanging patient information. Cami and Ashley were the only two people she really knew in her department.

She couldn't imagine why someone who for all intents and purposes was a complete stranger would have it in her for her. She hadn't crossed anyone, as far as she knew. The most she could've done was accidentally use the last of the coffee in the staff room—but even then, it was hardly grounds for total career sabotage. Whoever was doing this to her must *really* hate her.

It's not just Cami and Ashley, her subconscious whispered to her. There was someone else with whom she had regular dealings. Someone who was at the root of all of this.

It would make sense, but she still found herself

muttering, "Can't be Dr. Stevens," because there was no way. Couldn't be. The guy lived for his job; he wouldn't want to risk being exposed as a saboteur. It'd be the end of him. "He's a dick, but he wouldn't want to risk getting caught out."

"He thinks your dad's cleared a path for you to get the job you wanted," Cami pointed out.

"He doesn't like people who don't pay their dues," Ashley added.

Maggie thought about it a moment, then shook her head. Dr. Stevens was a total dick, but he was also a smart man. "Still can't see him doing it." She slumped a little, having exhausted her possibilities already, and flagged down the barman for another round. "Have there been any more incidents since I got suspended?"

Ashley and Cami exchanged a look, and then Ashley said with a visible apology, "No."

"God," said Maggie, groaning, flopping her forehead down onto the tabletop, "just kill me." And then another face floated into her mind, and she sat up so abruptly that Ashley jumped, splashing herself in the face with her own drink. "Ronald."

She couldn't believe she hadn't put him in the frame before. Of *course*, Ronald.

"What?" Ashley asked, mopping her face with a napkin.

"Ronald Mitchell. The resident I dated."

Cami's eyebrows lifted. "Really?"

And almost as quickly as the thought hit her,

doubt filtered in. No, not Ronald. He wasn't malicious—he was just weird. He wanted her all for himself, he'd made that perfectly clear, but he also cared deeply about having a respectable wife. There was no way he'd want to be involved with theft.

"No, not really," she said, slumping again. "I don't know." She scrubbed a hand over her brow, trying to find some believable logic in the Ronald theory. "He hates that I wouldn't bend to his relationship demands and chose to walk away instead. Maybe this is him lashing out."

"It's possible, I suppose," Cami said, voice full of doubt. "He *is* a bit creepy. Honestly, Mags, I never understood why you dated him in the first place."

Maggie lifted a shoulder. "He was a distraction." Which, of course, brought her mind straight back around to Declan—the man she was rebounding from when she agreed to go on that first date with Ronald. Her stomach fluttered with butterflies, such a wild juxtaposition to how this conversation was making her feel that she almost hiccuped a hysterical laugh. Trust thoughts of Declan to burst through the gloom and lift her spirits.

"Look, we can't do much to help with the investigation," Ashley said, oblivious to the sharp detour Maggie's thoughts had taken, "but we *can* dig around a bit at work, listen to the gossip. Maybe we'll pick up on something."

Cami reached out and squeezed Maggie's hand.

"Until then, try not to get too worked up about it. You'll be back at work in a couple days."

With a snort, Maggie said, "Unless they find a reason to extend my suspension," and whatever Cami wanted to counter with, she was forced into silence by the arrival of the barman, fresh drinks on his tray.

After he left, Ashley eyeing him up appreciatively, Cami said, "They can't do that unless they've got something concrete to go on, right? You'll be fine."

Sipping her drink, Maggie couldn't but feel as if she detected a hint of uncertainty in Cami's tone.

CHAPTER THREE
Maggie

Maggie twisted the bedsheets around her fingers and shoved her other hand into her hair, tilting her head back on the pillow as a wave of sharp pleasure shot through her groin. She moaned, a broken sound from deep in her throat, and spread her thighs wider, giving Declan more access.

Weak morning sunlight highlighted the slope of his shoulders from where he huddled between her legs, face buried against her pussy, midway towards giving her a morning orgasm she'd no doubt be feeling for the rest of the day.

His approach was thorough—two fingers pushed inside her, curved *just so* to make her shake all the way from her rapid heart down to her toes; tongue relentless on her clit, working it over with a single-minded focus that made her head spin, her skin light up with the fire of ecstasy, colors bursting into her vision, and she was gonna come—cresting higher and higher and, *God*, she couldn't breathe, pleasure flooding every inch of her body and seizing her lungs.

She trembled as she tipped over the edge into orgasm, hips convulsing and Declan groaning, removing his fingers to tongue at her entrance, taste the pleasure pouring from her as she clamped her thighs around his head and begged for mercy.

Then he was crawling up her body, throbbing cock in hand, his eyes dark and his cheeks flushed, forehead prickled with sweat and all of him, every part of this perfect man, radiating such powerful *need* that she couldn't help but whimper, part her lips, grip his thighs as he settled over her chest and fed his swollen member into her mouth.

Bracing one hand on the headboard behind her, he lifted up and angled his hips to better slide his cock over her tongue, using his other hand to grip a handful of her hair, and thrusting slowly, torturously into her mouth, starting a rhythm that made her want to cry with how arousal lit anew in her blood.

When it was over, after he groaned her name and spent himself, he settled beside her on the bed and pulled her to him, tugging her leg up over his still her sopping-wet pussy pressed against his softening cock. She shivered.

"You're amazing," he said to her, voice thick with the lingering aftershocks of his own orgasm.

"So are you." Her hips jolted with a spark of electric heat through her groin, making her suck in a sharp breath. "God, I'm still feeling it."

He hummed under his breath and took a moment to palm her breast, thumb a nipple, before they both settled into a comfortable silence, the only sounds their calming breaths and the soft strokes of his fingers over her skin.

A while later, he said, "I need to go into the office today."

She sighed, still full of contentment, her eyes shut and the warmth of his body lulling her into almost falling asleep. "Okay."

"Don't leave," he murmured, pulling her tight all of a sudden, pressing his mouth to the top of her head.

She huffed a tired laugh. "I have to go home at some point."

"I like coming back to you."

"My neighbors are gonna start thinking I've been kidnapped," she said, even as her stomach somersaulted at his words. "Mrs. Wilkins will *definitely* try to steal my parking space."

"Let me deal with Mrs. Wilkins," he said, and then he was moving, rolling her onto her back and leaning up on his elbow, smirking at her as he pushed his other hand down, slipping his fingers between the folds of her aching pussy.

She swallowed thickly. "I can't go again."

"Yeah, you can," he told her, eyes dark and intense, thumb flicking over her clit and making her gasp. "You will."

She was a hair's breadth away from spreading her legs and welcoming him back in when her phone beeped, and she reached for it on the nightstand, instinct overriding her desire for another earth-shattering round of pleasure. She'd been waiting for a particular text message for nearly twenty-four hours now, and she grinned when she saw her brother's name on the screen.

"Hold on…" she muttered vaguely, already opening the message as Declan sighed in mock irritation and flopped onto his back.

The message said: *1 p.m. @ Gio's*

The brevity of the text would've usually worried her, but she was so relieved to hear from him at all that she didn't let it set any worry or doubt in her mind.

"Just my brother," she said offhandedly to Declan, typing out a response, "give me a sec—"

He pushed up onto an elbow, looking at her with sudden alertness. "Grant?"

"Yeah." She blinked at him, at the crease between his brows. "We're having lunch today. What's wrong?"

Frown deepening, he opened his mouth, closed it, then said, "Nothing. Just—I've been trying to get a hold of him, that's all."

She hit send on her message response and

dropped the phone on the bed, rolled onto her side to give Declan her full attention, wanting to hear more. It wasn't like Grant to avoid communication from his friends—or, indeed, his sister. But it had taken him nearly a full day to answer her invitation to lunch, and now it turned out he was giving Declan the silent treatment, too. Her stomach twisted. "He's not answering your calls?" she asked Declan, and then, as an understatement: "That's weird."

He quirked a brow as if in resignation, took her hand between them, and laced their fingers together. He wasn't saying much, but she could feel the worry pouring off him. The tension.

"Should I tell him you're looking to hang out?"

He didn't answer her right away. A storm was developing in his eyes, putting her on edge, and she could almost sense the ocean of words he wanted to spill. Eventually he lifted her hand to his mouth, kissed the backs of her knuckles, and said in a voice dripping with veiled significance, "Tell him I need to catch up with him about that thing we'd discussed this past summer."

* * *

MAGGIE COULDN'T HELP THE GASP that escaped her as she rounded the corner and spotted Grant standing outside Gio's. He looked like an omen of death against a backdrop of colorful Italian cuisine—thin, hunched over, face gaunt and pale; and as she got closer, she saw eyes sunken, hair raggedy, temples clammy, and a hand that shook as he reached up to rub his ashen cheek.

She almost didn't want to catch his attention—there was a part of her, a part threatening to spill out on a sob, that so very desperately wanted to turn around and walk away, act like she'd never even seen this.

But she couldn't do that. He was her brother, and right now he needed her, even if the sight of him terrified her.

"Grant—"

He startled as she touched his arm, and then he turned around. This close, all she could see now was dead eyes and an unshaven jaw. "What time d'you call this?" he asked her. "Come on, let's go get a table. I'm craving that carbonara—" He was trying to pull her towards the door, but she couldn't go inside now and act like she was unaware of the state of him.

"Grant, stop. Look at me."

He paused, but didn't quite look at her. "What's up?"

"What's up? *What's up?*" She yanked her wrist out of his hold and grabbed him, forced him to look directly at her. "Have you looked in a mirror?"

"Oh. Yeah." He scrubbed a hand over his stubbly jaw, embarrassment twisting his mouth. "It's just this damn flu…"

"No, it's not," she said flatly. She wasn't going to let

him fob her off again. "You look like death. Please let me have a proper look at you. I think you need some serious help."

Something about her words angered him, because he shoved her away none too gently and thrust his hands into his pockets, hunching his shoulders and frowning deeply.

"Will you stop fussing, Jesus Christ. I'm fine."

"I'm worried about you!"

"Mind your own business!" It was obvious he immediately regretted his outburst, eyes widening as he said, "I'm sorry," with muttered contrition. "*Sis*," he added, when she hesitated in her response and considered walking away, "I'm sorry. I just…I feel like crap, okay? I can't handle arguing with you right now."

"We need to see a doctor."

"I told you, I've already seen one. He told me to get some rest and I'll be all right in a week or two."

"That was then," she said. "It's obviously progressed, whatever this is. I'm gonna call Dr. O'Malley." Digging around in her purse for her phone, she jumped slightly when his hand suddenly clamped around her forearm, halting her movements.

"I said no. All right?" There was an edge to him she hadn't seen before, and it scared her. Especially when he added, his tone harsh and unapologetic, "Deal with your own shit, Maggie, and keep your nose out of mine."

Slowly, she pulled her arm from his tight hold and stepped back. "What's that supposed to mean?"

"I know you're hooking up with him." He said it viciously, like he wanted to hurt her with his knowledge. Her stomach sank down to her toes.

"It's not like that."

"Don't come crying to me when it all goes wrong," he spat, face twisting aggressively, and Jesus Christ, who was this man? Because he wasn't her brother. Not even close.

She could've cried.

"What's happening to you?"

The broken note in her question reached some part of him that hadn't been taken over by this monster, and his face softened instantly, horror lighting up his features.

"I'm sorry," he said, reaching out for her. When she didn't accept his hand, continued to stare at him, he added, "Please, can you just leave it? Aren't you meant to be a nurse? You're acting like you've never seen a sick person before."

"You're my brother."

"I can look after myself."

They reached an impasse, staring at each other, Grant with an eyebrow raised as if in challenge. And suddenly Maggie was too tired to fight this. With everything going on in her life, she couldn't go to war with her brother, too. She just had to trust that he had a handle on things, that he'd let her in if it got too serious. She had to trust *him*.

Sighing, she gave a weary nod and gestured for him to enter the restaurant. Sounds of life filtered back into her awareness—passersby in the street, cars, a baby crying somewhere nearby. A man in an expensive suit swept past her, his watch glinting in the sunlight, and Maggie was reminded of what Declan had told her earlier.

"Oh, Declan had a message for you, by the way," she said to Grant's back, following him into the doorway of Gio's. "You're not answering his calls?"

He went stiff, pausing with his hand on the door handle. When he spoke, it was with careful precision. "What did he say?"

Maggie frowned. "Something to do with catching up with you about something you discussed this summer."

It took a moment for Grant to respond, and then he let out a weirdly strangled laugh. "Oh that. It's nothing," he said, releasing the door handle and turning to face her. Maggie was starting to wonder if they would ever make it inside this restaurant. "Just some stupid plan we made. Tell you the truth, Mags, I think I'll be better of just heading home to bed. D'you mind?" He wasn't looking at her—scratching his stubbly jaw in a vaguely agitated manner, staring at some point past her shoulder.

"I—no, of course not," Maggie said, blinking at

the abrupt turn of events. "Can I come with you? Maybe I can clean up your place a bit, get some fresh air in there."

"It's all right, the housekeeper's been taking care of me." He leaned forward and gave her a distracted kiss on the cheek, and said, "I'll call you," before disappearing off down the street, leaving Maggie in a spin, her mind trailing in the wake of the sudden abandonment.

That afternoon, rather than sit around feeling sorry for herself for yet another day, she decided to research. If Grant wasn't willing to figure out exactly what was wrong with him, then she could at least give it a go. She knew Dr. O'Malley couldn't speak to her about her brother's medical problems, so she decided against calling him directly and instead made an appointment for Grant for the following week. Maybe he'd be angry at her interfering, but it was better than him wasting away under the weight of whatever illness had taken hold of him.

He was usually so full of life—as the owner of a sports equipment franchise, he could often be found up on a slope or a climbing wall, or racing around a track and jumping hurdles. Grant Emerson did not like to sit still, not even after his accident last winter. He'd been in Vermont for a skiing trip with the guys—come to think of it, Maggie was pretty sure Declan had attended that trip, too—and he'd hit a bend the wrong way, catching his ski beneath him and managing to shatter his ankle. Watching how badly he took to bed rest for the next few weeks, she'd had to laugh at his attempts to sneak out and at least head to work. Not even a horrific fracture could take away his vibrancy, his thirst for action.

Only once had Maggie ever seen Grant in a bad state, and that was this past summer, when he'd had a stomach bug for a couple weeks. Back then, for a brief time, he looked much the same as he did now, only less deathly. But she'd hardly had time to worry about him before he bounced back to normal, healthy Grant—thanks to Declan, she knew, as he'd made it a priority to visit Grant almost daily, and no doubt made sure he was looking after himself. Not that she ever came face-to-face with Declan, still smarting from how soundly he'd dumped her during their second date some weeks previous.

This was different, though. This wasn't a simple stomach bug. It wasn't even the flu. She was pretty sure there was a much more serious problem going on here, and he was protecting her from it. With a sickening jolt in her gut, she thought of bigger illnesses—ones he might not be able to come back from. But she discarded those thoughts immediately. If he had something as serious as a disease, he'd tell her. She was sure of it.

Which left…about a hundred other possibilities, when taking his physical symptoms into account. There was nothing specific she could look up, just general human wear and tear. "Pale skin" and "losing weight" pointed to almost every illness in human existence.

It was hopeless. And, in the end, with frustration churning in her gut, she shut down the computer and headed to the kitchen, deciding to wait until she could speak to Dr. O'Malley. Now all she had to do was let Grant know about the appointment…and with how snappy and almost vicious he was being lately, that would surely mean he'd bite her head off about it. Still, she'd take it. She'd take anything if it meant getting better.

Declan arrived home earlier than she'd been expecting. *Home*. Like she'd moved into his penthouse. Like they *lived together*. It had only been a matter of days, and already she felt more comfortable here than she did at her own place. Which was dangerous thinking, especially with this man—she might have tipped herself fully into a physical relationship with him, and perhaps his knight-in-shining-armor act had a certain sentimental effect on her, but it didn't mean she was ready to forget his history. She wasn't ready to throw her whole heart into trusting him.

But she was entitled to some fun of her own, so long as it stayed on her terms.

"How was lunch?" he asked her, slipping off his jacket and loosening his tie, unbuttoning his top button and rolling up his shirt sleeves, exposing strong forearms and a bronzed collarbone and generally making her melt with how sexy he was.

She pushed her inappropriate thoughts aside and allowed an image of her brother to float miserably through her mind. "There's something wrong with him. He's so sick, but…I don't know. He says it's the flu."

Declan raised his eyebrows, coming to lean against the counter beside where she stood chopping carrots. "You don't believe him?"

"Something's not right."

He hummed a little, losing himself in thought for a moment, and then blinked down at the chopping board.

"I'm cooking," he said, taking the knife from her and gently pushing her aside. She tutted but went with it, reaching for a towel to wipe off her hands. "Did you give him my message?"

"Yeah." She decided against telling Declan how Grant had just laughed it off. "He'll probably call you when he's feeling a bit more up to it."

Bringing the knife down through a carrot, Declan said quietly, almost to himself, "I'll have to pay him a visit soon." And it hit her then, in that moment—Grant was Declan's oldest friend. They went back years, and it was Declan who'd been there for Grant when he last got sick. As much as all of this was affecting Maggie, it was likely bothering Declan just as much. No one liked to see a good friend suffer in any way.

"I'm sure he'd like that," she said softly, and rubbed his arm a moment.

They were silent for several seconds, the only sound Declan scraping his knife across the board, while Maggie watched him from behind, trying to appreciate his wide shoulders and strong back, but unable to quite banish the worrying image of her brother.

Abruptly, Declan dropped the knife and turned, reaching for her with the air of wanting to sweep aside all troubling thoughts. "You know what *I'd* like?" he said, falling back against the counter and pulling her close, until she settled between his legs with her hands on his shoulders, his around her waist. "A kiss."

She smiled, warmth filling her chest. She might not trust that this was a relationship she could depend on, but neither could she deny how Declan's proximity and fiery eyes made her feel. "Hmm, think I can manage that," she said, leaning in, her stomach flipping over at the dazzling grin he shot her in the instant before their lips met—

His phone rang.

"Excuse me," he said, and to her colossal surprise, he pushed her away. Didn't ignore the call or let it go to voice mail—didn't even let it ring a few times. The instance the sound pierced their intimate moment, he pushed her back and yanked the phone out of his pocket, glancing at the screen before answering and muttering, "Hold on," into it.

She blinked at him; the sensation of her heart sinking very slowly into her stomach made her want to wrap her arms around herself. "Work?"

"Uh—" He held the phone to his chest—shielding the screen, she realized—and looked at her with awkwardness. "I'll be back in a minute." Then he hurried out of the room.

She tried to be the bigger person, she really did, but her warring emotions got the better of her and she found herself tiptoeing towards the bedroom, in which Declan had secluded himself. Ear pressed against the door, she heard his muttered tones, but no distinct words. Whoever he was speaking to, he was making damn sure she couldn't figure it out.

The sickening, heavy weight of doubt and suspicion thudded into her gut and, absolutely unable to decide how she wanted to act, she headed back to the kitchen and waited, white noise buzzing in her ears and her blood burning hot through her face.

When he returned, he looked sheepish and shifty—two things she never wanted to face, because in most cases, it only meant one thing.

"I have to head out for a little while," he said. "Can we postpone dinner?"

She swallowed, trying to hitch a bland smile onto her face. "I'll get takeout."

"Sure? All right." He slipped on his jacket and smacked a kiss on her cheek simultaneously, then reached for his wallet and keys on the counter. "I'll be back as soon as I can." She nodded and he headed towards the door, before he abruptly stopped and turned back, walked up to her and seized her mouth in a bruising kiss. "You look beautiful tonight, by the way," he murmured, eyes dazzling, and then he was gone.

Unable to comprehend her whirlwind thoughts, Maggie slumped back against the counter and rubbed a hand over her face. A slice of carrot rolled desolately onto the floor.

CHAPTER FOUR
Declan

Declan was a man on a mission. He couldn't believe it when Grant's name flashed up on his phone—after a few days of radio silence, he's resigned himself to Grant avoiding him for the foreseeable future, his mind already working overtime to come up with a way of getting Maggie out of this mess without involving her brother. The problem was, from a legal standpoint, he could only see one solution here: redirect the investigation. But there was only one other direction it could go, and Declan was pretty sure Grant didn't suit orange.

So when Grant finally returned his many calls, it was the lifeline he needed—even if this particular lifeline didn't have a completely happy ending for everyone.

Grant had tried to brush him off, something about needing to catch up on a few days' of sleep, that maybe he'd call him next week, man, it's all good, *you know me, tough as nails...* But he'd let slip that he was at his apartment right now, and Declan wasn't waiting another minute.

"Hey Sam, how's the wife?" he asked the doorman of Grant's building as he swept past him towards the elevators.

"Still alive, dammit!"

Up sixteen flights to the floor occupied by Grant Emerson in the cooler months, Declan marched down the corridor with determination and then hammered on the dark-wood door.

No response.

He knocked again, and then leaned on the doorbell. Not even the housekeeper, let alone any other staff—Grant must've sent them all away.

Eventually, after Declan's repeated knocks, doorbell pressing, and calls on the phone, the door swung open, revealing Grant dressed in silk pants and an open robe—luxury loungewear to highlight quite how horrendous he looked.

The last time Declan had seen him had been at the wedding, when he'd looked the kind of rough he'd become all too familiar with in the summer. But this...he'd never seen him like this before.

For a moment, Declan found himself entirely speechless.

With a long-suffering sigh, Grant stepped aside to let him in. "I just wanted to be left alone for a while, man. I feel like hell."

"I'm surprised you finally returned a call," Declan said, snapping himself out of it and walking past Grant into his apartment. He didn't live in a penthouse like Declan, but his home still took up an entire floor, and the way he furnished it gave it an opulent feel, perhaps even more so than Declan's.

Although that wasn't the case today. It was obvious he hadn't used the services of his housekeeper in a good while—pizza boxes and beer bottles littered the surfaces, items of clothing draped over the backs of the white-leather couches. There was a suspicious stain on the rug and the curtains were drawn, shutting out daylight.

Declan swallowed, his stomach twisting sickeningly.

"You got Maggie on my case," Grant accused. "What was I supposed to do?"

Declan turned to face him, and he'd had a plan coming here—a plan to ease Grant into the situation, butter him up a bit, get him talking before digging deeper for the answers he needed. But seeing the state of Grant now, of Grant's entire life, Declan knew there was no point delaying the inevitable, beating around the bush. He observed a sunken-eyed Grant for a moment and said, "She doesn't know what's going on."

Grant stared at him. His dazed expression suggested he lacked understanding of *anything* right now, let alone what Declan was alluding to. "What?"

"You," Declan said, and then, ensuring he had

Grant's complete attention: "Framing her for the stealing."

It was as if an invisible frying pan had smacked into Grant's face. "Declan—"

"I didn't guess it, not straight away." He took a step towards Grant, scratched idly at his temple. "It wasn't until she got suspended and I spoke to that cop—did you know she's suspended, by the way?" he added, watching with a perverse sort of pleasure as Grant's eyes filled with undiluted horror. "She's under investigation."

Grant, shaking his head, horror-filled eyes opened wide, looked incapable of speech. "That…it wasn't supposed to go down that way."

"You left your DNA in that cabinet. And your DNA is her DNA, so I'm sure you don't need a lawyer to tell you how screwed she is."

Bringing a trembling hand to his forehead, Grant slumped back against the wall, looking for a brief moment like a frightened, vulnerable child. Declan's heart clenched for him—for his old friend, the one buried beneath this junkie veneer.

But then Grant muttered, "They can't get her on DNA alone," and Declan stopped feeling sorry for him in an instant.

"That's not all they've got," he said bitingly. "But you already know that. Why are you framing your own sister, Grant?"

"I'm not! Jesus." He shoved both hands into his

hair, dragged it back off his face. "It was just a few times. I didn't think—"

"Using her key code," Declan pointed out, holding up a finger, and then a second one when he added, "You do it every time she's on shift."

"Coincidence," Grant said, shaking his head almost manically. "*Fuck*. I've only seen her there once while I—"

"While you snuck in and stole pain meds. We talked about this, man." The words hurt to say, because he wasn't lying—he and Grant went through hell together in the summer, getting Grant off the painkillers. He'd become addicted to them after his shattered ankle wouldn't stop playing up, and Declan hadn't been able to stand by and watch his oldest friend self-destruct. So he'd come here every day, to this apartment, supported Grant all through the withdrawal period—a shoulder to cry on some days, a punching bag on others.

It hadn't been easy, and there were enough setbacks for them to consider rehab, but Grant pulled it together in the end, and after, when it was all over, they had a long chat about how he would never get himself in that situation again. And if he did, he would go to Declan and ask for help. He wouldn't suffer alone.

"I tried," Grant said, sounding so broken with it that Declan had the overwhelming urge to gather him in close and protect him from the world, just like he'd done in the summer. "I did. I tried so damn *hard*. But it's been worse lately. You don't know what it's like."

Speaking through the dryness in his throat, Declan said gently, "If the pain was that bad, your doctor would help you. It's not about pain, is it?" he added, all traces of anger filtering away. This wasn't a malicious, selfish act from one sibling to another. This was a man in desperate need of help. "You're addicted again. And an addict would throw anyone under the bus."

"*Fuck*, man, I didn't mean for any of this to happen."

"I believe you," Declan said. "Which is why I haven't turned you in yet." Relief washed over Grant's face and Declan let him enjoy it for a moment, but as much as it pained him to lay this on the shoulders of a friend in need, he couldn't see any other way this could go down: "*You're* going to do it."

Grant's eyes snapped back up to him. "What?"

"She's gonna lose everything, Grant. Her job, her reputation—she'll be struck off, left with no choice but to ask your parents for help. She won't take my money. You know that pride of hers."

"It won't go that far."

"It's already gone that far," Declan said. "She's been suspended, and the cops think they've got enough to throw the book at her."

Grant looked as if the whole weight of everything he'd done had hit him at once, expression of pure torment passing over his face. "Jesus Christ."

"I can't be the one to tell her that her own brother is ruining her life," Declan said, shaking his head. "She deserves more than that."

"Look, buddy—"

Declan could see the backtracking already, Grant's mind rapidly ticking over, looking for ways to get himself out of this mess without having to own up. But Declan wasn't going to allow that. Maggie needed to know, and aside from that—Grant, for his own benefit, needed to confess. The law acted far more favorably towards a remorseful man than one trying to act innocent.

"You're gonna face her," Declan said firmly, "and you're gonna tell her what you've done. And then you'll call Detective Sanders, and you'll say the same to him."

Grant's whole face was a picture of panic. "I could go to prison."

Doubtful, Declan was pretty sure, but Grant's statement left a bitter taste in his mouth all the same.

"You'd rather she did?"

"It was only supposed to be a couple times," Grant said desperately, pleadingly, but what did he want from Declan? For him to tell him it was all gonna be okay? Lying to him would help no one. "Just to take the edge off, you know?"

"That's how it starts. You're better than this, man."

He thought he'd hit his mark. Thought he'd gotten through. Assumed, by the clarity washing through Grant's eyes, that he'd reached the side of him that cared more for his sister than anything else in the world.

It made his heart stutter, therefore, to see Grant's expression harden. "I need some time," he said, looking up at him with steel in his gaze.

"What?"

"Look at me. I'm a wreck." He spoke calmly, robotically. Emotionless. He was cutting off decency.

He was letting the addict speak.

"I can't do this right now."

Declan could've choked on the sadness that rose in his throat. "What's happened to you?" he asked, something like an appeal in his voice. "Look at what those pills are doing. This isn't you."

For one heart-stopping instant, it looked as if the real Grant wanted to respond. But again, his face shut down, and he said coldly, "Just leave. Stay out of my business."

And suddenly, Declan was *furious*. He was actively withholding information from the woman who meant the world to him right now, all so he could give Grant the chance to do the right thing himself, and this was how the man in question reacted to finding out he was wrecking his sister's life?

Fine, he thought. *Fuck yourself over all you want, but I won't let you do it to Maggie.*

"You've got a week to pull your shit together and face this train wreck," he growled at him, stepping close, pretending he couldn't see the bloodshot eyes, the hollowed cheeks, all the signs saying Grant needed his help right now way more than his vitriol. This was no longer about what Grant needed. "One week, Grant, and then you'll leave me with no choice but to tell her myself." A twitch in Grant's jaw was the only sign he gave that Declan's words had any effect on him.

"Don't force me to turn in my oldest friend," Declan added. "Do the right thing."

Then he left Grant to stew in his own mess, his anger taking him all the way to the hospital. He hadn't intended on hitting two birds with the same stone today, but he was on the war path now, and *someone* was going to answer for what was happening to Maggie. There was no way Declan could go back to her empty handed.

"You'll be lifting Maggie Emerson's suspension tomorrow," he said as he barged his way into Dr. Stevens' office.

Stevens, caught entirely off guard, jumped in his chair and knocked his glasses askew.

Gathering his composure with rapid ease, he straightened his glasses and sniffed, "That matter is still undecided."

"I've decided it for you." Declan approached Stevens' desk and leaned forward on it, weight braced on his fists, invading Stevens' space and letting his teeth show a little as he said, "You've got nothing new, so you've got no grounds to keep her off work."

"If you don't mind, sir," Dr. Stevens said, straightening his cuff in an attempt to appear unconcerned by Declan's threatening behavior, even as his cheeks stained pink and his throat rolled with a dry swallow, "I can only have this conversation in the presence of my—"

"Screw your lawyer," Declan snarled, punching his fist down on the desk, sending papers fluttering. Dr. Stevens jerked backwards. "I'm the only lawyer you need to worry about. She'll be back here tomorrow," he said, "and you're not gonna give her a hard time. In fact, you'll be downright *welcoming*. Otherwise, you know what I'll do? Actually," he added, straightening up and pulling a business card from his shirt pocket, which he tossed onto Stevens' keyboard, "look me up. See what happens to people who think they can win against me."

Then, flashing a twisted smirk, he left the office, left Dr. Stevens looking alarmed, and headed home to Maggie with the certainty that he'd achieved something for her today, even if he hadn't yet been able to end her nightmare completely.

Dr. Stevens would only need to spend five minutes with Declan's name in a google search before realizing it was in his best interests to do exactly what he was told.

CHAPTER FIVE
Maggie

Maggie might've still been in a mess, she might've had some troubling doubts about her relationship with Declan, but right now, she was on cloud nine million and nothing, *nothing* was going to dent that. She half wanted to find the nearest hilltop and sing on it.

Instead, she pounced on Declan when he came through the door. "Dr. Stevens just called me," she said breathlessly, arms hooked around his neck after squeezing the life out of him with a hug.

She didn't know where he'd been for the past two hours, but right now she didn't much care. He was wearing the tired look of someone who'd been through a hard time and she didn't want that, not when her own mood had rocketed skyward.

His drawn expression split into a smile. "Really?"

"Didn't sound *too* happy about it," she said, nodding, "but it seems he's got no choice—I can go back tomorrow!"

He lifted an eyebrow. "You mean I don't get to have you waiting at home for me every day anymore? I'm not sure about this."

"Asshole," she said with a laugh, tapping his cheek. He caught her hand and kissed it.

"Congratulations," he said. "Although we knew he didn't have enough on you to extend the suspension."

"You might've been sure of it, but I definitely wasn't. For a while there, I felt like I'd lost it all."

"I know," he murmured. "But it's gonna be okay." He kissed the tip of her nose and brushed the hair off her forehead. "Give it a couple weeks and this whole thing will just be a bad memory."

"I hope you're right." God, did she hope.

"I'm always right."

She grinned at him, before leaning away from his hold and clapping her hands together. "Let's celebrate."

"What did you have in mind?"

"Dinner. Italian. Wine," she said, butterflies tickling her belly. She could hardly believe it—she was going back to work! "Well, one glass of wine. I can't go in hungover tomorrow."

"Takeout?"

"You kidding?" She laughed and shoved his shoulder. "You're taking *me* out, baby."

His eyes twinkled, gazing at her as if she was a

vision. "I've missed this version of you," he said softly, pulling her close again.

"Me too," she admitted.

This was the first time she'd felt like her old self in such a long time that she wasn't even quite sure if she could trust it, half afraid it would all rip away from her in an instant. But even those foreboding thoughts weren't enough to dent her spirits and she let out another breathless laugh, floating high on giddiness while he looked at her with sparkling eyes. "I'm gonna head home to get ready. Pick me up in an hour?"

"Hmm, just one thing first—" he said, then kissed her soundly, backed her up until she hit the wall. The breath knocked out of her, and her mind spun as he wasted no time shoving her legs apart with his thigh. She could feel the crackle in the air, the moment it turned from fervent kissing to the start of something, and nearly whimpered when he broke the kiss to press his fingers into her mouth, on her tongue, saying, "Get them wet for me," as he used his other hand to hike up the front of her dress. Then he slid his wet fingers into her panties, and she groaned.

His middle finger slipped into her, and his thumb pressed down on her clit and she was grinding against his hand all of a sudden, losing total control of herself—grinding on him and taking the assault on her mouth and whimpering in her throat as he quickly, efficiently, and expertly worked her to orgasm.

She could hardly believe it happened when it was

over, slumped against him, her whole body trembling and her mouth squished against his shoulder. She huffed a laugh.

"What the hell."

"Couldn't help myself," he murmured, stroking her back. "You're so damn *alive* right now." And then he added, mildly, "Turn around for me now," and her gut flooded with more heat.

She did as she was told—turned around on unsteady legs, leaned forward slightly, hands braced on the wall for balance as he lifted the back of her dress and pulled her dripping-wet panties to the side, fondling her pussy lips a little and sliding a finger back inside her briefly.

She heard the rustle of a condom wrapper, thrilled he now kept one in his wallet at all times, and then his cock pressed against her entrance, his hands clamping around her hips. He pushed in, releasing a groan, and she stuttered a sigh as her overstimulated nerves lit up with renewed fire.

"You're so good for me," he said, before pulling back and slamming in again. She cried out. "So warm, taking me deep…" He leaned over her, one hand coming round to palm her breast while he rocked into her, building up a breathless rhythm that had her whimpering on each thrust, pleasure building in her gut again, sending her towards the edge.

His other hand drifted down over her rounded belly and lower, into the front of her panties and finding her clit. She choked out a moan and spread her legs wider, arching her back into a low slope to angle her ass higher, take him deeper, shuddering as he pinched her swollen nub and rubbed at it, other hand plucking at her nipple through her dress and sending shockwaves of pleasure back down to her pussy.

She came with a silent cry as he suddenly increased his speed to a relentless pace and then he shoved her flat against the wall, pinned her hands up above her head, bent his knees to get that perfect angle and gave it to her hard and fast and deep, fingers still clamped on her clit and then sliding through the slick of her folds, making her convulse with overstimulation.

They didn't climax simultaneously, but it was close enough, and after they stayed squashed together against the wall, Declan's considerable weight leaning on her until she had to give an unladylike grunt and elbow him off. He chuckled breathlessly and slipped out of her, disappearing for a moment too dispose of the condom and clean up, while she righted her clothing and considered getting another shower before they headed out for their celebratory meal.

Deciding that was *exactly* what she wanted to do—and not alone, either—she practically skipped after Declan towards the bathroom, heart swelling with giddiness over how perfect everything was right now.

Until she walked in on Declan in the bathroom

and found him hurriedly shoving his phone into his pocket like he didn't want her to see who he'd just been communicating with on it.

CHAPTER SIX
Maggie

Her first day back at work, as it happened, felt just like any other. Like she hadn't been away at all. Completely anticlimactic, and she was thrilled about it. Aside from a few whispers as she passed by the resident hospital gossips, no one even mentioned her absence. It was like a collective decision had been made to let her feel as normal as possible, and all day she'd felt random rushes of affection for her colleagues, even the ones she barely knew.

She almost bumped right into Cami on her way out of the staff room, laughing as she gripped her friend by the arms to stop them from colliding in the doorway.

"Hey you!" Cami said once they'd gathered themselves. "It went good, right? Dr. Stevens didn't give you a hard time?"

"He was surprisingly…pleasant?" She couldn't believe she was saying it, but it was the truth. Dr. Stevens had been fine with her—to a point. Granted, his smile to welcome her back had been thin and clearly pained, and he'd decided against directly including her when briefing the whole team, but he hadn't been outright nasty to her at all. And while she would prefer a nicer working environment, she'd settle for bearable. "Okay, maybe not pleasant," she conceded, and they shared another laugh. "You heading home?"

"Yep." Cami bounced on her toes, eyes lighting up brighter than the stars on a clear night. "Drew's on his way back."

Maggie grimaced playfully. "You're disgusting."

"Shut up," Cami joked, whacking her on the shoulder. "Like you're not all crazy about Declan right now!"

"I'm not." She said it on instinct, and her stomach twisted with conflicting emotions. Now was not the time to bring those thoughts back to the forefront of her mind, not when right now she was feeling lighter than she had in days. Cami looked supremely disbelieving, so she added, "Really, I'm not."

"Oh, Maggie," Cami said, some of that twinkle in her eye dying as she looked at her friend with pity. "You have to let someone in. Why not him?"

It was a good question, and the fact was, she didn't have anything concrete on Declan—nothing solid to make her doubtful feelings justifiable. But that didn't change the swell of foreboding in her gut when images of his secretive behavior floated into her mind, and she found herself admitting it to Cami.

"Something doesn't feel right. I don't know, just a warning bell." She tapped her temple to indicate where a warning bell would live in her head, mouth flattening into a grim smile.

Cami stared at her for a long moment, and then said abruptly, "You know what, Drew can wait one more evening. Let's go out, okay? You and me."

The absolute last thing Maggie wanted to do was take away from Cami's happiness and excitement today. Just because her own relationship was slowly sinking beneath doubt, it didn't mean Cami's had to suffer, too. Not after everything Cami and Drew had been through to be together.

"No, God, don't be stupid," she said, giving Cami's shoulder a squeeze. "I'm fine. Really. Just a bit overwhelmed right now with everything going on." With that, she pushed a hand into her unruly hair and swept it away from her face, attempting to convey through expression alone that she was making an effort to get her shit together.

Cami looked torn, but it was obvious her desire to see Drew was strong enough to have her wavering. "You sure?"

"Definitely," Maggie said breezily, moving to brush past Cami and patting her again on the shoulder as she did. "Enjoy your night and I'll catch up with you tomorrow."

When no other protestations came, Maggie left Cami to get changed and—purse slung over her shoulder and chest full of contentment at a job well done today—she headed towards the exit.

Outside, with the wind kicking up and setting a chill across her skin, she shivered a little as she dug in her purse for her car keys. The staff parking lot was empty, and only one of the two streetlights was currently working. The rustle of leaves in the shadows made an icy tingle spread down her spine and she cursed as she couldn't quite get a grip on her keys.

"It's a shame how quickly you've fallen."

The voice in the darkness made her jump and whip around, staring into the gloom. "What?"

Emerging from the shadows like something out of a terrible horror movie, Ronald wore a smirk that made dread settle into the pit of her stomach.

"You and I split up, and a few months later you're being investigated," he said delicately, "suspended, accused…"

Maggie scowled at him, trying to appear as if he was of no consequence to her—even as her gut churned with alarm. She'd never seen that sinister look in his eyes before. "None of this has anything to do with you."

He observed her for an uncomfortably long moment, and then stepped closer, glancing at an invisible watch on his wrist. "I've told you before. You need a man's influence in your life, Maggie. Someone to guide you." He met her eye again, paused, then smiled in a way that showed his teeth, but not like a grin. Something much worse than that. "Show you where you can improve your behavior."

"Improve my behavior."

"None of this would've happened if we were still together."

"No, you're right," she said, and for one brief instant, she allowed anger to overtake her sense of self-preservation. "Because I wouldn't even have a job, would I? You wanted to make me quit." Because he might be currently exhibiting signs of instability, but she wouldn't give him the idea that she in any way agreed with his twisted ideas of a balanced relationship.

"And would it have been so bad?" he pressed. "Look at the mess you're in. Maggie, sweetheart," he said, stepping closer still, until she could see the unhinged gleam in his eye. "You need a man to take care of you." He reached out to tuck a lock of hair away from her face, and she stepped back, dodging his touch.

"Got one, thank you," she snapped at him. "Although his idea of *taking care of me* is a hell of a lot different to yours."

"You mean that lawyer?" Something that screamed danger to her flashed across his face. "What happened to not liking wealth, hmm? What happened to your *principles*?"

He was getting rapidly worked up, a tick developing in his jaw, a ruddiness appearing on his cheeks visible to her even in this shadowed light. Her heart kickstarted a panicked rhythm.

"We're done here," she said, and made to leave.

"We're done when I say we're done," he growled, grabbing her arm and yanking her back. She gasped, shock and fear colliding in her chest and seizing her lungs, while he snarled, "*Don't* you walk away from—" and then, in a chilling tone: "What's that?"

"Get your hands off me." She wrenched herself out of his hold but he kept coming, reaching for her hair now, her jacket collar, ignoring her attempts to brush him off and pulling everything to the side to expose her neck. The hickey on her neck.

The instant he recognized it for what it was, absolute outrage lit up his face. "You're coming into work with his *marks* all over you? You're not *fit* to—"

"Get off me!"

She broke away with a choked-off sob, furious with herself for allowing panic to get the better of her emotions even as she put everything into getting somewhere safe. But she'd only made it a half dozen hurried footsteps away before his hands clamped down on her again, and she found herself abruptly and violently thrown against the side of the building, Ronald's hateful face inches from her own. Her stomach plummeted as icy fingers of terror curled around her heart, and Ronald bared his teeth at her, spitting,

"I said don't you walk away from me, you filthy—"

"Hey!" a new voice bellowed, and Ronald's eyes went wide in the instant before he was unceremoniously flung backwards, away from Maggie, revealing Declan, beautiful Declan, wearing an expression of fury, his chest heaving with labored breaths, wide shoulders rising and falling. He was looking at Ronald like he was moments away from ripping his throat out, and when he spoke, his voice came out strangled and full of venom. "You put your hands on her again," he said, stepping up to a now-panicked Ronald, getting right in his face, "and I will *end* you."

Maggie peeled herself away from the wall, observing the situation, feeling as if one sudden move would make Declan attack, like he was a wolf with its hackles up. "Declan."

"Am I making myself clear?" Declan pressed, speaking through gritted teeth, his hands curled into tight fists by his side—radiating, with total intensity, the barely controlled rage of a caged animal. Ronald, for his part, could only nod, his eyes still wide, arms up in front of himself for protection. "If I find out you've been anywhere near her—"

Declan stepped forward, directly into Ronald's space, and Maggie couldn't stand by and watch Declan commit an act they'd all regret—not for her. Not because of *Ronald*.

"Declan! He's got the message," she said, gingerly approaching him, putting a hand on his arm.

"You've scared him. Come on…"

It felt like forever, waiting…waiting for Declan to tear his eyes away from a cowering Ronald and look at her. When he finally did, when he took in the sight of her and lifted a shaking hand to touch her cheek, she took the opportunity to glance at Ronald and nod. Ronald took his cue and scurried away like an alley rat.

"Are you okay?" Declan muttered. He was still shaking. His chest still heaved with breaths of anger. He was still, despite the calming of the situation, full of that same fire that almost had him ripping Ronald to pieces. It scared Maggie to see him like this.

Scared her, and aroused her.

"Yes, I'm fine," she said. "What're you doing here?"

It was like he hadn't quite come back into himself yet—eyes glassy, fingers trailing over her skin, a heat emanating from him that made her want to hug him tight almost as much as it made her panties wet.

"Did he hurt you?"

"*No*," she said vehemently, not wanting to incite that fury again. Ronald wouldn't be far enough away yet. "He's just a creep. Are—are *you* okay? You're shaking."

She'd apparently failed, because something about her question made fire spark in his eyes again and he looked over his shoulder, staring out into the shadows of the night, jaw tense. "I'll kill him."

She swallowed thickly and said, "Come on," taking him by the arm and making an attempt at steering him away. "Where's your car?" She'd intended on driving her own car home tonight, but that seemed highly insignificant now. She'd get a cab back here, pick it up later, after she'd taken Declan back to his penthouse and made him forget he wanted to murder her ex-boyfriend. One who, while not exactly normal, had never really shown signs of violence or instability until this evening. She shuddered as she remembered the look in his eyes.

"My driver brought me. I wanted to surprise you with reservations…"

"I'm surprised," she said. "Very surprised. Let's go."

Once they settled in the limo—stretch, the kind she hadn't set foot in for many years—she expected Declan to calm down. But while he no longer looked moments away from exploding, his face suggested he was still imagining all the ways he could teach Ronald a painful lesson.

"Tell me if he gives you any more trouble, okay?" he said, fingers twitchy, breathing deeply as he looked her hard in the eye, searching out her promise.

"I will," she said. "Look at me." She took his face in her hands, ran her thumbs over the tight lines around his mouth, felt his feverish skin and shifted closer, wanting to cover herself in some of that heat—cover herself in this man. Her groin was tingling, the adrenaline of the situation shifting into arousal. He'd been so *animalistic.*

"He won't touch me again," she continued, and then, shifting closer still, she lifted his tense hand and pressed it flat against the center of her chest. "You're the only man who gets to put his hand on me from now on."

His hand drifted lower until the heel settled on her flushed cleavage and he swallowed thickly, the roll of his throat slow and glistening with sweat, his eyes darkening as he tangled his other hand in her hair, dragging her head back to expose her neck. She gasped, parted her lips.

"I'd never hurt you," he said, dipping close like he wanted to breathe her in.

"I know." Her legs drifted open, her heart hammering against her ribs. She knew he wouldn't hurt her, but she wanted to see him take some of that power he used to warn off Ronald and *ruin* her with it. "I didn't mean that."

"Show me," he said, hand fisting in her hair. "Show me how you want me to touch you."

The limo jolted into motion as her breath faltered in her throat, and she had half a mind to refuse him, or at least ask to wait until they were somewhere more private. But the electricity lighting her veins at the sight of the veiled desperation in his eyes made her bite her lip and glance at the partition, check the driver didn't have a view.

Then she captured Declan's gaze again, slowly trailed her fingers up her own torso—pushed her jacket aside and thumbed open the top buttons of her blouse, tugged down a bra cup to expose her breast and dragged his hand over to cover it.

"Like this," she whispered as his jaw went tight, as he clenched his fingers on her breast and moved to circle her nipple with his thumb. "This," she added, and feeling bold, feeling so painfully aroused, she dragged him in by his tie, arched her back, and guided his mouth to her breast.

He released her hair, splayed both hands around her ribs, breathing a muted sound of relief in the instant before he closed his teeth around her pebbled nipple, then his lips, sucking as he flicked his tongue over the sensitive peak and her pussy clenched, *Jesus*, her clit throbbing.

"Declan," she muttered, eyes fluttering shut. He hummed around her nipple in response and her legs drifted open even further, straining her skirt around her thighs and offering him an invitation, everything within her screaming at him to take it.

And he did—pressed his face between both breasts, pushing them together with his hands so he could breathe her in, thumbs plucking her nipples, and then he slipped onto the wide expanse of the limo floor between her spread thighs, straightened up to look her in the eye, his hair in disarray and his eyes blazing. Then he gripped her by the swell of her buttocks and yanked her forward until she sat right on the edge of the seat, shoved her skirt up her hips and then, in one teeth-gritted move that was almost primal, tore away her panties. She cried out, her pussy flooding with her arousal, reached for him to pull him in for a kiss but he resisted. Pressed a hand to the base of her throat and pushed her back, the look in his eye telling her she better not move.

"No one else gets to touch this," he said, growled almost, as he dragged a thumb through her slick folds, pressing hard on her clit. She hissed, back arching high, exposed breasts pushing out and she grabbed them, tugged on her own nipples, a torturous distraction as he played with her pussy, teasing her, pinching her clit and spreading her folds and getting his fingers wet with her juices. "You hear me? I'm the only one who gets to make you feel like this. D'you want to come?"

"Yes," she gasped, hips rolling with his continued assault.

He hummed under his breath, tilting his head to get a good look at her throbbing pussy. "Hmm, not yet," he said, then he spread her thighs painfully wide and hunched over to bury his face in her wet folds.

She bit off a scream, fingers clamping down on her handfuls of breast, eyes rolling back in her head as he attacked her clit with tongue and lips, relentlessly, blissfully aggressive, making her see stars and sending her hurtling towards the brink, so overwhelmed with pleasure that she couldn't even speak—just broken moans and gasps of panting breath, until she hung on the edge, desperate to tip over, and he abruptly pulled away.

"God, please—"

"Shh," he said, stuffing two fingers in her twitching hole as he wiped the back of his other hand across his mouth. He fingered her for a moment, thumb pressing on her clit, watching the perfect agony pass over her face. Then he lifted her legs and pushed her knees back against her chest and took her swollen nub back into his mouth, sucking on it quick and without pause until she was shuddering, her pussy spasming, a scream caught in her chest and her toes curling.

She could barely see straight when he let go, put one knee on the seat beside her hip, released his cock, and stroked it rough and desperate, enough time for her to drag in a labored breath or two before he came across her bare breasts, painting them white and making her moan his name in exquisite satisfaction.

She felt so blissfully good in that moment, elevated high on pleasure and intimacy, that she didn't understand why, in the exact instant Declan pulled her in for a kiss, her throat seized up with apprehension and made her choke down the urge to run away.

* * *

IT WAS TOO MUCH. ALL of it. From her sick brother to the investigation and Dr. Stevens, Ronald's newfound maliciousness and the dark side of Declan—everything piling up on her all at once and it didn't help that she was falling in love amongst it all, that all of her feelings of doubt and fear and dread about everything in her life warred with the emotional weight of developing love.

And she couldn't help thinking that she was setting herself up for a fall, lining up the pieces for the game Declan couldn't help but play. Because that was what he was. A player. She knew it, and Grant had warned her, and still she'd jumped head first into this *thing* with him, the thing that was growing too big for her to handle. There was every chance he couldn't change his ways, no matter how hard he tried. She didn't want to be an experiment.

But he looked at her with such sincerity. His voice, when he spoke to her in their intimate, private moments, was full of affection. She felt it from him, whenever he touched her—that intangible thing that said this wasn't just a game to him.

Whatever was between them, it was *big*.

And she wasn't ready.

CHAPTER SEVEN
Declan

In the days following the Ronald event—or, as Declan liked to put it: that time he nearly beat the shit out of a slimy little creep—things were tense. Maggie spent more time at her own place than with him and he wasn't sure what to make of it—if she was just seeking space enough to clear her head, or if she was distancing herself from him. He knew he'd lost his temper with that bastard ex of hers, but how else would anyone expect him to react to seeing a man assault a woman—any woman, let alone Declan's girlfriend.

And Maggie was his girlfriend, at least in his eyes. He had no intention of seeing anyone else, and wanted nothing more than to come home to the welcoming sight of her beautiful face every day for the rest of his life. Trouble was, she seemed to be pulling in the opposite direction.

There was no movement on the Grant thing—at

least as far as he knew. He was quickly losing patience with his old friend, although he was torn on how to handle it. A massive part of him wanted to tell Maggie everything; he was already full of guilt at how long he'd kept quiet.

On the other hand, he was desperate to give his friend a chance. Surely, beneath the addiction, underneath all that mess, there was some decency left within Grant strong enough to make him do the right thing? It was a hope to which Declan clung with determination. There was no way Grant Emerson wouldn't come through in the end. He was too much of a good man. Maybe he just needed a little extra time to find the courage. And Declan would give it to him, but not for much longer. He couldn't let Maggie continue thinking her career was in danger.

Just like their relationship.

He could feel it, how she was pulling away from him. Returning his calls less and less, only spending one night at his in the past few days. He saw her yesterday, but he already missed her terribly.

Sick of the uncertainty, he did the only thing that made sense: he went to see her, bouquet of roses in hand and a hopeful smile on his face as she answered the door.

She was wearing threadbare pajamas with little penguins on, her wild hair piled up on top of her head, big fuzzy socks pulled up to her knees, and not a single lick of makeup. She was, in that moment, the most beautiful thing he'd ever seen. The breath punched out of him.

Her smile was tight, a little bit apologetic. "Hello," she said, her eyes glittering.

"Hi." He held out the flowers. "For you."

She took them, although the smile dimmed a little. "I thought I said I'd see you on Friday."

"I know. Hear me out. You're not working tomorrow, are you?"

She hesitated. And then, slowly: "No…"

"I've got a cabin, a couple hours away. It's in a real pretty spot. Lots of trees." He rearranged his face into something he hoped conveyed how much her agreement would mean to him. "I can have you home early Friday morning?"

She lifted an eyebrow. "You want to take me to some secluded cabin in the woods?"

"No murder, promise," he said, lifting his hands, and shared a laugh with her. He watched, with his heart leaping into his throat, as her expression softened. She brought the flowers to her nose, smelled them, glancing up at him through her lashes.

Thirty minutes later, they sat together in the back of the limo, Declan wishing he could've had the foresight to take a different car—this was the very seat they'd put to use after the Ronald incident, the day everything started going intangibly wrong for them.

The silence in the car was thick with tension, so bad that Declan was beginning to wonder why she'd agreed to come on this little trip with him at all. And then she turned to him abruptly and said, "Look—" just as he said, "Maggie, listen—" and they stopped, laughed, the tension easing a little.

"I was just going to say," Maggie continued, "that I know I've been a bit off with you. It's not—there's no particular reason for it. I just...I don't know if I trust this. Trust *you*. And then you were so aggressive to Ronald, and it was fine, I mean—I'm glad you showed up when you did. But I'd never seen you so angry before and...I don't know. It threw me. And on top of everything else, with work and Grant and all the things weighing me down right now, I guess—I guess I just couldn't be *here*, you know? In the moment. With you." She stopped, blew out a breath. "I needed a break." She grimaced, her makeup-free face scrunching up adorably, and added, "I'm sorry."

He wanted to hug her, squeeze her tight, tell her everything was fine, that he understood. But he was stuck on one thing in her tumble of words, and his heart thudded painfully behind his ribs. *I don't know if I trust this.* She wasn't sure of him, of what they had. She was *scared*.

He took her hand, swiped his thumb over her knuckles. "This trip is gonna be exactly what you need," he said, and made a silent vow to remove that fear she had for them.

He started with the journey. Two hours sitting in the back of a limo, nothing to distract them but their own thoughts—and he knew how dangerous that could be. He asked the driver to put the radio on and settled in close to her, asking her questions about her job and her friends, getting her to talk, to relax, a conversation they carried all the way up to the cabin.

She already seemed lighter when they stepped out of the limo, and her eyes lit up as she took in the sight of the cabin—all polished wood and wraparound porch, situated in a secluded woodland clearing like something straight out of a picture book.

"Declan, this is beautiful," she said breathlessly, gazing at the ivy, the white shutters. He smiled, thought, *You put it to shame*, and led her inside.

After putting their things in the bedroom and giving her a brief tour, he took advantage of the last drop of sunlight and took her for a walk around the surrounding pathways, held her hand and talked to her about his memories coming here as a kid, how he'd brought Grant here once, the two of them climbing trees and chasing badgers. Talk of her brother dulled her sparkle a little so he quickly changed the subject, tucked his arm around her shoulders and kissed her temple, reminded her of better times.

That evening they ate soup with warmed bread and drank wine by the fire, and she kissed him in the light of the dying embers and removed his clothes, and then her own, the amber glow highlighting every swell and curve of her body, making him want to kiss every inch.

She let him—laid back on the hearth rug with a pleasurable sigh, arms resting above her head, body splayed out entirely unselfconsciously, and he hoped she looked in the mirror and saw the perfection he beheld right now, because he hardly believed something could be so beautiful. For an age, he kissed her, trailed his lips and tongue across hips, thighs, stomach, breasts. Kissed her until her skin glimmered with a rosy flush, until her breath escaped her in broken stutters, her fingers twisting in the fibers of the rug and her legs drifting open, the scent of her arousal kickstarting his own urgency.

They made love for an hour, warmly and without hurry, learning each other in a way they hadn't yet taken the time to do. He whispered words of sentimental nonsense and kissed her plush lips and buried his face in her breast, held on tight as wave after wave of climax crashed through him, her orgasmic gasps lighting him up on the inside.

After relocating to the bed, they slept until dawn, tangled up together and waking up once to pull each other close again and touch until they trembled. Morning came bright and Maggie's smile beamed brighter, and Declan looked at her over the breakfast bar and thought with sudden clarity, *Careful, buddy, or she'll have your whole heart.* But he didn't want to be careful. He didn't want to give her anything less than everything.

He took the old Jag out of the garage and fired it

up, surprised at the life that roared through it, and he and Maggie spent the day in the small neighboring town, whiling away hours in the quaint book store and tea shop and a cozy dress boutique. He wanted to buy her the lacy number he caught her eyeing up but she wouldn't allow it, suggesting he buy her lunch instead. They took it late at a quirky café that sold tea on saucers and gave cake for free, and by the time they encouraged the old, stalling Jag back up to the cabin, the sun had set and Maggie was breathless with laughter.

After cracking open another bottle of wine, Declan dug out an ancient TV/DVD combo from a closet in the back bedroom, found a stash of movies in a box behind it, and that evening they watched *The Holiday* and *Notting Hill* on the creaky sofa in front of the fire, Declan spending half the time wondering who the hell brought these DVDs to his cabin, and the other half wondering how he got so lucky to have Maggie Emerson curled against his side right now.

When Maggie became more yawn than alertness, her eyes pushing shut, he carried her to bed and kissed her goodnight, tucked her in tight and headed back into the living room, grabbed his phone and called Grant. He didn't answer, but he had voice mail.

"I'm not waiting any longer," Declan said quietly. "I can't lie to her anymore. You've got until the end of this week." He paused, and then added, "Don't let me down."

Then he went to bed and held her all night.

The limo arrived early the next morning, before the sun had truly risen, and the journey back was quiet but comfortable. Once back in the city, he stepped out to walk her to her door, dropped her bag in her hall, and kissed her on the doorstep.

"Thank you," she said, smiling up at him, arms around his neck. "This was exactly what I needed."

He kissed the tip of her nose. "Will you come over tonight?" he asked her, and waited with breathless anticipation for her response. Her answer now would determine how successful this little mini-break had really been—if he was back in her affections, or if she planned to distance herself again.

"I can't," she said, and his heart sank to his shoes. But then she added, "I'm working a double shift. I can come tomorrow—spend the weekend?" And he could've powered all fifty states with the elation that rushed through him.

"I'll look forward to it," he murmured, kissing her again, and then again when heat overtook them. They were moments away from committing a public indecency crime when she broke away gasping, laughing, pushing at him and telling him to *get out of here*.

Declan stopped off at Grant's on the way to the office, but got no response. Sam the doorman said he hadn't seen him in a few days, and worry coiled in Declan's gut. Empty apartment, unanswered calls... No drugs had gone missing since before Maggie's suspension, which meant Declan was getting them elsewhere. Or worse—he wasn't getting them from anywhere, and the withdrawal had him knocked out and on the brink somewhere.

Declan had no fucking idea what to do. He *needed* Grant to come clean himself—a confession would limit the legal consequences, and there was a chance they could all put this whole sorry mess behind them before the year's end. The longer Grant stayed in the dark, left Maggie under suspicion, the worse he would make things for himself.

The warm glow of the mini-break fading under the weight of his concern, Declan pounded the treadmill that night, shoved on headphones and cranked up the music and ran and ran and ran, until his mind washed clear of everything except pleasurable exhaustion.

But still he felt amped up, unable to settle, and he eyed the weight benches on the far side of the gym, considering how much usable energy he had left in him.

"You feel like a little competition?" a voice said behind him after he switched off his music, and he turned with a smile on his face.

"Trixie." She wore figure-flattering gym gear and all of her makeup, a towel over her shoulder and a bottle of water in hand. She'd caught the eye of most men currently working out in the room, and some of the women, and Declan understood it. Because she was stunning—slim, tall, blonde, perfectly made up. But he'd never really seen her that way, aside from one disastrous date a million years ago when they first met. Comparing Trixie's aesthetic perfection now to Maggie's soft-figured, makeup-free, wild-haired company these past couple days, and it was easy to figure out what he preferred. It wasn't even a close finish.

Still, Trixie was beautiful to him in other ways—her kindness, her compassion, her wicked sense of humor. She was one of his best friends, and even though Maggie had gotten the wrong idea about them, he wasn't going to cut Trixie out of his life. He hoped, one day, that the two women might become friends.

He hugged Trixie now, sweat and all, laughing as she squealed in disgust and pushed him away.

"You *stink*," she told him, wrinkling her nose. "How long have you been here?"

He shrugged, rubbing his hair with a towel. "An hour, maybe. I hit it pretty hard."

"Yeah?" Eyebrow quirked, she looked at him with an expression of concern. "Everything okay?"

He could tell her—about Maggie, Grant, his conflict over the whole thing. She would keep it to herself, there was no doubt about that. He could tell her he'd murdered someone, and her only response would be to help hide the body.

And yet, he hesitated. Trixie knew of the Emersons. Everyone did. Which meant she wouldn't be hearing a story about some stranger. She would discover that Grant Emerson was a thief and an addict, that Maggie Emerson was currently being investigated by the police, and tomorrow she'd have lunch at the club with Mrs. Emerson, unable to say anything. It wasn't fair to anyone—to Grant and Maggie for telling their secrets, and to Trixie for putting her in that position.

So he smiled and said, "Yeah, just a long week at work. You want a spot?"

"You got time?"

"Always, for you," he said, hooking an arm around her neck and yanking her in close again as he steered them towards the weight benches. She yelled at him and he laughed, and behind the cheerful veneer, his stomach churned with foreboding.

Time was running out. He could feel it.

CHAPTER EIGHT
Maggie

Working a double shift had its downsides, but the worst by far was not having time to get a proper dinner. Maggie was definitely not someone who could go hours without food, so she grabbed the thirty minutes between shifts and headed down to the cafeteria, determined to inhale a sandwich at least.

She met Ashley there, who'd taken up residence in the corner, slumped over the table with the world's largest coffee clasped between both hands.

"These night shifts are killing me," she groaned, before sitting up and scrubbing a hand over her bare face. "I just can't sleep during the day no matter how tired I am."

"What time are you on till?"

"Eight A.M."

Maggie checked her watch and winced. It was

only seven P.M. now—Ashley had a whole thirteen hours before she could collapse back in bed. And then she'd lie there unable to sleep, like she'd probably done all of today, before rolling into work now with enough coffee to power a regular person for a week.

"I can cover you," Maggie said, "if you want to skip tonight."

Ashley responded through a yawn. "Nah, it's okay. I've only got two more and then I'm back on days. How are you doing?" she added, running a fingertip over a watery eye and gazing at Maggie. "Declan treating you good?"

Smiling, Maggie told her all about their little break these past couple days, leaving no detail private. Ashley raised a hand to stop her, a grimace twisting her lovely face.

"Stop, I'm too single for this," she said, looking queasy. "I swear, between you and Cami—"

"Let me set you up. I bet I can find a man or two willing to take a chance."

Ashley snorted. "I'd rather die alone, surrounded by cats. But thanks," she added dryly, getting to her feet. "Nice to know you also think I'm a hopeless case."

"I didn't mean that!"

"Hush," said Ashley. "Drink this coffee. I'm gonna vibrate into the next dimension if I have any more."

Sadly, Maggie didn't have time to sit and leisurely drink Ashley's secondhand, rapidly cooling coffee.

Twenty minutes of her thirty-minute break had already gone, and she hadn't yet even opened her sandwich packet. Sighing, she stood and wandered off in Ashley's wake, the two of them heading in different directions upstairs as Ashley went off to get changed into her uniform, and Maggie took her sandwich and cold coffee to the break room.

She's only made it partway through one half of her sandwich when the door opened and Ronald entered, making her freeze mid-chew, her whole body snapping taut with wary alertness. She hadn't seen him since the incident in the parking lot earlier in the week, and she had no idea how he'd react now.

But rather than bring up the incident, he smiled sort of sharply and gestured at the ancient coffee machine. "Just getting some fuel."

"Okay..." she said around her mouthful, and then swallowed it down thickly. The room felt charged, the air crackling, Ronald's every step and every breath as he approached the coffee machine deafening in the thick silence.

He glanced down at her as he switched on the machine, and then at her half-eaten sandwich.

"Do you really think that was the best choice?" he asked her, and then sniffed with apparent disinterest and turned back to the coffee machine.

Glancing at her sandwich in confusion, she said, quite eloquently, "What?"

"I just mean, you know, with your weight problem

and all." He said *weight problem* delicately, like it was a sensitive subject, and he was making a mockery out of not wanting to offend her.

Maggie cleared her throat, trying to ignore the white noise filling her ears. "My weight problem?"

"Yes," he said casually. "You really shouldn't eat bread, or..." He squinted at her sandwich. "Is that mayonnaise?"

"Yep." She flopped the sandwich down onto the paper and brushed off her hands. "Tell me more about my weight problem, Ronald," she said, standing up. "I'd really love to know your opinion on it."

"Hey, don't get angry." He raised his hands in a placating gesture. "I'm just being a doctor here. You do know I'm a doctor, don't you?"

"Of course, I know." What kind of question was that?

"I mean, I wouldn't blame you for getting confused—you do get paid more than me right now, after all." He snorted, reached for a coffee mug on the shelf. "A nurse earning more than a doctor," he added in a mutter, his voice dripping with bitterness.

"You're a resident," she pointed out.

His response spilled out of him like he'd been bottling it up for a long time. "Doesn't matter," he snarled, turning to stare at her again, his face darkening with that same dangerous glint he'd worn the other evening. Maggie's stomach swooped. "You're a nurse and you're a woman and now you're a *thief*. In what *universe* does that entitle you to more money than me?" He prowled closer, his jaw clenching in random anger, and Maggie could only back up, not make any sudden movements—get to the door before he had chance to twist his rage back on her again.

This man was shockingly unstable, and she couldn't believe she hadn't seen it before—that he'd managed to hide it so well when they dated, right up until the end, when his views on women in the workplace started coming to the surface and setting off alarm bells.

"And you're a goddamn *mess*," he continued, furious with her, completely unfathomably. "You won't get in shape and you drink too much coffee and as for how you conduct yourself with men—"

"What's that supposed to mean?" she snapped at him, forgetting her fear for the moment. She hit the wall behind and started feeling for the door, keeping him firmly in her sights.

"You're a whore," he said bluntly, scathingly. And then suddenly he was too close; she could smell his breath on her face, the heat of his body. For a heart-stopping instant, she was paralyzed. "There's only one way to treat a whore."

"Ronald, think about what you're doing—"

He reached for her, hand outstretched. She batted him away. Undeterred, he tried to grab her arms, and she shoved his chest. When she turned to get away, he pushed her flat against the wall, forcing the breath out of her lungs as he pressed in close behind. Then he murmured, "There's no one here to save you this time," and slithered a hand around her waist, beneath the hem of her shirt.

At the first brush of his touch, she sucked the air back into her lungs and flung her head backwards, making contact with Ronald's face, a sickening *crunch* reverberating around the room, joined immediately by Ronald's cry.

When she turned, she found him hunched over, holding his face, blood gushing through his fingers as he whimpered.

She didn't pause for his retaliation. Racing out of the room with her heart in her throat, she sprinted her way down the corridor, away from the break room, desperately trying to keep a lid on her emotions as she rounded the corner and ran smack into Ashley.

"Woah—hey! What—"

"I have to go," Maggie gasped. "I can't explain but I—I need you to cover for me with Stevens—"

"Okay." Ashley didn't pose a question, a demand for an explanation. Her eyes were deep with concern and she nodded. "I'll call you tonight," she said, the only indication that she didn't plan on letting Maggie keep silent about it. "Go."

Maggie went, didn't even stop to get changed. Just made sure her car keys were in her pocket and booked it out of there. A few minutes later, she found herself pulling up outside Declan's building without any awareness of having made the decision to go there.

His face lit up with total surprise when he opened the door to find her standing there.

"I thought I wasn't seeing you until tomor—"

She rushed forward and buried herself in his chest, clinging on to the front of his shirt and squeezing her eyes shut. *Just hold me,* she thought, unable to speak, and somehow he understood her, because his arms came up to envelope her in safety and, for the first time since she'd felt Ronald's touch against the bare skin beneath her shirt, the steel band around her chest eased and she drew in a calm breath.

CHAPTER NINE
Maggie

Minutes later, rubbing her back, Declan murmured, "What happened?" in a voice full of compassion.

Maggie sniffed and pulled back a little. "Nothing."

"Maggie."

Declan's tone had switched from compassion to intolerance in the space of one heartbeat, as if he'd anticipated her attempts at keeping quiet. But it appeared he wasn't going to stand for her brushing him off, not when she'd flung herself at him so emotionally.

Truth was, after Ronald in the break room, she'd just wanted to go somewhere she felt safe. And there was nowhere safer to her than Declan's arms. She would have to accept it at some point—she loved him, and she needed him. No amount of denial could squash down the swelling of her heart.

And she couldn't lie to him, either. Not when he looked at her so intently, so full of concern.

"It's Ronald," she mumbled, and predictably, his whole body stiffened, his arms around her tightening, his eye glinting in the low light of his expensive lamps.

"What about him?" It was remarkable, really, how he could speak through such clenched teeth.

With a shuddery sigh, Maggie uttered the one thought that had raced around her brain the entire journey over here. "He's the one framing me for the drugs."

It was all so clear to her now, because who else could it be? Dr. Stevens' investigation had stalled—and if it had been him, surely he would've planted more evidence to move things along?

No one else at the hospital was bothered by her.

She certainly wasn't taking the drugs.

So who did that leave? Ronald Mitchell, a man she'd mostly felt sorry for all this time, convinced he was inherently good, if massively misguided in his views on women. He'd never treated her badly during their brief relationship. Their dates were enjoyable, the conversations sparkling. Even their intimate moments, when they eventually began, felt warm and inviting. He was the perfect doctor boyfriend every mother wanted for her daughter.

Until things started feeling a little bit too serious, and he began making noises about her quitting her job. "You'd have so much less to worry about," he would tell her. "You can focus on our home, make more time for hobbies… You mentioned how much you wanted to learn how to cook more exotic dishes, didn't you? Move in with me and hand in your notice at work, and I'll look after you. Home is the best place for a woman…"

It didn't take her long to say goodbye to *that* proposition, and while things certainly soured between them at work, he was never malicious.

Not until now, after she'd returned to work following her suspension. And the reason for it was startlingly clear.

His plan hadn't worked. He wanted to punish her for walking away from him, but all she received was a week-long suspension before being allowed back to work. And the failure of it all had tripped that twisted part of his brain he'd managed to conceal until now. Seeing her back in her uniform, defiantly going against everything he wanted, had made him crazy.

He'd shown his hand.

Declan stared at her, his face washed off all emotion. Suddenly he was impossible to read. "He's what?" he said with an odd, indecipherable note to his voice.

Maggie nodded. "I'm sure of it." Then she sighed again and pulled out of his hold, buried a hand in her hair. "I'll have to call Detective Sanders," she added, feeling very strange. Part of her was still reeling from the event in the break room; and yet, she felt weirdly light. As if the black clouds had cleared, and suddenly everything was brighter.

"I'll do it now before I lose my nerve," she muttered, mostly to herself, pulling her phone from her pocket.

Declan's hand landed on hers, stalling her. "Uh," he said, blinking an odd look out of his eyes. She frowned at him. "Just breathe for a minute. Why don't we sit down and you can tell me—"

"I have to do it, Declan," she said, and she couldn't work out why he was so hesitant. Shouldn't he be glad to know she had found the guy responsible? "I've got to at least report him for the attack. I mean, how many more times am I gonna let it happen before I—"

It was like a crack of lightning flashed through his eyes, and his hand tightened on hers, almost making her drop the phone.

"What?"

Instantly, she realized her mistake. She'd never intended on telling Declan what had happened today, knew how much it would rile him up—but she'd let it slip now, the fact that there'd been more than one occasion, and she winced.

"Don't worry about it," she said, but he raised a hand to halt her.

Very precisely, the words chipping out of him, he said, "What did he do, Maggie?"

With apprehension swirling in her gut, Maggie told him, briefly and without much detail. She left out the part about how he'd touched the bare skin of her waist, convinced it would be the one detail to turn Declan into a murderer. Instead she focused on how he'd insulted her weight, and then her character, and ended up getting a little forceful as she'd tried to leave.

"Because he's furious," she said, as Declan stood stoically still, jaw tighter than a vice. "His plan failed and now he's lashing out at me. Do you see it?" She so desperately needed him to see it, if only to distract him from the red flood of rage she knew was currently rushing through his mind.

Declan left her words lingering in the air, and then said in the darkest voice she'd ever heard from him, "Where is he now?"

"No." She put her hands on his chest, gripped his shirt a little. "No, you're not going to do that. Look at me."

He did, but with unseeing eyes.

"Declan. I'm fine. Okay? He hasn't hurt me. In fact, he's *freed* me. Don't you understand that?" She tugged on his shirt. "This is a good thing."

His throat rolled with a very thick swallow, and it was painfully clear how hard he was working to push through his murderous thoughts and find the thread of her logic. "Don't call Sanders yet," he said tightly. He reached up and took hold of her hands on his chest. His own hands were shaking. "Let's sleep on it, get your thoughts together. And then tomorrow we'll go to the station; I'll be there as your lawyer."

She couldn't help but think there was a lot more to his suggestion than he was letting on, but right now she was so relieved that she'd managed to pull him back from the brink of violence towards Ronald that she was willing to go along with it. Either way, it didn't matter. Tomorrow this would all be over.

The only thing putting the slightest dent in her certainty was the troubled look in Declan's eyes.

* * *

She awoke with a throat dryer than the Sahara and edged out of the bed, careful not to jostle it too much and disturb Declan. He looked completely passed out, even snoring a little, mouth hanging open and arms flinging above his head, completely at ease in his deep sleep. She couldn't help but smile, forgetting her worries for a moment and taking the time to look at him, just look, and appreciate how the sight of him made her feel. Warm, protected…in love.

In the dead of night, with silence all around her, it was easy to think of love and not freak out. It was like she was surrounded by a dreamlike little bubble, that her thoughts could remain abstract, everything a little hazy and unreal. She could be in love with Declan Archibald at three in the morning while he slept. It was safe.

She tiptoed to the kitchen and filled a glass with water, standing silently against the counter and drinking her fill, quite at peace with the world. It was like a small weight had been lifted off her shoulders—the nightmare not over yet, but she had a lead now, something she could go on to get this all over with. Ronald Mitchell would not be ruining her life for much longer.

Satisfied, she put the glass in the sink and headed towards the bedroom, pausing when she saw a flash of light coming from somewhere in the living room. It turned out to be Declan's phone, left on the coffee table, and it was flashing a voice mail message. She didn't recognize the number—somewhere international, probably a client of his.

But she did recognize the name attached to the text message beneath it, one that had arrived early in the evening. It remained unread, because Declan had spent the evening in bed with Maggie. Made love to Maggie while *Trixie Lane* sent him a text message that couldn't be any clearer if a neon light appeared in the room, blaring "Declan's cheating on you!"

The message highlighted on the screen. There for her to see without pressing a single button, was like a sledgehammer to the chest:

I'm still aching from last night. You still know how to hit that spot so good. ;) Call me later, stud.

And just like that, in the space of a phone screen at three in the morning, Maggie's whole world tipped up beneath her feet.

CHAPTER TEN
Declan

The sunlight spilling across Declan's face, escaping through blinds left open last night, roused him from sleep. He kept his eyes shut for a moment and yawned, stretching his back, and then turned over to wake up Maggie in the best way possible.

She wasn't there.

Frowning in mild confusion, he checked the time. Surely she wouldn't be up already, so early on a weekend? Maybe she'd just gone to the bathroom, and he lay there a while, waiting, drifting in and out of a doze.

When he eventually realized he'd not heard a sound since waking up, he blinked some sleep out of his eyes and pushed himself out of bed, padding naked down the hall, checking every room.

She wasn't just missing from his bed—she'd disappeared from his entire apartment. Even her shoes were gone.

He looked around for a note, for some sign that she'd had to slip out early, but she'd told him she would spend the whole weekend with him, didn't she? That must've meant she had no other plans, so unless an emergency had come up…

Swallowing down a rise of mild concern, he located his phone and lit up the screen, intent on checking to see if she'd left him a text message or a voice mail, letting him know what had called her away. Whatever it was, he wanted to help.

She hadn't left him a message, but Trixie had, and it took Declan the whole of half a second to figure out what had happened.

Maggie had seen this message somehow and immediately thought the worst.

Which he couldn't blame her for—this message from Trixie was all sorts of shady. She was referring to their session at the gym, of course, in her usual overly friendly way, but Maggie wouldn't know that—and Trixie was already a sore subject for them.

"Shit," he said to the empty room, before rushing back to his bedroom for some pants. "Fuck." He couldn't deal with this naked.

Shit. This was a disaster. After everything, the last thing Maggie needed was to feel as if all her previous reservations about him were true, that she should've trusted her instincts. She'd said it to him, back at the wedding—told him he had a reputation for this. And he *did*, he was the first one to admit that, but not now—not since Maggie Emerson came into his life. Not since he fell in love.

All of his calls went straight to her voice mail and he left multiple messages throughout the morning, increasingly desperate after heading to her place and finding her missing from there, too.

"No, I haven't seen her," Drew told him when he called, thinking perhaps she'd gone to Cami for comfort. "Cami and I are just heading out to this family thing—"

"No worries, thanks," Declan said, hanging up, sitting in his idling car in the street by Maggie's apartment, casting about for some idea of what to do.

He called Grant, got no response there either, and then called the hospital. "She's not working today," said the woman on the other end of the line. "Scheduled for Monday."

He didn't know what else to do, short of calling her family. But he was pretty sure she wouldn't have gone to them, and he was certain that she'd be absolutely furious to hear he'd brought them into their business. Her mother maybe, but if her aunts got wind of this…

"*Think*," he snapped at himself, thumping his forehead on the steering wheel. Who else was she close to?

The girls.

It was never just Cami, whenever Maggie went out. It was always "the girls". Cami and…

Ashley!

Jesus, he should've thought of her before. Of course, she worked at the hospital too, and she was friends with Cami—Declan had met her a few times at Drew's various functions. It made sense that Maggie was a part of that little group, too. Only problem was, Declan didn't have her number.

He called Drew again.

"I need to speak to Cami," he said, wasting no time.

"Ah, we're just getting in the car, buddy…running late…"

"Please," he said through clenched teeth, and he heard Cami in the background enquiring about the call.

"Declan Archibald," Drew muttered to her, and the next second there was a bit of a rustle, before Cami's sweet voice came through the line.

"Declan? Is Maggie okay?"

"I…yeah. I need Ashley's number."

"Ashley? Hold *on*, Drew. Let me just—" There was a pause, and when Cami next spoke, her voice had a slight echo, liked she'd slipped into an empty room. "What do you want with Ashley?"

He pressed a fist to the center of his forehead, screwing up his eyes. Considered lying, but knew any lie right now would come back to bite him on the ass. After blowing out a breath of composure, he said, "Maggie and I have had a…misunderstanding. And I think she's with Ashley now."

"A misunderstanding."

With a resigned sigh, he said flatly, "She thinks I've cheated on her."

"Have you?" The response came at once, arched and sharp.

"No! Jesus. Like I said, it's a misunderstanding. And I'd really like to get it straightened out."

Cami hesitated. "I mean…if she wanted to speak to you, then she would. Right?"

Loyal until the end. Declan laughed mirthlessly.

"Please," he said, entirely without shame. "I'll beg if I have to."

"Why don't you leave Maggie a voice mail?"

"She'll delete it. She'll screen all my calls. All calls from unknown numbers. Everything. There's no way I'll be able to get through to her today. I'm pretty sure she's blocked my number too."

"Then wait—"

"I *can't*," he said, wrapping a white-knuckled grip around the steering wheel. "I love her." And then, quieter, almost a whisper: "I love her."

It took Cami a while, and when she did speak, there was a slight tremble to her voice. "She's gonna hate me."

"She won't," Declan rushed to tell her, sensing some hope. "Once she knows the truth, I promise—"

"Declan," she said, and he waited, but she went very quiet. *Thinking*, he realized. Thinking about how best to help her friend. Then she said, "I'll text it to you," and he ran a shaking hand through his hair.

"Thank you."

"I'm not doing it for you. This—you and her… I'll text it to you."

Ten minutes later, armed with Ashley's number, he considered his next move. He could call, beg to speak with Maggie. He could call and leave a voice mail, explaining everything to a machine. He could text, ask Ashley to make sure Maggie read it.

All of these things seemed wildly underwhelming.

In the end, he called, but he offered no explanation.

"This is Declan Archibald," he said, and listened to Ashley's sharp intake of breath.

"She won't want—"

He cut her off. There was no point wasting anyone's time here. "Tell Maggie to meet me at the hospital tomorrow, at noon. I've got the answers she needs." Then he hung up abruptly, confident his message would be passed on.

He wasn't going to offer some lame explanation. She deserved more than his pathetic attempts to explain away a dodgy text message.

She deserved something he should've done from the start: put an end to her misery at work. He had the solution to lift all the weight of the world off her shoulders and until now he'd failed, caught in some misguided loyalty for an old friend.

His affection for Grant went back decades, but his love for Maggie was stronger. And really, at the end of the day, he would be doing the best thing for both of them—Grant couldn't live in this bubble of denial forever, and when he finally did break his way out of it, he'd feel wretched for having put Maggie through so much pain.

To save Maggie from this nightmare, and to limit Grant's despair once he got his shit together, Declan could do only one thing.

He was going to have to blow a hole in their worlds.

the Reckless Secret

BOOK THREE

CHAPTER ONE
Maggie

Maggie drove around aimlessly for hours. No destination in mind; no thought to the roads she took, a left here, a right there. She could've driven all the way to the ocean for all she knew.

The only thing she could think about was that message.

I'm still aching from last night. You still know how to hit that spot so good. ;) Call me later, stud.

The message, sent to Declan at some point while he and Maggie had been in bed together, with Trixie Lane's name attached to it—it could only mean one thing. There was no other interpretation of those words. *...still aching...hit that spot so good...*

Maggie felt sick.

Declan had told her that Trixie was just a friend, and she'd believed him, and she was glad for it. Because if Declan's type was tall, leggy blondes, then she stood no chance. With her wild dark hair, short frame, and generous curves, she was as far from the glamorous society girl look as it was possible to get.

But Trixie was just a friend, apparently, and Maggie was the one he wanted in his bed.

Lies, all of it.

She couldn't believe he'd taken her away for the most romantic stay in a woodland cabin, made her think she could trust him, *rely* on him to always do right by her, and then the day he dropped her home, hours after they'd kissed goodbye, he found his way into Trixie's arms…between Trixie's *legs*, it seemed…

God, she could kill him. Actually tear him apart. The rage burning through her blood made her shake, made her want to scream. But all she could do was cry, because beneath the burning, consuming rage, she was a wreck of devastation.

She'd thought he cared about her. She thought what they had was *real*.

Turned out all he cared about was fucking anything that moved. And she'd let herself be a target.

A player will play, and you made yourself a game…

Everything she went against, the whole reason she had trust issues in the first place, it all came down to the betrayal of a man. Her father, decades ago, living his double life of too much alcohol and too many other women, tearing his family's world apart. And she'd sworn to herself that she would never put herself in that situation. That if she didn't trust a man one hundred percent, then she would walk away from him.

She'd had her doubts about Declan from day one, but still, she remained with him—because he lit her up like nothing else, spoke to the very soul of her. She never quite trusted him, but she wanted to, so badly. Wanted to have all of him, every day, forever.

She should've listened to her instincts. Once a player, always a player. What was she thinking, betting on Declan changing for her? He wouldn't change for anyone.

Eventually, with the sun rising and her tears running dry, she found herself outside Ashley's little house. She couldn't go home; that would be the first place Declan would look for her. And she needed space from him right now—time enough to pull herself together. She wasn't going to face him when she was such a wreck. She wouldn't let him have the satisfaction of knowing quite how much he'd shattered her.

Before getting out of the car, she took a moment to text her mom, letting her know she'd be unavailable for phone calls that day, and then turned her phone off. He wouldn't even be able to call her. She wanted to give him total radio silence—it was the least he deserved.

Then she went and sat on Ashley's porch and

waited for her to come home from the night shift. With a start, Maggie remembered how Ashley had also covered her shift yesterday on top of her own responsibilities—Maggie had been so swept away by the drama of everything that she'd forgotten she'd abandoned work in the middle of her split shift. *God*, the last thing she needed now was for Dr. Stevens to find a reason to reprimand her. Hopefully Ashley had covered for her well. Maggie would definitely be buying her a gift and taking a few of her shifts to say thank you.

The first thing Ashley said, when she climbed out of her little car and spotted Maggie on her porch, was: "Jesus, what happened?" Which was a testament to how upset Maggie must've looked. No way could she face that asshole while so obviously affected by his actions.

"Declan's sleeping with someone else," she said bluntly, and Ashley stumbled to a stop.

She paused, blinking up at Maggie, then said, "I've got vodka in the fridge."

Maggie snorted. "It's nine A.M."

"We'll put orange juice in it."

* * *

THEY DIDN'T HAVE VODKA, BUT they did have a long chat, and at some point Maggie made an embarrassing show of herself by breaking down with emotion. Ashley just hugged her tight and rubbed her back and waited until she'd pulled herself together. Then, tears dried and mind cleared, the anger came back full force.

"I can't believe I let that *asshole—*" Maggie was spitting mid-tirade, when she noticed Ashley's bloodshot eyes and pale skin. Instantly, guilt overrode the anger. "God, Ash, I'm so sorry. Here I am ranting on, and you haven't had any sleep yet."

Ashley tried to wave it off, pretend she was fine, but eventually, she gave in and plodded off to bed and told Maggie not to leave yet.

Maggie had no intention of going anywhere. This was the only place she felt vaguely safe. And it wasn't as if she was scared of Declan—it wasn't that kind of safety she needed. She was scared of her own reactions if he got in touch with her. Right now she was furious with him, wanted nothing more than to rip his balls off and stomp on them in her sharpest stilettos. But there was also the part of her that had dived head first into a relationship with him even after her brother's warning, after knowing herself how Declan was bad news. Apparently, when it came to Declan Archibald, she couldn't trust herself to make the smartest decisions.

And so she planned to hang out here at Ashley's tiny house for as long as possible—at least until she had a handle on herself, and knew she would be able to face Declan without allowing his charm and her own desire to take her over.

Ashley hadn't long lived in this house, and as far as Maggie knew, she and Declan weren't exactly friends—Ash just knew of him. The chances of him knowing her address were slim.

Safe in her hiding spot here, and with a full day stretched out before her, Maggie decided to get a little sleep, after her interrupted night and all the aimless driving. She settled on the couch with a cozy knitted blanket she found draped over the back of it, and closed her eyes.

The message swam through her mind, images of Trixie Lane, the two of them together, how they would look in bed, twisted around each other, full of pleasure…

She threw the blanket aside and got up. Stretched her back and ruffled her wild hair a moment. And then, cracking a yawn, it was like the torment of everything lifted slightly, enough for her to look around this house properly for the first time since she got here. And what she saw made her feel awful for Ashley.

The place was a mess. The string of night shifts had obviously taken their toll on Ashley, because she was never this unkempt. Against the backdrop of shabby-chic décor was an abundance of takeout containers, dirty mugs, laundry tipped here and there, mail piled up…signs, all of it, of a woman with too much on her plate. And now Maggie knew exactly how she could pay Ashley back for covering her shift.

Arming herself with rubber gloves and her hair tied back, Maggie got to work, trying to stay as quiet as possible so as not to disturb Ashley from her much-needed sleep.

By the time she was finished, her stomach informed her it was about lunchtime, and the house looked as shiny and charmingly shabby as it usually did. Maggie observed it with her hands on her hips, smiling at a job well done.

"Wow," Ashley said, stumbling into the room, rubbing one eye, her hair plastered to her left cheek and one pajama leg bunched up. "You've saved me a job here."

Maggie lifted a shoulder. "I owed you one. What're you doing up already? You've only had an hour or so…"

Ashley grunted a reply and staggered into the kitchen.

And now Maggie had nothing left to do, no more distractions; those conflicting emotions she'd managed to smother with a pair of rubber gloves and house chores now reared their ugly heads again. She sighed shakily and took a seat on the edge of the couch, waiting for Ashley to make herself coffee. Tried to fool herself into thinking everything was fine…she was just visiting a friend…nothing odd going on here…

Ashley's phone rang on the coffee table, lighting up and trilling like a siren of panic. Declan's name didn't show on the screen, but his number did, and Maggie knew it instantly.

She and Ashley locked eyes when Ashley came into the room, frozen in a moment of *oh-shit-what-do-we-do*.

Maggie swallowed and nodded, and watched with her heart in a throat as Ashley had a very short, terse conversation on the phone.

"That was him," Ashley said after, gazing at Maggie with uncertainty.

Maggie already knew that, but it still made her stomach swoop. "How did he even get your number?"

"Don't worry about that now." She took a seat beside Maggie on the couch, impatiently shoving hair off her face. "He wants you to meet him at the hospital tomorrow."

"Of course, he does." Maggie felt sick again, although she wasn't entirely sure why. The shock of the message had worn off, and now there was a strange sort of sadness washing through her.

Declan hadn't begged to speak to Maggie, to see her, to explain his side of things. The conversation had been brief. Concise. Businesslike.

He didn't care enough to plead his case.

Ashley continued, oblivious to Maggie torment: "Says he's got the answers you need."

"He means lies," Maggie said, sounding to her own ears as if her voice was coming from a great distance. Her tone was empty, dry. Ashley stared at her.

"This isn't about Trixie Lane."

"What?"

"He's asked you to attend a meeting at the hospital tomorrow," Ashley said steadily. "He wasn't calling to beg for you back. He's arranging a meeting as your lawyer. He's got answers."

There was a weird buzzing going on in Maggie's head, like the static of an old radio. " But I already know who did it."

"Maybe he's got some different information for you." Ashley grabbed her hands, squeezed them, looked her deep in the eye. And the buzzing faded long enough for Maggie to take in her next words.

"You've got to go, Mags. This is your future."

Her employment future. Not her future with Declan.

That future no longer existed—if it ever did.

CHAPTER TWO
Maggie

She wasn't sure why she was doing this, couldn't help thinking she was making a massive mistake. There was something about walking down this corridor towards her meeting with Declan that inspired a sensation akin to foreboding in her gut. Every part of her was screaming she would regret this.

Still, her curiosity had won out. She wanted to know what Declan had to say.

But that didn't mean she wasn't freaking out. Halfway towards the meeting room, attempting a strong-and-sassy kind of demeanor, she promptly stopped and turned back, heading towards the staff room instead. She needed a minute, *God*, just a minute, to get control of herself.

She was about to see him. Look in his face and see his guilt. Or, worse—see no guilt at all. He'd already proven that he didn't care.

Cami was in the staff room, sitting at the table, idly sipping from a cup of coffee and flipping through a stack of photographs. She looked up at Maggie and said, "What're you doing here?" and there was an oddness to her tone, something awkward.

"Meeting," said Maggie. She took a seat. "What do you have there?"

"Someone at my wedding had a Polaroid camera and she's just found the pictures still in the purse she wore that day." Cami shuffled closer to share the photos with Maggie, the scent of her sweet floral perfume floating pleasantly in the air. "Can you believe that? Who takes a ton of pictures and then *forgets* them. Anyway, she thought I might like to see them, so she sent them over this morning."

She flipped through a few of the photos, each one a snapshot of perfection and glowing happiness. Maggie couldn't help but smile.

"Oh, Cami. You look beautiful in these."

Cami wore a soft smile of her own. "The whole day was beautiful."

"It really was."

"When're we gonna get you up the aisle, hmm?" Cami asked, nudging Maggie playfully.

"Yeah, I don't know," said Maggie, snorting. "If I ever did, it wouldn't be like this. Look at all those people staring at you. I'd be terrified." She was terrified just *thinking* about it, a shudder running up at her spine at the image of her entire extended family, plus everyone from the club and random society leeches, all watching her awkwardly mumble her vows. She'd be so aware of everyone's attention on her that she wouldn't be able to fully enjoy the experience of marrying the man she loved.

Not that it was ever likely to happen anyway, she thought forlornly, shoulders slumping.

"So you'd do the whole small, intimate thing?"

"Yeah, definitely," Maggie said, allowing, just for a moment, the fantasy to pass through her mind, like a fluttering sheet of silk in the wind. "In the evening, I think. Candlelight. Rose petals down the aisle."

Cami gave her a considering look. "I can see you in a Vera Wang."

"You think?" Maggie asked, perking up a little, but she didn't have time to picture it herself, as Cami spoke again, all in a rush, and with the air of someone confessing to something heinous.

"I gave Declan Ashley's number. I'm sorry," she said, scrunching up her adorable face. "I just…I feel like you two are so *right* for each other." She made fists as she said it, clearly impassioned, and Maggie wondered about it—what it was about her and Declan that made Cami believe in them so completely. She hadn't even seen them together. "I shouldn't interfere, though. I've felt awful since yesterday."

Maggie smiled wanly. "He's been cheating on me."

"No, he hasn't," Cami said at once, voice full of conviction. Maggie blinked at her. "Trust me."

"Why?" Maggie responded on a mirthless laugh. "Because he told you he didn't?" She assumed that was the case, that Declan had filled Cami in on what had happened, told his side of the story—or whatever lies he could rustle up, anyway. She couldn't help the sarcasm. "Oh, then obviously we have to believe him."

The look on Cami's face spoke of sadness, and out of nowhere, it hitched a lump into Maggie's throat. *God, this hurts,* she thought. She'd spent her whole life avoiding a broken heart, and here she sat, the shattered remains of it piercing through her chest.

"I heard it in his voice," Cami said. And then she said the one thing Maggie couldn't hear, the one lie she couldn't brush away and pretend didn't affect her: "He loves you."

Maggie almost choked on her response. "The only person he loves is himself."

"He told me," Cami said, with a compassionate nod, and Maggie's world lurched around her.

"What?" Her voice was very faint, her whole body going hot all over with something like panic. He *couldn't* love her. There was no way. She swallowed and tried to adopt a nonchalant expression, then mumbled, "Well, whatever. It doesn't change anything. I've seen the proof of it."

"Have you?" said Cami. "Or are you letting your past rule your heart now?"

Maggie stood up abruptly, chair scraping loud enough to rival the deafening pounding of her heart.

Her stomach lurched with nausea, and she couldn't even run away from this.

"I've got to go. Declan's here, and I need to get it over with."

"Listen to him, okay?" Cami implored, grabbing Maggie's wrist before she could hurry off. Her eyes were deep wells of sadness, echoing the feelings churning in Maggie's gut. "You don't have to make any decisions, but…listen to him."

She listened to him before. She listened when he made her feel as if he would change for her. She listened when he made her think he *cared*. She listened, and it cost her a heart she'd kept guarded for so long. After allowing him the privilege of being the first man to push past her barriers, she listened, and he wrecked her.

She would listen today, to what he had to say. And then she would make him listen as she said goodbye for the final time.

CHAPTER THREE
Maggie

Maggie took a deep breath, hand on the door, and then pushed. She expected emotion to bombard her at the sight of Declan sat at the head of the conference table, to fight her instinct to crumble and run away. What she didn't expect to feel was surprise.

Declan was there, of course. But so was Dr. Stevens. And they were both looking at her with twin expressions of what she could only describe as guilt.

Declan's guilt, she could understand, even if she was pretty sure it was fake. But Dr. Stevens…?

"What's going on?"

Dr. Stevens cleared his throat. "Ms. Emerson, please have a seat."

Gingerly, she did as she was told. "Is this about my suspension?"

"Your lawyer here has informed me of a number of troubling things," he said after a beat, gesturing to

Declan. Maggie refused to look at him. Not yet. "One of which, I'm sorry to say, is Dr. Ronald Mitchell's behavior towards you."

The floor jolted beneath her seat. "Okay."

"Now I've called him here—ah." There was a knock on the door, and a new helping of panic welled in Maggie's chest. "Come in," Dr. Stevens called, and in walked Ronald, looking just as confused as Maggie no doubt did when she'd entered. Out the corner of her eye, she saw Declan lean forward onto his elbows, his body set in stiff lines. All of a sudden, the air in the room filled with a different kind of tension, and Maggie's skin buzzed with it.

"Dr. Mitchell, please take a seat."

"I'm in the middle of my rounds, sir."

"This won't take long."

Maggie, trying to swallow down her thumping heartbeat, addressed Dr. Stevens as she said, "What's he doing here?"

Dr. Stevens paused. "He's here about you." His voice was delicately careful.

"Maggie, are you all right?" Ronald asked, frowning, looking for all the world like a man concerned for a friend's welfare. "You were so distressed yesterday."

He couldn't be serious. Was he actually going to pretend he hadn't attempted to attack her? She snorted bitterly. "Oh, I wonder why?" she said, and his frown deepened.

Beside her, Declan shifted his weight. She could almost feel hot waves radiating from him, and she had to make a fist beneath the table to help contain her emotions.

"Ms. Emerson," Dr. Stevens said, opening a notepad, his tone changing to something more businesslike, "can you please tell me, in your own words, about Dr. Mitchell's behavior towards you these past few days?"

Maggie blinked. The lump in her throat had swelled, blocking her voice, and she couldn't look away from the three sets of eyes pinned on her. Dr. Stevens, always so hateful, now watching her with compassion. Ronald, his scowl full of malicious challenge, daring her to speak, and Declan—she hadn't looked at him, but she could feel his gaze on her like a brand.

Then, gathering her courage, she met his eye. And the look on his face hit her like a truck to the heart. He nodded gently. "It's all right," he said, and somehow, those three little words gave her enough strength to face Ronald and Dr. Stevens head on and tell her side of things.

"He, uh…" she said, then cleared her throat, strengthened her voice. "Just aggressive, really."

"Physically?"

"Yes," she said, while Ronald released a harsh noise of disbelief. "Mostly verbal, but yes, some physical aggressiveness too."

Ronald slammed a hand down on the table, making both Maggie and Dr. Stevens jump and look at him with alarm. "What happens between me and Maggie has nothing to do with anyone here."

Declan didn't move a single inch, not even at the sudden slam of Ronald's hand.

Like a tiger in the brush, biding his time, watching…

"It happened on hospital grounds," Dr. Stevens said steadily, "and to one of my employees."

Ronald huffed out a sigh of immense exasperation, and then looked at Maggie with appeal in his eyes. "Maggie—"

"Ms. Emerson, do you wish to make a formal complaint?"

"I…" Her hesitation hung in the air. This wasn't what she wanted to string up Ronald for—her case against him was much bigger than a couple of aggressive confrontations. She couldn't help but think that making a formal complaint now would distract everyone from what the real problem was—that Ronald had been setting her up for the stealing. Yet she couldn't bring that up yet, not without some solid proof. She had to speak to Sanders before she started flinging the accusation around a boardroom.

Suddenly, making all three of them startle to attention, Declan stood up. "Can I have a moment alone with my client, please?" He bit the words out, and looked at only Dr. Stevens.

"Of course."

Declan nodded, then pushed his chair away and walked around to Maggie. "Come with me," he said quietly, and didn't wait for her response before striding over to the door.

Maggie spent three seconds contemplating her options before deciding to do as he asked. It was either that, or sit alone in a room with Dr. Stevens and Ronald, and that was something she wasn't willing to do without Declan present.

She guessed that made him some kind of safety blanket for her. Sadly.

Outside the room, in the harshly lit corridor, she found Declan pacing.

"What the hell is this?" she hissed at him.

Declan stopped in front of her, lifted a hand to touch her, and then aborted the movement. There was absolute fire in his eyes. "He has to pay for the way he's treated you."

"He will pay. He's the thief—I'm gonna string him up for way more than feeling me up in a staff room."

Instantly, she realized her mistake, and she winced.

Declan's face went very dangerously sharp.

"Feeling—feeling you up?"

"I mean…pushing me around," she attempted, but it was too late. His teeth were bared, and he was ready for the kill.

"Maggie."

She sighed deeply and with great irritation. "All right. Yes. He tried to…force himself on me, okay? Didn't get very far, though."

His fiery eyes flashed, and he made a noise that sounded something like a growl from deep in his chest as he looked at the door, like he was looking *through* the door and at the man he was going to tear apart.

And just like that, Maggie was *done*.

"Oh, you can cut that out," she snapped. "We both know you don't really give a damn about me."

The look he shot her was downright *incendiary*.

"Maggie, what you think you saw—"

"I know what I saw."

"I can explain it," he said at once, stepping towards her. She crossed her arms over her chest and tried to look unconcerned, but the intensity radiating from him was intoxicating. "I would never want to put my hands on any other woman," he added fiercely. "Ever." Then he stepped closer still, close enough for her to see every line of sincerity on his face. "You're *everything*."

She couldn't do anything but stare back at him, her mind free-falling, her heart thudding a bruising rhythm against her ribs.

"If we're ready to proceed?" Dr. Stevens asked, poking his head through the door and wearing an expression of impatience.

Maggie cleared her throat and said in a weak voice, "Yes, sir."

Declan was still staring intently at her, deeply, as if trying to see through to the very bones of her. "Make the formal complaint," he said. "Get him punished for it. He's not the thief."

She was shaking, she realized. Her hands trembled as she pushed locks of hair off her face. "How do you know?"

"Trust me."

Biting her lip, she said, "I already tried that once."

He took her by the shoulders, a firm grip, making her startle; then he dragged those hands across the slope of her shoulders and to her neck, cradling her jaw in his palms and stroking thumbs beneath her cheekbones. His eyes were glittering at her, captivating every ounce of her attention, and his touch on her skin was like sitting an inch too close to a roaring fireplace. "*Trust* me," he said, and by God, she did. On this, she did.

She swallowed and nodded, and he kissed her forehead before letting her go, making her flutter her eyelids and almost cling on to him in the moments before she headed back towards the door, towards reality.

Dr. Stevens and Ronald watched her with precise focus as she took a seat again, no doubt trying to read her face, get an idea of what she would say. She waited for Declan to sit beside her and then opened her mouth, speaking in strong tones.

"I want to make an official complaint against Dr. Mitchell regarding the physical and verbal assault—"

"This is ridiculous!" Ronald exploded, launching himself to his feet, arms waving wildly. He looked desperately at all three of them before settling on Dr. Stevens, and implored, "Maggie and I used to be in a relationship, sir, and what happened between us this week was little more than a spat between lovers—" Maggie raised her hand and opened her mouth to interrupt, and Ronald said, "Former lovers! It's a personal matter, sir."

"Not while it happens in my hospital, to my employee, and after a formal complaint has been made. And this isn't the first, Ronald."

The whole room fell silent at that, abruptly and sharp, and for half a moment Maggie and Ronald shared a look of mutual disbelief.

"What?" Ronald mumbled finally.

Dr. Stevens nodded. "Two other complaints have been made about you in the last month. We've been investigating, but we can no longer sit on this." He paused, while Ronald sputtered with extreme indignation and Maggie blinked in confusion, and Declan, saying nothing, remained a tight line of tension to her right. Then Dr. Stevens added, "You are suspended effective immediately, pending full dismissal," and Ronald erupted into animated fury once again.

"You can't be serious!"

"I'm afraid I am."

"Suspend *her*," he yelled manically, stabbing a finger in Maggie's direction. "She's the one stealing from you! You can't fire me! I'm the best resident in this hospital!"

"That, I'm sure, is debatable," Dr. Stevens said idly, straightening his cuffs. "Please collect your belongings and leave the premises. Unless you'd like me to ask security to escort you?"

What happened next occurred so quickly that Maggie barely had time to blink, let alone prepare for it. Ronald launched himself at her, spitting, "This is all your fault—" and his fingers closed around the air centimeters from her face in the instant before there was a crash somewhere in the room, and Ronald was propelled back from her, and then all of a sudden, he was flat against the wall beside the door, pinned there by a seething Declan.

"What did I say to you about touching her again?"

"See this?" Ronald wailed, trying to indicate to Dr. Stevens behind Declan's shoulder while simultaneously—and futilely—attempting to push Declan away. "*This* is physical assault!"

"Yes, but he is not my employee…"

Maggie, gathering herself after the initial shock, got to her feet. She approached Declan and put her hand on his heaving back. The man was staring into Ronald's face like a murderer in waiting. "Let him go, Declan." And then, to Ronald, "Just leave, before this gets any worse."

He made a face that quite clearly said "*How?*" and she gently pulled Declan away from him. Slowly, and with much obvious reluctance, Declan let him go, sucking in air through his teeth and still clenching his fists, and Ronald, knowing a lifeline when he saw one, scurried out of the room with his cheeks flushing almost purple.

Maggie heaved a deep breath and turned to Dr. Stevens.

"Can I go?" she asked. "Are we done here?" She'd reached her fill of drama today, and Declan's proximity was muddying her mind. She needed to go home and decompress, figure out how she felt about the day's events. Get control of herself before choosing how to deal with the Declan situation—which was more unclear now than it had ever been. He'd sounded so sincere out in the hallway, *looked* sincere, and now with him stood so near to her, that sensation of anger she'd been carrying for two days was strangely absent.

"Not quite," Dr. Stevens said. His tone had changed—while with the Ronald incident he'd been calm, businesslike, he now sounded…almost apologetic. Uneasiness settled in Maggie's gut as she waited for him to elaborate.

"As I said, your lawyer has informed me of some troubling facts. Now *that* one has been taken care of…" At this, he looked at Declan, who—having gained control of himself—sighed and nodded. The atmosphere in the room seemed to have been plunged in ice.

"I'll go collect him," Declan said, and then abruptly pulled Maggie to him, cupped her face, while her mind swam in total confusion. "Look at me," he said, and she did, caught in a moment of apprehension. "I want you to remember how sorry I am. I tried to make him tell you a long time ago."

"Who?" she said. "Tell me what?" But he merely shook his head sadly and let her go, giving her one last heavy look before leaving the room, leaving her completely in the dark.

It was like the world was spiraling around her, and the one thing she could hold onto had just walked out the room.

She whirled on Dr. Stevens. "What's this about?"

He, too, projected something like sadness, and Maggie was starting to feel like she'd been dropped into some kind of surreal, tense dream. "It seems I may have been wrong about you," he admitted, and with such ease that she had to sit down before her knees gave way with shock. "It doesn't happen often, but… there we are."

She swallowed dryly. "Wrong about what?"

It took him a moment to speak, and when he did, he looked her right in the eye as he said the words she'd longed to hear from him since this all began. "You were not the one stealing the drugs."

"I know that," she choked out. "I tried to tell *you* that."

"You can see how I would think it was you, though, can't you? Your DNA, your keypad code... I was left with very little choice." He sighed, rubbing a hand over his forehead and throwing his hair like a man in distress. Like a man with *feelings*. Feelings like guilt. "I'm not fond of you, Ms. Emerson. It's no secret. But it's personal, and I shouldn't allow it to be. Your father is the reason why I've been stuck in this role for the past decade," he revealed with a heavy tone. "I should've been Chief of Medicine many years ago, and no one would argue that I'm more than qualified for it... But your father likes to put his friends in high places, you know? Even the ones who haven't earned it. I've earned it a dozen times over, but I'm not his friend, and therefore I'm stuck here."

He seemed so incredibly human to her all of a sudden that she felt a shock of empathy for him. Duke Emerson had affected Dr. Stevens just like he had Maggie—manifested in different ways, sure, but they both carried the same scars. They had a common enemy, and that made them something like friends.

"Whatever my father has done to you," she said levelly to him, "it's not my fault."

"I know that." He smiled thinly, mirthlessly, a hint of self-deprecation hidden in it. "I never was very good at separating my personal feelings," he admitted with uncharacteristic rawness. There was a part of her, buried deep below propriety and her tumultuous history with this man, that wanted to offer him a hug.

"But I apologize now, Ms. Emerson. I've been unfair to you. Although a lot of evidence *did* point to you, we must be honest now."

"I don't know why, sir," she said. "I've been trying to wrap my head around it for so long—"

"The answer, I'm sorry to say, is about to become very clear." He sighed again, very deeply, and gave her a look full of overwhelming apology. "I would prepare yourself, if I were you."

"Prepare myself?" she said blankly, her stomach twisting. "For what?"

The reason became horrendously clear seconds later when the door opened and Declan came through, and trailing behind him, wearing a guilty, self-hating expression that revealed *everything*, was her brother.

Her brother, the thief.

CHAPTER FOUR
Maggie

White noise rushed in her ears, the walls closing in on her, the floor swaying beneath her feet, and when did she stand up? Because she didn't remember moving an inch.

"No."

Grant stretched a hand out to her. "Sis—"

"*No.*"

"Let's sit down," Declan said, sounding maddeningly calm, somewhere to her right. She couldn't tear her eyes from her brother.

Her *brother*.

A gaping hole formed in the pit of her stomach, aching and hollow.

"I'll stand, thanks," she said numbly.

She knew exactly what was coming, and she didn't want to hear it—both Grant's utter betrayal, and Declan's hand in it. A dual-edged knife slicing right through the heart of her, and she couldn't breathe, couldn't *think*.

Everyone else remained standing with her and she didn't like it, felt closed in by these towering figures of pain, looming over her as the walls drew in, and it was getting darker, she was sure of it, the room around her dimming into shadow…

She sucked in a breath and grabbed the back of a chair, then closed her eyes as her stomach spun like she'd had too many drinks. Someone touched her arm and she snapped her eyes open, finding Declan looking at her with concern. She shrugged him off with a grimace and stood straight.

Faced her brother.

Prepared herself, like Dr. Stevens told her to. Of the three men in this room, right now, Dr. Stevens was the only one she could trust. And that…that was something she could almost laugh about, hysterically and pained.

Jesus Christ.

"I'm so sorry," Grant whispered, his eyes watery, his jaw holding a minute tremble. He was either scared or upset—neither gave Maggie much comfort. Grant's guilt did little to help her. It didn't take away what had happened.

"I didn't mean—it was never meant to go this far," Grant continued—empty words in an empty apology. She didn't answer. Didn't even know how she was supposed to get words through the swelling in her throat, the rapid beat of her heart.

How the hell was she supposed to deal with any of this?

Grant was still looking at her, still with that same watery, sorry expression. But this time there was an edge of pain in his gaze. More than pain—agony. "I've got a problem," he said quietly, and Maggie staggered into a seat at last.

The three men followed suit—Dr. Stevens opposite her, watching her face with total compassion, so much so that she almost wanted to go sit directly beside him and take comfort from his newfound concern for her. Declan to her right, stoic and straight-faced, his eyes sparking with a fire that always spoke of his intensity. And Grant to her left, agonized and sorry. There was the weight of a hundred lies settling over this table and she wanted to crumble from it.

These two men on either side of her were breaking her—the two men who were supposed to care about her the most. She could hardly stand the taste of the air in this room.

"Just explain it all to her," Declan said, his voice sounding heavier than it'd ever been to her. "She needs to hear everything."

She didn't. She didn't want to. She had a fairly good idea already, and hearing the details wouldn't make her feel better.

But there was a twisted side of her that wanted

to know *exactly* how her brother and her boyfriend had betrayed her. The precise details of it all. What went through their minds when they looked at her and knew that they were slowly destroying her.

If they *enjoyed* it.

"Painkillers," Grant said, bringing her back to the room, away from the free-falling thoughts her bitter mind was trying to conjure. "I got addicted to them during the summer after my ankle wouldn't stop acting up. Got myself completely dependent on them. Declan, he—he got me through it."

She swallowed. "You had a stomach bug." Her voice came out shaky and she hated it, the weakness she displayed.

After a moment, he said thickly, "No."

Breath rushed out of her all at once. "Oh my God." She'd believed it—believed it so faithfully. Felt *sorry* for him, all through the summer; spent so much of her time worrying about him. And all along… All along he'd been an addict, lied to her face, and *Declan* had hidden it.

"I thought I was over it," Grant continued. "That it wouldn't be a problem anymore. But the pain came back and I…I took the pills again. Dr. O'Malley stopped giving them to me, said we needed to start looking at other ways to manage my ankle—mentioned surgery. But by then it was too late." He stopped, drew in a rattling lungful of air. "I knew you had them here, and I knew your access code…"

She could do nothing but mutely shake her head.

"It was like the part of my mind that knew how wrong it was had switched off," he said, his face cracking with the pain of it. "I couldn't control myself. All I could see were the pills. I didn't know how to stop it." His voice broke at the end, wavered and splintered, drenched in desperation, and suddenly, her bone-deep fury at his betrayal pushed aside, and from beneath it emerged something else entirely.

Her heart started to break for him.

"I have to go," she said, scraping her chair back and getting to her feet.

Dr. Stevens, who'd sat in silence through the explanation with a crease between his brows, startled at her sudden movement and stood with her, like a gentleman ripped from the pages of *Pride and Prejudice*.

"Maggie," Declan said, and she whirled on him, veins crackling with adrenaline, her tumbled mix of emotions making her blood burn—rage, pain, compassion...

"How long have you known?"

Declan looked at her steadily. "Since the day you got suspended," he confessed, his tone strong and clear.

"You can't blame him," Grant piped up, but she couldn't turn and look at him again. Couldn't allow the devastation of his life right now to cloud her feelings. She wanted to be furious with him. She didn't want to feel the urge to help him. "He tried to make me tell you. I was just too stupid to listen."

"*You* could've told me," she spat at Declan, because this was worse—worse than what Grant had done to her. Her brother had a serious problem, driven by addiction, and she would hate him for it for a long time, but there was no denying that the pills dictated the man here, and that the man did not decide one day to randomly fuck up his sister's whole life.

But Declan—he had no excuse. Even if his expression right now told a whole other story.

"I couldn't be the one to break your heart like that," he said quietly, as if she were the only one in the room with him. "I'm a coward. And you needed to hear it from him."

She stared at him, locked eyes with him for what felt like an eternity, torn between the desire to rush forward and bury herself in his arms, in his safety—and the desire to slap that look of heartache right off his face.

She turned to Dr. Stevens. "I assume this means the investigation on me will be dropped?"

He started again at suddenly finding himself the focus of attention, and then cleared his throat. "Yes."

"Good," she said. "I'm going." She shot one last scathing look at the man she loved, and muttered, "You can sort this mess out on your own," and then swept towards the door with, what she hoped, was a modicum of dignity. She could feel her defenses rapidly falling, shattering into a million shards at her feet, and if she stayed here for one moment longer, she'd break.

"Sis, wait—" Grant grabbed her arm as she passed, and his touch sparked something within her that made anger suddenly rear up in her chest like a beast, causing her to spin and land a hard slap on her brother's cheek. The sound echoed through the room, off the startled faces of all three men, through the pained sound of her heavy breathing and the sob that came after.

"You were the one who was never supposed to hurt me," she said, her voice high with emotion, her heart falling low into her gut, heavy and dying. "The only man I could ever trust."

He blinked watery eyes, his throat rolling convulsively. "I'm so sorry."

"Yeah." She sniffed, brushing hair off her face. "Me too," she said, and then walked away from them all.

CHAPTER FIVE
Declan

Silence reigned where heartbreak had moments ago nearly smothered them all, and Declan couldn't allow himself a spare three seconds to think about quite how thoroughly he'd just helped destroy the woman he loved most in the world.

"I need to go after her," Grant said desperately, and Declan shot him a firm look.

"Sit down," he ordered, then turned to the other man in the room. "Dr. Stevens. I know I'm putting you in an impossible position here, but I'm going to ask you not to follow this up."

Dr. Stevens blinked at him. "You want me to drop the whole thing?"

"Yes. He doesn't need a criminal investigation. He needs rehab."

"Be that as it may—"

"Look at him," Declan said, waving a hand at the pathetic figure of Grant, who looked as though he couldn't care less about his own fate in that moment. He was too busy beating himself up. "He's not malicious. He's not a criminal, for Christ's sake. He's a man in need of help. I'm asking you to please look beyond the protocol and let me put an end to this quietly."

Dr. Stevens observed him a moment, and then turned to consider Grant. He cleared his throat, then said sniffily, "Your father wouldn't be happy to know he's got a thief for a son."

Grant's face twisted with bitterness. "My father can go to hell for all I care."

Dr. Stevens, in apparent shock, raised his eyebrows. "You don't get along?"

"I'd turn myself in just for the pleasure of humiliating him."

"Hmm," Dr. Stevens said, looking at Grant for a few seconds of strange, contemplative silence.

Worried, Declan said nervously, "How about we don't talk about handing anyone in?" but it seemed his mind was on a different track to Dr. Stevens'.

"I know of an excellent rehabilitation program," the doctor said. "I would probably be able to get a place for you."

Grant blinked at him, looked at Declan wildly, and then back to Dr. Stevens. He had to swallow twice before he could speak. "Are you saying—"

"And afterwards," Dr. Stevens said, steamrolling over him, straightening his cuffs, "there's a fair amount of fixing-up needed in this hospital. We don't really have the budget."

Clever, Declan thought proudly, feeling a new-found affinity for the odd doctor.

Grant nodded eagerly, looking every bit like a puppy who'd just been told he was going on a walk. "I'll do it all— whatever you need. I'll be at your service."

Dr. Stevens sniffed again and got to his feet, giving off the distinct vibe that he found this whole saccharine, emotive display of gratitude rather displeasing and probably a bit embarrassing.

"If you'll excuse me," he said. "I have an investigation to call off."

Declan could almost feel Grant's relief, and if it was anything like his own, then it must've been making the man lightheaded.

He wasn't quite sure what he'd been expecting when making this plan—deciding to bring everyone together and blow the whole thing open had been a risky move, but he'd run out of all other options. Grant had reached rock bottom, and Maggie…well. His heart twinged at the thought of her.

Dr. Stevens paused beside Grant, considered him a moment, and then offered his hand. "Meet me in my office at four P.M."

"I'll be there, sir," Grant said, shaking the doctor's hand vigorously. "Thank you so much. I'm so sorry for everything I've done. I know it's hard to believe, but this really isn't like me. I'm not this guy."

He wasn't lying. Grant hooked on painkillers was like an entirely different Grant to the one Declan knew and grew up with. That Grant was smart, confident, powerful, full of charm. This Grant, this pathetic lump of a man currently on the verge of tears, was little more than a weak shadow. A healthy Grant rivaled Declan's status as most eligible bachelor in society.

Declan's *former* status. He was a taken man now, no matter how much he had to fight for it.

Mouth straining into an approximation of a smile, Dr. Stevens patted Grant's shoulder. "And you won't be this guy anymore."

"Thank you."

"Thank me by getting clean," said Dr. Stevens, before offering Declan a tip of his head and then leaving the room.

Grant blew out a long breath. "Now all I have to do is spend the next…rest of my life, probably? Making it up to Maggie." He shook his head, scrubbing a hand over his face. "Not that I deserve to make it up to her."

"You're an asshole," Declan agreed, and Grant nodded.

"What're you gonna do now?"

Good question. Logic told him to lie low a while, let the dust settle, let people calm down. And then, maybe, begin to tentatively reach out again, start patching things up where he could.

His instinct, however, was pulling him in the complete opposite direction.

"I'm gonna tell your sister I love her," he said.

Grant stared at him. "Sounds like a plan."

"You approve?"

"I might."

Declan's heart lept into his throat at that—not that he would admit it to Grant. Truth was, no one knew Declan like Grant did, which meant no one but Grant was aware of quite how prevalent his "player" ways had been in the past. The fact that Grant now gave his blessing to date his sister meant something to Declan—that maybe he'd become a better man despite himself. That he was worthy of the love of an incredible woman like Maggie.

And that maybe Maggie thought so too.

Swallowing down the rush of emotion, he grabbed Grant's shoulder and said, "I'll meet you at his office at four," looking firmly in his eyes as he uttered it. It was important—vital, even—that Grant not fuck this up now. He'd been given a lifeline, and if he didn't take it, Declan would kill him personally. "Don't be late."

"I won't," Grant said fiercely. And then, suddenly, and without a hint of awkwardness, he pulled Declan in for a hug. "Good luck," he murmured into his ear, and Declan could do little else but hold on and squeeze a bit tighter.

* * *

Without really having a clue how he knew she'd be there, Declan headed straight for Maggie's apartment. Logically, she would've been back at Ashley's, or hiding out somewhere unknown, away from the men who hurt her. But she was in her own apartment, and she answered the door on the first knock, and the devastation on her face was enough to shatter Declan's heart anew.

"I don't even know what to say," he muttered thickly, taking in the sight of her swollen, bloodshot eyes, the tear tracks on her smooth, plump cheeks, the red stains on her bitten lips. Her gaze was almost dead as she looked at him, and she was trembling like she'd been crying for days.

She sniffled, rubbing a sleeve against the edge of her nose. "I'm okay. Come in."

She wasn't okay, clearly. She was far beyond okay. And what he felt for himself in that moment went beyond hatred—he *detested* himself.

He closed the door softly behind and followed her to the living room. "Gotta admit, I wasn't expecting you to let me in so easily."

Shrugging a shoulder, she turned to him with something like resignation written all over her face. "I don't have the strength for a fight right now."

"God." His chest felt cleaved in two, a hot iron speared through his ribs and plunged right into the center of his heart. "What can I do? I want to make it bett—"

"You can't," she said shortly.

"Maggie." The desperation in his voice chipped into the air between them like shards of ice.

She stared at him for a long moment, and there was so much he wanted to say—*sorry*, and *please*, and *I love you*. But he didn't say them. He didn't say anything at all. Because he didn't know how, and she was broken, and he might have thought himself worthy before, but now he couldn't imagine a man less deserving of such an incredible woman's forgiveness.

Then she sniffed and stepped forward, and he froze, waiting, watching her, his chest thumping a mile a minute against his ribs and his blood running hot.

She put her hands on his chest, and she looked into his eyes, and then she leaned up on tiptoes and his breath caught in his throat in the instant before her lips touched his.

"Please," she said against his mouth, voice splintered with pain. "Please, I just need to—I need you to make me feel something else."

Desire shot through him—desire laced with sadness. She was moments from crying again; he could see it as he gently pushed her back an inch or so, raked his fingers through her hair, tried to catch her eye, but she had them closed, her throat rolling with a thick swallow, face etched in lines of hurt. Hurt that he caused—or at least helped with. If only he'd been honest with her from the start, filled her in on Grant's problems, then maybe now she wouldn't feel so doubly betrayed. And yet, if he'd done that, he would've betrayed his oldest friend. Between a rock and a hard place—that was where he'd been living these past few weeks.

But this wasn't about him. She needed him now, clinging to the front of his shirt, lips parted slightly. She needed him, and he'd give her anything.

"Please," she said again, eyes fluttering open. "Declan. I need you to—"

"Okay," he said. "Okay." And he took her to bed.

CHAPTER SIX
Maggie

She let him strip her clothing, slowly and reverently. He kissed every revealed inch of her skin until she trembled, and she sighed, and she caught his lips when he reached her face and kissed him deeply, tasting his adoration of her on his tongue.

He removed his own clothes, and then they lay together, on their sides, kissing and kissing, with her thigh hooked up over his hip and his hand roaming, searching, feeling every rise and fall of her body, leaving a tingling path of fire in his wake, lighting her up from the inside and making her whimper as he teased—trailing fingers across her pelvis and up her inner thigh and beneath the swell of her breast but never close enough, never where she needed him.

"Declan…" The word came out on a breathy whisper on his bottom lip, and he smiled, just slightly, knowing exactly what he was doing.

"Lie back."

She did, and he kissed her throat, kissed the curve of her shoulder, trailed a tongue across the rise of her breast and then pulled a nipple between his lips. She gasped and held the back of his head, and he sucked her to a peak just the right side of painful.

Lower, ghosting over her ribs and across the softness of her tummy, grabbing handfuls of her hips like he wanted to worship them, he kissed where the skin swelled between his thumb and forefinger, burying his face in her pelvis.

She parted her legs, expectant, but he didn't go down—instead he came back up, and he pushed a hand down, and he parted her folds with his fingers as he licked into her mouth and then he breached her entrance, and he thumbed her clit, and she moaned for him. "You're so beautiful," he whispered to her, pulling back enough to look her in the eye, his face so devastatingly handsome and his eyes shining for her. And she thought, *I love you, god, I love you* but she didn't say it, couldn't say anything. She took his face in her hands and she brought him in for a kiss and she arched her back when he pinched her clit and made her shiver.

Things accelerated quickly, his desire so clearly winning over his need to take it slowly, and she encouraged him along when he started shifting his own hips closer, when his cock jutted out thick and hard and throbbing. She took hold of it, stroked it, rubbed the head of it against her clit and they both moaned, his eyes squeezing shut, and then he leaned down to bite her nipple and he thrust forward, his member sliding through the slick folds of her pussy. She dug nails into his back and said something that sounded like a plea and he lifted off her, returning moments later with a condom and with reverence in his eyes.

She wanted to capture that look forever, keep it locked in her mind, and with a rush of sadness she realized she may never see another man look at her that way again—never see Declan wear that expression of pure adoration for her anymore. Not after this, her final farewell to what they had together.

She fought back the swollen lump of dismay in her throat and welcomed him back onto her body, between her legs, watched him smile warmly at her as he prepared himself, and her heart broke for how he had no idea that these were their final moments together.

And then he pushed inside her and gathered her close, and there was scarcely a whisper of space between their sweat-slick bodies as he developed a slow, torturous rhythm, and she rolled her hips up to meet him and they kissed the sounds from each other, until they could do little more than pant open-mouthed and cling lips and swipe tongues. And then Maggie tilted her head back and caught a gasp in her throat and shuddered right deep down to her bones as climax rushed through her.

Ten minutes later, she stood on the balcony, a sheet wrapped around her, breathing in the cold air and letting her mind race with every agonizing thought she'd kept at bay since her world imploded today.

Her brother had betrayed her, set her up, almost ruined her whole life.

Declan, the man she loved despite everything, had known all along.

And then, still there in the back of it all, that as-yet-unexplained message from Trixie Lane.

She felt like she was choking, didn't even know where to start. If she wanted to scream at her brother or hug him tight, hurting for what he'd been going through alone, but now so devastated by what he had done to her. A part of her felt nothing more than the deepest sympathy for him. The rest of her couldn't stomach the barefaced betrayal.

The fact that he had come into her place of work, used her keycode, stolen drugs she alone was responsible for—it was calculated. It wasn't an accident. He'd known exactly what he had been doing, regardless of his apology now. He must've known how badly he'd mess up her life for it.

And yet, he had an addiction. He hadn't asked for any of this, just like she hadn't. He didn't wake up one morning and suddenly think what a good idea it would be to fuck up his sister's entire world.

But that didn't change what had happened, and neither did it explain Declan's hand in this.

He could've told her. It would've meant betraying Grant's trust, but the alternative was to lie to her face and watch her world crumble. And he had lied to her, when she thought he'd been working on her case. He'd known all along who it was.

God, she couldn't cope with any of this. She needed space to breathe. Needed time—

"You must be cold out here."

He'd put his clothes back on and stepped up beside her now with his hands in his pockets, his shoulders slightly raised like he expected a frosty welcome, even after what they'd just done together.

She hadn't stopped to cuddle with him afterwards, invite him to hold her. He'd released with a groan after her own climax faded, and he stayed inside her for a moment or two before pulling out, and she'd got up immediately, taking the bed sheet with her. The only sound she heard from him was a soft sigh, and then nothing until now, here on this balcony.

"I'm fine," she said, and looked away from him to stare back out across the mid-afternoon sky.

"I have to go back to the hospital. Grant has a meeting with Dr. Stevens at four, and I said I'd be there for him." He paused, and then added, "Dr. Stevens is dropping the investigation. We're gonna get Grant in a rehab program instead."

Relief washed through her, bittersweet. Regardless of her current feelings towards her brother, she would never want to see him in prison. It would've destroyed them both.

She couldn't let Declan see that relief, though. Couldn't let him think it was all okay now.

He hesitated at her lack of response, then said, "I could come back here afterwards?"

"You could," she replied quietly, then she drew a deep breath and turned to face him. They'd reached the moment—the moment when she had to tell him how things would be between them now. She had a suspicion he wouldn't like it. "But I won't be here."

He frowned. "What?"

"I'm going away," she said, speaking calmly, levelly. There was a kind of numbness settling in her, smothering the pain and making it easy for her to speak to him like this. To make this decision. "I don't know how long for. But I—you and me, we're not—"

"I love you," he said forcefully. He stepped into her space and cupped her face in his hands, his movements so quick that she didn't have chance to contemplate moving out of his reach. "You're not gonna do this, okay?"

She blinked slowly, bringing her hands up to hold his wrists. "I haven't said what I'm doing."

"You're ending it." He brushed thumbs over her cheekbones, just beneath her eyes. Moistness dampened her skin there as if he'd wiped away a tear. "You think I'm no good for you, and you're running away from it."

"I'm not running away from anything." The numbness remained, but a spike of anger pushed through, and she wrenched his hands off her face and shoved him until he stumbled back a pace. "I can't even *look* at either of you right now. Do you get that?" They'd both broken her, like a tag team from hell. Her hands shook.

"The message," he said, agony washing over his face, "from Trixie. We'd been to the gym and I spotted her on the weights. You can ask her—ask the gym—I don't know, but I didn't—"

"I know." She'd known it all along, if she was honest with herself. After the initial shock had worn off, and she'd been able to think with a level head, and then she'd seen the sincerity in his eyes at the hospital—she'd known instinctively that he hadn't betrayed her in that way. Little did she know at the time that he'd betrayed her in another way entirely—a worse way. "But don't you see? The fact that I instantly thought you did—that you *could*—what does that tell you?"

"It tells me I have a lot of work to do to prove to you that I love you, and that I've changed. But I do love you," he said, dropping his voice lower, stepping close again and she let him, didn't resist when he reached out and gently took her hands. "Do you believe that, at least?"

She wanted to, but right now, she was struggling to feel much of anything. Coldness had filled the empty corners of her body since she'd left the warmth of the bed, and the hole at the pit of her stomach had widened. She wanted so badly to believe that he loved her, that he respected her, that he'd changed for her—but when she couldn't feel anything now, she couldn't trust it. And she couldn't trust him.

"I have to go," she said, slipping her hands out of his hold and backing away towards the door. "I can't talk about any of this now."

"Maggie—" He stopped her, again with his hands around her wrists, and again she let him. It was like there was a part of her that didn't want him to let her leave. "I'm sorry for everything. For that message—for Grant—"

"You should've told me," she whispered, and *now* she felt something. Pain. She felt a flood of pain in her chest, rising up and coiling around her heart. It hurt to even look at him, to see a man she'd chosen to love, and to know he'd so easily lied to her.

"I know. *God*, I know. I can't even—there aren't words for how sorry I am. I didn't know how to—" He stopped, released her wrists, dragged hands through his hair in frustration. Or maybe desperation. "I didn't know what to do," he said after a pause, sounding as broken as she felt. "I didn't know what was best."

He was human. Humans made mistakes. But this mistake had been made at the expense of her heart, and she needed now, so completely, for him to go away and let her *think*.

"Please, can you go," she asked him, pulling her sheet tighter around herself. "I need space."

He looked at her for a long moment, heartbreak written all over his face. "How long will you be gone for?"

She ached for him. Even now, she ached to fall into his arms.

She stepped back.

"I don't know." Panic was welling up in her, sudden and inexplicable. She needed to be alone right now, before she suffocated under the weight of all the pain. "Please, just go."

Then she left him standing on the balcony, wrecked and alone in the afternoon sunlight.

CHAPTER SEVEN
Maggie

What Maggie wanted, more than anything else in the world, was her mom. A hug from her mom, some comfort, a long chat about everything... Well, maybe not the Grant thing. But she could confide in her mom about her pain right now, seek some advice. And, more importantly, bundle herself up in maternal care. Because her mom was a society girl, but she was always a mother first and foremost—Maggie and Grant hadn't been raised by a team of nannies; they'd always known their mother's love and attention. She was Mom—a good mom, and the one person Maggie needed right now. Like a child with a scraped knee.

Only problem was, she didn't exactly know where her mom was at the moment.

Gillian Emerson had found herself a boyfriend recently—a Fancyman, as they called him—her first romance in over a decade. He was a man from the club, naturally, widowed some years previous and his children all grown. He worked in wealth management, although Maggie didn't know the details, and his tan was a little too orange. But he made Mom smile again, and blush, and do that twinkly little giggle she used to do in her younger years, before the weight of life forced it out of her.

A few weeks ago, Mom and Simon the Fancyman had embarked on a long adventure around Europe, something Maggie knew her mom had wanted to do for years, but had postponed until her children no longer needed her.

And Maggie needed her now. So did Grant, in truth, but that wasn't Maggie's secret to tell.

Which made her exactly like Declan. She decided to not think about it. (*Hypocrite*, her subconscious said. She squashed it.)

It took a while, but Maggie eventually managed to get her mom on the phone and find out where she was.

"Oh, we're in London, honey," said Gillian. "It's lovely here. A bit cold…"

"Can I come and see you?"

Gillian paused. "You want to come here?"

"Yes," said Maggie, with a thick swallow.

"I…of course, honey. I'll get you a room." No questions, no accusations…no *judgement*. So perfectly accepting that Maggie could've cried.

She didn't cry, but she did book herself a last-minute flight and pack a few essentials. Mom and Simon would be in London for the next four weeks, and that sounded like absolute perfection to Maggie. Away from this apartment, the hospital, this town, this whole country… Away from Declan and Grant, and the splinters of her broken heart.

She found herself sitting beside a lovely gentleman on the flight over. He introduced himself as Billy and shook her hand, and bought her a white wine to go with his whisky. They chatted and passed the time together, and then shared a movie in the last hours before Maggie fell asleep. She awoke to a blanket on her and the lit-up sign telling her to fasten her seatbelt for landing, and Billy smiled at her and asked for her number, and she almost considered it, for half a moment, but then declined. It felt like cheating.

She wasn't even in a relationship anymore, but it still felt *wrong*.

Her mom surprised her by waiting for her in Arrivals—Maggie had been expecting an anonymous driver and a town car, but instead she had her mother's warm hug and then a concerned expression.

"What's happened?" Mom asked, brushing a hand over Maggie's cheek and frowning.

Maggie laughed mirthlessly. "Man trouble. What else?"

"Oh, Maggie," said Mom, because she got it. Out of everyone, she got it the most. They shared a look of fierce understanding.

But Maggie didn't want to talk about it now, not after a long flight, feeling groggy and a bit gross, in need of a good shower and a proper bed.

Her emotions were curiously absent. They had been that way since she'd booked the flight. It was as if the prospect of escaping the country had numbed what remained of her heart, and she struggled now to feel much of anything at all.

She supposed that was better.

Her mom took her to the hotel, a five-star monstrosity of luxury, and gave her a few hours to get herself together and rest awhile before dinner. She watched Maggie with concern all through dinner, although she was prevented from asking much by Simon, who seemed absolutely thrilled to have Maggie join them for this leg of their journey.

"You'll be coming with us to the museums tomorrow, I hope?" he asked, his squashy face going red with good wine. "I've got my eye on an exhibit in the—"

"Now, dear, I'm sure Maggie has her own plans."

Simon smiled and put his hand atop her mother's, and her mom smiled that soft smile and looked at him with such warmth in her eyes, and for a moment, a tiny moment, Maggie was jealous of her.

"I don't, actually," Maggie said, pushing her salad around the plate. She hadn't eaten much. "But I'll leave you two to the museums, if you don't mind. I'm thinking a stroll through one of the parks."

"That sounds lovely," Mom said, with the air of one wanting to wrap up the conversation. And minutes later, Maggie found herself bundled into an elevator with her mom, having been prodded away from the table under the guise of Mom thinking she needed more rest. ("She looks tired, doesn't she, Simon? Heavy under the eyes.")

"You're going to tell me everything," Mom said to her now, enclosed in this elevator, some unidentifiably bland music leaking from the speakers above. "Because you can't fool me, girl. I can see it in you." She paused, narrowing her eyes at her daughter. "You didn't fly all this way just to see me. This man trouble of yours is bigger than you're letting on."

"Yes," Maggie said, and suddenly she was choking on it—every compartmentalized emotion. All of it reared up, expanded through her chest, coiled around her ribcage, and squeezed her throat. She couldn't breathe. Her vision swam. "Oh, Mom…" she sobbed, and then her mom was hugging her, and she was crying, soaking tears into Mom's cashmere and making dreadful noises, and the elevator stopped, and a couple waited to get on, and Maggie would've blushed had she not been so overtaken by pain.

"Come on," Mom muttered to her, and Maggie allowed herself to be steered to her hotel room, to hold her mom's hand. To feel like a heartbroken child, just for a little while.

"You're going to be all right," her mom murmured

to her in a soothing tone, stroking her hair as they sat together an hour later on the huge couch and breathed. Maggie had told her everything—as much as she could, anyway. How she'd found a man, the most amazing man—handsome and kind and charming and, yes, *he's wealthy, Mom, you'd approve...* She'd found him, and she'd let him into her heart, because she'd thought him worthy, just for a little while.

For a short time there, she thought he'd protect her heart like it was the most precious thing in the world. But he hadn't. He'd betrayed her. She didn't say how, but she explained the scale of it, how it was *big*, too big to brush away—*but he didn't cheat, if that's what you're thinking; it wasn't anything like that*, she added, just in case, because she didn't want her mom to think of Declan as unfaithful. He wasn't like Dad.

And now here she was, heartbroken and alone.

Maggie wanted to believe her mom, that's she'd be okay, but right now, she didn't feel as if anything would be all right ever again.

CHAPTER EIGHT
Declan

Declan Archibald was a man of simple pleasures—give him a good whisky, a bloody steak, and some great company, and he was set.

He had all three of those things right now, and yet he felt hollow. He'd felt hollow since that day—*that day*. The day he lost everything that mattered.

"Come on, man," Grant said, putting his steak knife down with a sigh. "You can't mope around forever."

"I'm not moping."

He was definitely moping. Lovesick, they called it. *Pining*. He loved a woman who, it seemed, didn't love him back. Who'd run away from him. Who wanted to be so far away from him that she'd left the damn country.

She'd gone to London. He only knew that because Grant had gotten overly emotional when he left rehab and started rambling on about calling his mom in London, seeing if Maggie would agree to speak to him.

Declan had immediately considered trying to get in touch with her himself, but he didn't. Because he'd made a pact with himself. He would wait for her to come to him—not because he felt she should be the one to make an effort, but because he didn't want to invade her space anymore. Force his presence on her. If she wanted him in her life, she'd let him know, and the least he could do was allow her time to make that decision herself.

"She'll be back soon."

Declan shrugged morosely. "Doesn't mean she'll want anything to do with me."

Grant sighed again, raking a hand through his hair. "I'm sorry."

"It's not your fault."

He didn't blame Grant, not really. It had been Declan's choice not to tell Maggie what had been going on. And now he was paying for it, just like he deserved.

"Of course, it is," Grant said heavily. "If I'd never—if I'd been honest with her from the start… She left you because you were keeping *my* secret."

"No. She left me because I lied to her." Declan put his own cutlery down as a lost cause and reached for his glass. "Can't really blame her."

"So you're giving up?"

"What else can I do?"

"Oh, I don't know," Grant said, looking angry at Declan all of a sudden. "Fight for her?"

Declan huffed a mirthless laugh. "This isn't some mushy movie, Grant. This is real life. And the fact is, I betrayed her." He took a big gulp of his drink, feeling the burn down his throat. "We both did."

The words hurtled Grant straight back into his bubble of self-hatred, his face clouding over and his eyes drooping with depression. Declan was almost apologetic, if he wasn't so busy feeling sorry for himself.

"I still can't believe what I did," Grant muttered. "D'you think she'll ever forgive me?"

"Yes." There was no doubt in Declan's mind. Grant and Maggie had a sibling bond like he'd never seen before, and nothing would ever permanently come between them—not even this. It was a bump in the road, and Maggie might struggle to find that forgiveness, but they'd get there in the end. He wished with all his heart that he could say the same for himself. "Me, on the other hand…"

"She loves you," Grant said, not for the first time. He kept telling Declan in these sad moments, trying to give him some hope. Declan stopped believing it days ago—if he ever truly believed it at all. Seeing the flatness of Declan's face, Grant said bracingly, "Man, come on. She left the country."

Declan snorted bitterly. "No need to remind me."

"But don't you see what that means?" Grant asked, using his hands like an impassioned politician. "You and her, that was *big* to her. So big that she had to disappear halfway across the world to be away from it. She didn't just split up with you, man," he said pointedly, his eyes fierce with some kind of determination. "She had to leave behind everything connected to you."

The words twanged his heartstrings, made him think, just for a moment, that there was something worth holding on to in what Grant was saying.

Then the dark cloud of truth hit him again, and he slumped his shoulders. "I've hurt her too badly."

"Maybe," said Grant, nodding. "But I know she understands it. She knows why you did what you did, and that's all on me, not you. She's in London because it hurts her too much to be here. Near you."

He couldn't deny it—there was a lot of sense in Grant's words. Why *did* Maggie go all the way to London? Go to that effort of asking for time off work, booking flights, flying halfway across the world… No woman went to those extremes when a fling ended. She hadn't even skipped town when she separated from Ronald, let alone left the country…

Could he be arrogant enough to assume she did it because it was too painful to be near him? Because she…felt too much when she was around him?

Or maybe it was because, as she'd told him, she couldn't even look at him. But she didn't have to look at him. She could've gone to Ashley's. She could've gone to the Emersons' second home in Vermont. She could've simply switched off her phone and got on with her life.

She left the whole country. The whole *continent*.

He swallowed and looked up at Grant.

"She loves me?"

Grant's face split wide with a dazzling grin. "Yeah, she does," he said, and Declan felt himself buoying up at his enthusiasm.

It was *possible*. Grant could be talking out of his ass; Maggie could've left because she hated Declan. None of this could come to anything. But there was a *possibility*, a possibility that he and Maggie should be together, and here he was, feeling sorry for himself, moping, expecting *her* to make the first move?

What kind of man did he think he was?

You want your girl, his subconscious growled at him, like it had just woken up from the coma he'd put it in with his depression, *then you get out there and fight for her.*

Like he should've done from the beginning.

The one woman in all the world he loved more than anything, and he was half a planet away from her.

"You got the number?" he asked Grant, chucking his napkin onto his plate and scraping his chair back. "The hotel?"

Grant followed suit, the both of them moving

with purpose now, a *determination*. "Don't really think that's gonna cut it, y'know? A phone call."

"I was actually gonna call for a room," Declan said, flipping a wad of cash onto the table and flagging down a waiter for his coat. "Fly over."

Grant tutted. "Think bigger."

Declan stumbled to a stop and looked his best friend in the face, saw the stem of an idea written in his blazing eyes.

And yes, *of course*. Flying over to face her was never going to cut it. Not when he could put his whole goddamn heart on the line for her.

He looked at Grant hard, feeling his eyes widening. "You sure?"

"This means something to you, right?" said Grant. "You and her?"

"Means everything."

"Then go big or go home."

And Declan was just desperate enough to do something so crazy. It would either work, and he'd be the happiest man on the whole planet… Or it'd fail miserably, and she'd tear his heart out of his chest. No matter which way the chips fell, it'd be the perfect result, because one ending gave him the woman he loved, and the other ending gave him a punishment he severely deserved.

And both endings, no matter which one prevailed, allowed him to see her perfect face again, if only for a few minutes, and for the final time in his life.

There was no time to lose, though, and he was already sending a message to his assistant, telling her to cancel his upcoming appointments.

"Can you rally everyone?" he asked Grant as they left the restaurant. "Have them meet me at my place tomorrow?"

"You mean, Cami, Ashley…?"

"Yeah. And we need to go shopping," he said, stepping out to the street and hailing a cab. As the car drew close, and the wind blew against the bare skin at the nape of his neck, Declan felt a frisson of doubt. He swallowed and looked at Grant. "Do you think this is gonna work?"

Grant smiled, soft and warm, in a moment of compassionate understanding. He put a hand on Declan's shoulder. "You're meant to be together. If she doesn't want it, then at least you can say you gave it your all. And she deserves your all, Declan."

Truer words had never been spoken.

He opened the cab door and gestured for Grant to go first. "And more," he said, mind busy drawing up lists of everything he needed to do to make this happen, his stomach squirming with cautious anticipation.

CHAPTER NINE
Maggie

Maggie was in love.

She'd given up trying to deny it, to squash it, to kill it off.

She loved Declan Archibald. The man owned her whole heart. He was the first thing she thought of when she woke up, and the last image to drift through her mind before she fell asleep. She'd almost called him a half dozen times, then lost her nerve. Drafted four different emails, but had no real idea what to say to him.

She did want to be with him, but she was unsure of him.

He'd betrayed her, there was no getting away from that—yet the pain of it had started fading almost immediately. He didn't lie to her through malice. He wasn't trying to hurt her. He was doing the opposite—trying to *spare* her. He *didn't* want to hurt her, and he felt it was better that she hear the truth from her brother himself, and he'd been right. She never would've believed him, for a start, and when she finally did, she would've been completely floored by the fact that her brother was still trying to conceal his deception from her.

And his loyalty to Grant had put him in an even more impossible position. Either way, he had to betray someone, and while she'd taken the hit in the end, it hadn't been because he'd chosen Grant over her. In actual fact, he'd put her feelings above what her brother wanted.

She couldn't quite say she was over what had happened, but she no longer hated him for it. She understood him.

And yet, she was unsure of him, enough to prevent her from calling him. And it was because of one stupid, pathetic reason: he hadn't called her. He hadn't even tried to contact her, not since she'd ordered him out of her apartment.

She had a horrible, heavy, black feeling deep in her gut that he was no longer particularly interested in her. And she'd been humiliated enough—there was no way she was going to chase him.

But that wasn't to say it didn't hurt like a bitch, though.

She sighed as she came to a stop beside a flowerbed in the heart of Hyde Park, her fourth or fifth visit to this beautiful landmark in the four weeks she'd been here in London. The weather was playing along today, even offering a wash of sunlight through the clouds, but the breeze was cold enough to sink into her skin and create that odd sort of lonely feeling she often got in miserable weather.

She was lonely, here in England's capital. Even her mother had a man to love.

Her phone rang as she took a seat on a nearby bench, and she gazed with vague bitterness at a loved-up couple sitting beneath a tree while she ignored the trilling, not in the mood to speak to anyone. It was most likely just her mom anyway, asking what she was planning to do for dinner.

It stopped ringing, and the silence allowed the sounds of nature to creep back in—the wind rustling the trees, birds chirping, a dog somewhere in the distance, barking excitedly. This part of the park wasn't too busy, but there was enough activity to hold her attention, zone out as she watched people take their strolls, stop to admire the beauty.

Her phone rang again. With a sigh, she slipped it out of her pocket, already preparing to grump at her mom. Only it wasn't her mom's name on the screen—it was Cami's.

Frowning, she answered, and Cami's high-pitched voice came through, sounding very far away.

"Mags?"

"Cami?"

"Hey! How are you?"

"I'm…I'm good," she said truthfully. She wasn't full of despair anymore, at least. "Yeah. Doing much better."

"I'm so glad to hear that." Cami paused, then: "You ready to come home?"

Home. It sounded good. Her own bed, work, her friends…

Declan.

She swallowed. "I don't know, Cam. Things are still a bit…"

"Raw?"

"Yeah."

"Heartbreak's a bitch, isn't it?"

Maggie laughed, short and quiet. "You're telling me."

After a moment, Cami said cautiously, "You thought about contacting him?"

Oh, if she only knew.

"Pretty sure if he cared all that much, he would've called me by now."

"Maybe he thinks you need space."

"By now he's probably back out on the town, Mr. Most Eligible Bachelor once again." It was a thought she hadn't been able to get rid of, infecting her mind and splintering her heart. She couldn't bear the idea of it, him flirting with other women, charming them, taking them home…

She felt sick.

"Oh, Maggie," Cami said heavily.

"It's fine," Maggie said, and it was, for the most part. Except for the one thing that really mattered. "I'm fine."

"Look, it's a two-way street. Just because he hasn't called you, it doesn't mean you can't call *him*. Life's too short. If you find something you want, you've got to grab it with both hands."

Spoken like a true woman in love.

"Yeah." Maggie had given herself that very same lecture daily since she'd decided she was no longer angry with him, but her nerves had prevented her from following through. No matter what she tried, she couldn't shake the image of him coldly sending her through to voice mail—or worse, answering, and then brushing her off while she laid her heart out for him. "I don't know. I guess I just feel like that boat's passed."

Cami snorted a laugh as if Maggie's words had taken her by surprise. "You can't be serious."

"I don't know what I'm feeling, to be honest," Maggie admitted, and then said it out loud, the one thing she'd kept to herself all through this: "I love him."

It made her chest tight, and she closed her eyes, focusing on not letting the emotion bubble up and overtake her once more.

"I know you do," Cami said sympathetically. "You've had a lot of time to think."

"Yeah."

"And?"

"It doesn't matter."

There was no point going into it, telling Cami all about the twisted paths her mind had taken these past four of weeks. It wouldn't help anything, and repeating it all, putting it out there, would only remind Maggie of what she could no longer have.

Cami must have sensed her reluctance, because she drew in a breath and neatly changed the subject.

"Well listen, I know you're not planning on missing my birthday party this weekend."

Oh God, Cami's birthday had completely slipped Maggie's mind—although, to be fair, she didn't actually know there would be a party. But she'd been out of the country and therefore away from her social scene, so she couldn't really blame Cami for the short notice. She had a quick think about the logistics of it—flying home, jet lag, buying a gift…

"I totally forgot," she said. "I'm so sorry." If she got a flight tonight, she'd arrive tomorrow morning and have the day to catch up on some sleep.

"Psshh. Don't apologize. Just get your butt back here!"

It sounded good, Maggie had to admit. Seeing her friends again, laughing, maybe having a drink or two and letting go a little. Her mother was great company, but more of the TV-and-tea type, and what Maggie needed right now was a really long appointment with her girlfriends and a bottle or three of wine.

But a party, though. It wouldn't just be the girls. It was likely she'd see one or two other people in particular…

Her throat tightening, she asked, "Have you spoken to Grant?"

Cami's voice softened as she responded. "He's doing really well. The rehab program worked wonders and he seems back on track. Working, helping out at the hospital… You'd be proud of him."

Maggie smiled, her eyes watering up. *God*, she missed her brother. Above everything, she felt the separation from Grant like one of her own limbs had been severed.

"I already am," she said quietly, and allowed silence to fall between her and Cami for a moment.

"You've gotta face this sometime," Cami said after a while, speaking gently, her voice sounding like a warm hug Maggie desperately wanted to bury herself in.

She sniffed and hitched a smile onto her face. "Birthday party, you said?"

"Yep. Drew's gone all out. It's gonna be amazing."

"Then of course, I wouldn't miss it."

CHAPTER TEN
Maggie

Her mom had been sorry to see her go. "I've really enjoyed having you with us," she said soppily in the hotel lobby, pushing Maggie's hair out of her eyes and smiling in a sort of wet fashion at her.

"I need to get back to my life," Maggie said. She pulled her mom into a squeeze. "But thank you. This has been such a help."

She promised to call as soon as she landed, and then accepted Simon's kiss on the cheek before heading out to the town car her mom insisted she take to the airport.

The flight was long, and Maggie was too full of nervous adrenaline to sleep much. She couldn't stop thinking about seeing everyone—Ash, Cami… Grant…

Declan…

Even the thought of seeing Dr. Stevens again

made her a bit anxious. They hadn't communicated since she'd asked for a leave of absence to go to London. Their heart-to-heart conversation in the meeting room that day hadn't been referenced since, and she wondered if he was as embarrassed as she was at the open display of honesty they'd given each other.

By the time her flight landed, she'd had maybe an hour's sleep in total, and she'd worked herself up into such a frenzy of nerves that she'd pretty much cancelled it out, and she now felt like a zombie walking through baggage claim.

There was a suited man waiting for her in arrivals, holding up a plastic card with her name on. "Ms. Emerson?"

Maggie blinked at him, over-tiredness making everything seem surreal. "Yes."

"Follow me, please."

"What's going on?"

"Your friend sent a car to collect you."

"Oh…"

The car, of course, was a limo, because why would Cami ever do anything by half measures? The windows were blacked out, muting the midday sun outside, and ten minutes into the drive, Maggie's eyes started forcing themselves shut, and she let herself drift off, mind pleasantly numb for once…

When she woke up, she knew, instinctively, that a lot of time had passed—way more than the distance from the airport to her apartment.

She sat up blinking, feeling the car rumble to a stop, and was about to ask the driver what the hell was going on, vaguely concerned she was stepping into a horror film, when her door swung open.

Declan.

He was like an angel, standing there, with the sunlight beaming down on him, looking at her with dazzling eyes, his face cut in perfect lines and his hand outstretched, offering.

Maggie forgot how to breathe.

In a daze, she took his hand, letting him help her out of the car—which chose that moment to drive off quietly, leaving her alone here. With Declan.

"You look beautiful," he murmured, a slight tremor to his voice.

"I look like I've just slept in the back of a car for five hours after a transatlantic flight," she retorted, smoothing down her hair nervously, heart hammering, throat swelling, blood rushing and God, *God*, Declan was here.

His smile, when he managed it, was wobbly. "You're always beautiful to me."

She couldn't—she couldn't look right at him. Couldn't cope. Needed a moment to compose herself and—

Oh my God.

She was at the cabin. His family cabin in the woods that he'd brought her to for the most romantic two days of her life.

She swallowed, but it was no use. The tears were coming.

"What's going on?" she asked thickly, and then watched with her heart lodged in her throat as he released her hand, brushed a hand over his face, and then got down on one knee.

"Oh my God," she said, near hysterical. "Oh my God, Declan. What are you doing?"

She still couldn't remember how to breathe. What the hell was this? Was she—was this a dream? This couldn't be happening. There was no way she was looking at Declan Archibald, in front of this romantic cabin, on his knee for her.

She needed a drink.

She needed him to speak.

"Maggie," he said brokenly, then he swallowed and cleared his throat, and she could feel his nerves like a brand. "I've hurt you," he continued, stronger this time. "I betrayed you. I don't deserve one ounce of your trust or affection ever again. But I'm asking for it anyway. Because I love you." He took her hands, holding them warmly in his. "I'm always going to love you. There will never be anyone else for me. You're everything."

She was crying already. She knew she was. Her eyes wet and tingling, her throat a swollen mess of emotion. "Declan…"

"I'll spend my whole life loving you how you deserve to be loved, cherishing you, treating you like the most important thing in the world. Because you are," he said. "To me, you are. And I'm so sorry." He brought the back of one hand to his mouth, pressed his lips there, eyes closing for a moment before looking up at her again. "Maggie, I'm sorry. I am. It was never my intention to hurt you, and I've hated myself every day since—"

"No." She didn't want that. God, she *never* wanted that. She didn't hate him—far from it; the complete opposite, in fact—so the last thing she wanted was for him to hate himself.

It broke her heart to think about it.

"I'm on my knees now," he said, "hoping for your forgiveness. For your love." He paused, swallowed again, and there was something like an electric spark in this moment, an anticipation… He released one of her hands and reached into his pocket, and from it he pulled out a small, blue box. "For your hand."

Her head was spinning, her free hand flying to cover her mouth as everything within her crashed together in pure elation. Pure *love*. "Oh my God…"

He took a breath and looked her steadily in the eye. "Maggie Emerson, will you do me the honor of giving me another chance? And of being my wife?" And then he opened the box to reveal the most perfect, shimmering, yet understated diamond ring.

This was a dream come true. This was everything she'd been fantasizing about in her wildest, loneliest moments in London. She couldn't believe she was actually standing here, with Declan Archibald proposing to her. That he loved her enough to give her his whole life.

Her heart had expanded so much, she didn't know how it still fit in her chest.

She drew in some air to compose herself enough to speak.

"You betrayed me," she said shakily, watching his face splinter a little. "I didn't know if I'd ever be able to get past it. But these four weeks have been so hard." She fell to her own knees, level with him, his eyes widening. Took his face in her hands and sobbed through a smile. "Being without you is torture. I love you. And I want to trust that you'd never lie to me again—"

"I won't," he said, pressing his hand against one of hers on his face. "God, I won't. I swear on my life, I'll never hurt you again."

She sniffed, laughed, giddy with joy. "I want you in my life forever. I can't deny it. I don't *want* to deny it. You're the man for me, Declan Archibald. You always will be." She leaned forward, rested her forehead against his, looked at his watering eyes and then shut her own, smiling so deeply she could feel it in her very soul. "Yes, I'll marry you."

She found herself swept up on her feet, in his arms, his face buried in her neck and then his searing kiss on her lips.

"I love you," he said into the kiss. "God, I love you."

When he finally let her breathe, she couldn't help but laugh as he slid the ring onto her finger. Perfect fit. "Aunt Connie's gonna be *thrilled* when she hears about this wedding." This was better than her own daughter's. Maggie, marrying an Archibald? She'd take out a full-page ad in the society pages.

"She'll be furious she missed it," Declan said, an odd note in his voice.

Maggie blinked at him. "What?"

Declan winced, giving her an expression that quite clearly said *don't get mad*. "I've been thinking of wedding dates…" he said cautiously. "Hoping, you know." Then he gulped and squeezed her hand, his thumb fiddling with the engagement ring. "How do you feel about…now?"

Maggie's whole mind went completely blank. "Now?"

And suddenly, making her jump near out of her skin, the front door of the cabin burst open and Cami and Ashley rushed out, running towards her with twin grins splitting their faces.

"Oh my God, Maggie!"

"We've got your dress, makeup, everything—"

"I'm sorry I lied about the birthday party thing, we just didn't know how else to get you here—"

"Everything's set up, exactly how you'd like it—"

"It's *so* beautiful, oh my God—"

"Whoa, whoa…" Maggie raised her hands, preventing the girls from throwing themselves at her,

her stomach doing a very slow somersault at what she *thought* was happening right now... But no, he couldn't be serious. Could he? "What's going on?"

The girls' grins slipped into grimaces of anxiety, and Declan took her hands again, pulled her around to look at him. "I want to marry you today," he said fiercely, his eyes bright and shining for her. "I don't want to wait."

"I—" Maggie couldn't think, couldn't *comprehend*... Was she absolutely sure this wasn't all a dream?

"How?" she asked, at a total loss for what else to say.

"Here," he said. "Around the back." Then he licked his lips in a nervous gesture and tried a smile on for size. "We've been making arrangements for days."

"You planned a whole wedding, brought me here... What would you've done if I said no?"

"Cried," piped up Ashley. "Big ugly man-tears."

He paid her no mind, kept his attention firmly on Maggie. "What d'you say?" he asked her quietly.

There wasn't one single part of her that wanted to say no.

A rush of pure, bright, overwhelming excitement flooded every corner of her body, and she couldn't help but stutter out a giddy laugh.

"Yes," she said, and Declan's face lit up like Christmas. "Oh my God, yes! I can't believe this."

She didn't get a chance to bask in the glow of her

shared happiness with Declan, because the girls lassoed her with their arms and started dragging her away, chatting excitedly.

"Come and take a look at everything—

"Honestly, Mags, it's so perfect—"

"She'll meet you down the aisle in a couple hours, Decl—"

She was suddenly yanked back, out of the girls' arms, and right into Declan's chest. "Not so fast," he murmured, then brought her into a deep, searching kiss that made her feel like she was floating.

"Now, now," she whispered to him a moment later, her skin tingling where he'd slipped his fingers beneath her shirt, "I only kiss my husband like that."

His eyes twinkled. "He's a lucky man."

"Ugh, come on," Ashley said, bulldozing in and sweeping Maggie away. "She'll be all yours in a while, Declan, and oh, by the way, we're commandeering the second bedroom. We've got everything set up in there," she added as an aside to Maggie. "Brought all your makeup and everything up from the city."

But Maggie wasn't listening. She was too busy gazing over her shoulder at Declan, feeling entirely lovestruck by the look of total adoration in his eyes as he watched her go.

She was so high up on cloud nine billion, that the bump of crashing back down to earth at what awaited her inside the cabin was enough to punch the breath out of her.

Grant was standing in the middle of the living room, his hands in the pockets of his suit, his face shadowed and unsure as he looked at her.

"Hey, sis," he said cautiously, and it was like Ashley and Cami disappeared, and nothing else existed except her brother, now, looking at her like he expected nothing but savagery in her greeting.

He looked better. *So* much better. Like the brother she knew, the one she loved—the one who would never try to hurt her.

The Grant Emerson who existed before the pills took him over and controlled his life.

"Hello," she said, or at least tried to—the word caught in her throat, hitched on a sob, because she'd missed him so much it hurt to even think about it. She'd worried about him, kept herself awake long into the nights, so scared he wouldn't be able to get better, that he was in pain, that he needed her and she'd abandoned him.

He recognized the break in her voice and his face crumpled, and she rushed to him, hurried across the room, him striding forward to meet her in the middle and they crashed together in an all-encompassing hug that had her crying into his shoulder.

"Maggie, I'm so sorry—"

"No," she muttered, holding him tightly. "No. We're not doing that." She sniffed and pulled back, her hands on his shoulders, looked into his healthy face. "You're okay?"

"I am," he said thickly, bringing a hand up to rub one eye. "I really think I am."

"Then that's all that matters."

She was ready to put it all behind her now. To move on. It happened, and it had pained her so deeply, but no one had acted out of any kind of intention to hurt her. One had been governed by a vicious addiction, and the other had been stuck between two impossible solutions. They both loved her, and she—them, more than she could ever put into words. And nothing else held any significance.

They would put it to bed now, and today she would marry the man she loved, with her beloved brother by her side. And she would be the happiest woman in the whole world.

CHAPTER ELEVEN
Maggie

It had, of course, been perfect. The girls had been left to decide everything on Maggie's behalf—the dress, the hair, the makeup, the jewelry. Even her lingerie had been chosen by Cami.

They'd locked themselves away in the second bedroom—although Maggie wasn't entirely sure why they couldn't use the main bedroom, suspecting perhaps that the groomsmen had commandeered it. The second bedroom was beautiful, though, with old wood and lace, a pale blue décor and an antique dresser that made Maggie feel like a princess as she sat before it.

The dress was exactly as she'd imagined her wedding dress would be—Vera Wang, elegant, long lines, and not a pouf in sight. Both girls gasped as she stepped out into the room wearing it, a mid-length veil atop her teased hair, a teardrop necklace complementing the diamond flashing on her finger. Ashley even cried a little.

With another hour to kill, they sipped champagne and Maggie got them to fill her in on the past few days, how Declan had pulled all of this together, got them all rallied around. Until they were interrupted by a knock on the door, and Maggie's jaw hit the floor as her mother swept in.

"Surprise!" she trilled gaily, whipping Maggie and the girls into a whirlwind of hugs and kisses.

"Mom—what—"

"I was on the same flight as you," her mom said, laughing, grabbing a random champagne glass from the dresser. "Made sure you didn't see us. We were in coach!" She seemed weirdly proud of this fact—and it explained why her mom had been so adamant Maggie fly first class back to the States.

"God, Mom, I don't know what to say." She was tearing up again, and the girls started flapping around her, panicking about her eye makeup.

The ceremony itself…Maggie had no words. Cami had listened, that day in the staff room at work, and Maggie and Declan said their vows at twilight in the woodland clearing, with flickering pillar candles around them, a small collection of their closest friends and family surrounding their bubble of happiness. Declan stumbled over his words, emotion getting the better of him, and it made Maggie cry again and then her mom was crying, and the ceremony had to take a pause while everyone had a little chuckle at the romanticism of it all.

"Wait, wait," Declan said hours later, mid-laugh, in that funny, hushed sort of drunken voice everyone did when trying to be inconspicuous. "I need to carry you through."

They'd somehow made it to the end of the evening and everyone had left in various stages of drunkenness—Ashley with Declan's friend Preston, and wasn't *that* going to be a story Maggie wanted to hear about in the morning. Now it was just the two of them, here at some time around three A.M., with the soft glow of the house around them and a wedding band each on their ring fingers. Maggie could've died of happiness.

Instead, she snorted.

"Okay, you are too drunk and I'm too heavy for that to be a possibility."

Declan made a noise that sounded something like "Pffsshaw" and made Maggie hiccup another laugh, and then he bent to hook an arm beneath her legs. "C'mon."

"Whoa, hold on, *no*."

"It's fine, we've got this."

She stared at him. "You're gonna regret it."

"See this?" he said, flexing his arms and showing off his guns. "You married all man, baby."

"Oh my God."

He flashed her a grin. "I'm kidding. You weigh nothing. I've had you on top of me *many* times and the only thing I felt—"

"All right, shut up." She blushed a little. "Go ahead then," she said sort of mock grumpily, throwing her arms wide in invitation.

He wiggled his eyebrows, stooped low, and swept her up in his arms so smoothly and with such ease, wearing a wicked smirk and sparkling eyes, that Maggie probably would've swooned, if she hadn't been too busy getting aroused.

"Wow," she murmured.

He winked. "Oh yeah."

She wrapped her arms around his neck. "Take me to bed," she said in her most sultry voice.

"Uh, you need to get the door first."

"Oh. Right."

She unhooked her arms from around his neck, mildly embarrassed, and reached down to open the door. And then gasped when he carried her over the threshold.

It wasn't her first time in this room, having spent those couple of days with him here before, but back then it didn't look like this. Candles, silk, petals… "This is amazing."

"I'm gonna be honest," Declan said, blinking around the room and still showing absolutely no strain at holding her up for this long, "I had no idea it'd be like this."

"Cami and Ashley?"

"Probably."

"Well, I love it," Maggie said. "Although those

petals look like they might be a bit inconvenient…"

Declan stared over at the bed. "Yeah, let's get those off," he agreed, before plonking her down on her feet and helping her sweep the petals off the bedspread.

Not the most romantic start to their wedding night, Maggie had to admit, although just being here with Declan… She looked up at him from across the bed and found him gazing at her, his eyes full of warmth.

She felt shy all of a sudden.

"What?"

"Nothing," he said, smiling softly. "Just….you're my wife."

Her stomach did a pleasant squirm. "Yeah, I am."

"How'd I get so lucky?" he asked with a fluttering breath.

She narrowed her eyes at him playfully, even as butterflies spread through her torso and her heart kicked up a gear. "You drunk?"

"Oh, very," he said, making her laugh. Then his face straightened, and he said with breathtakingly open sincerity, "But I'm also completely in love with you." He put one knee on the bed. "Mrs. Archibald," he added, crooking a finger at her as he crawled to the center.

She feigned coyness. "You are?"

"Mmm-hmm." He reached out and grabbed the front of her dress, yanking her close so she had to lean forward over the bed and brace her hands on it for balance. "And you're going to let me show you," he murmured, pressing a kiss to the corner of her mouth. Then to the other corner—"Show you hard..."—and to the edge of her jaw—"Show you deep..."—over the flutter of her pulse—"Until you're begging me..."

She drew in a shaky breath, tangled her fingers in his hair. "I don't beg."

In one sudden, smooth move, he looped an arm around her waist, pulled her onto the bed, flat on her back, and lowered himself on top of her. "You'll beg," he promised, and then kissed her breath away.

She lost herself in it for minutes, in the slick sweep of his tongue in her mouth, the rumbling groans in his chest as she intensified the kiss and pulled him closer, bent her legs to let him fall between her thighs.

Then he slipped one hand up beneath her and unzipped the party dress she'd changed into after the wedding, pulled it apart and kissed the skin as he revealed it.

"I can't believe," he said, dropping the dress on the floor and then pausing to look at her, "that I get to have this for the rest of my life."

She tried to press her thighs together, put some pressure on her aching pussy, heat seeping through her groin at his open inspection of her. "How about you concentrate on having it now," she said, with an attempt at keeping her voice level.

He smirked. "That sounded a little like begging to me."

"Shut up," she said, reaching for his tie. "And come here."

"Hmm." He resisted her pull, remained kneeling. "Maybe I'll wait."

"You know, it's not too late to annul this marriage."

He laughed. "All right, point taken." He fell forward, kissed her smiling mouth, then murmured, "How do you want me?"

She expected to blush; she expected to feel shy. But her need for this man was too strong, and instead she swallowed and said, "Down."

His mouth twisted in a smirk of pleasure in the moment before he slithered down her body.

She gasped in anticipation, spread her legs wide, twisted her fingers in the bedsheets and curved her back off the mattress as he pulled her wet panties aside and tongued her throbbing clit.

"Oh God, Declan," she said breathlessly, and he hummed against her, causing a shock of pleasure to shoot through her groin.

He took her to the very edge, in those minutes; worked her clit until she was a trembling mess, moments from begging, sobbing out her moans and yanking on the bedsheets and clamping her thighs around his head. He didn't use his fingers, but he didn't need to—his attention on her swollen clit was enough, got her strung up high enough that she could scream with it, staring down at him working her over, and there was something deliciously filthy about it, of him fully dressed, holding her panties aside, face buried in her sopping-wet pussy…

She cried out as a wave of near-bliss rolled through her, as her sex spasmed, as she came inches from orgasm…and then he stopped, and she whimpered, reaching for him, trying to press his face back against her.

"Patience," he groaned in a voice thick with arousal, and all of a sudden, he flipped her onto her belly, took the skin of her shoulder between his teeth for an instant before pulling on her hips, bringing her up onto her knees. "Stay like that," he instructed darkly, then the sound of material ripping filled the room, the remnants of her panties hitting the floor beside the bed…her bra unhooking, falling away…two fingers, suddenly and without warning, burying deep inside her pussy…

"Good girl," he said, thrusting those fingers in and out of her at a steady, deep pace. "My beautiful wife." She moaned, pushed her face down in the bedspread, took his assault on her sex as she listened to the sounds of his clothes rustling…

Then she felt the unmistakable press of his cock against her, and she whimpered, spread her legs wider, her anticipation of it lighting her up on the inside.

But he didn't push into her, not yet. He removed his fingers and rubbed the head of his cock through her folds, up and down, over her clit, until she'd soaked him with her juices and her hips were shaking, and she was so desperate to be filled that she sobbed and said, "Please, Declan…" and wasn't even irritated that he'd made her beg in the end, she'd beg for hours if she had to—

"Shh," he said, reaching forward to gather her hair and drape it over one shoulder. He leaned down, kissed the side of her exposed neck, fondled her breasts as he teased her pussy with his bare cock. His skin was burning heat, his movements a little stilted, obvious signs that he was as affected as she was…barely holding onto his control…

"I need to go get something," he whispered to her, lips against her throat. "I'll be right back."

"No." She grabbed his wrist, held him close against her, heart hammering as her mind spun. "No." It was a knee-jerk decision, but one she wanted so badly. "Don't…"

He hesitated. "You don't want me to use—"

"No," she said again, like a mantra. "Declan, please." She squeezed her eyes shut, pushed her hips back against him, made him bite off a groan.

"You know what this might mean," he said, his voice strained and raw, and she nodded.

She knew it, and there wasn't one single part of her that wanted to prevent it. If they created something out of this night, if they ever created something so special together, she'd be the happiest woman alive.

"Please," she whispered again, and he drew in a deep, shuddery breath.

"God, I love you," he said fiercely, then pulled her face to the side so he could press a bruising kiss to her mouth.

Then he released her lips, lined himself up, and entered her.

The bareness of it, the rawness, took her breath away, and she found herself hurtling towards the edge with barely any movement from him. She'd never felt so close to someone, so connected, so deeply ingrained in the existence of another person, and she couldn't control her emotions, her feelings, her *pleasure*...

He rocked into her with stuttering thrusts and held her tight, his own moans choking out of him, and she had to hold the headboard, hold onto *something*, pleasure spiraling higher and higher within her and making her sob with it, real tears falling from her eyes at the perfection of this moment, joined so intensely with the man she loved—

Orgasm hit her like a freight train, and she screamed, clenched the headboard, heard him somewhere in the vague edges of her consciousness as he joined her in this moment of ecstasy, his hips jolting as pleasure overtook him, as she floated on a crest of bliss, tumbled over it and collapsed, shuddering, breathless.

He took her hand, shaking, linking their fingers

together, and their wedding rings connected. A symbol of their unity, of their lives shared forever.

Maggie didn't even know it was possible to be so happy, and her heart swelled with emotional joy as Declan pulled her close into the curve of his body, still buried inside her, still connected so deeply, and murmured, "I love you, Mrs. Archibald."

The End

*Have you read **The Stubborn Suitor**, another hot romance by Alexa Wilder? This is a story about Cami and Drew, so if you haven't had a chance to grab it, here is your sneak peek:*

SNEAK PEEK: THE STUBBORN SUITOR
Chapter One: Cami

"Hey, Cami," Ashley said, leaning over the counter of the nurses' station. "It's slow right now. Why don't you go ahead and take your lunch break?"

Cami glanced at her watch and was surprised to find that it was already after noon. She was over halfway through her ten-hour shift and well past due for a break. The Emergency Room of Sacred Heart Hospital, where Cami Hendricks worked as a nurse, had been unusually busy for a Tuesday morning, and the time had gotten away from her.

"Sure," Cami said with a smile, knowing that Ashley wouldn't be able to take her own break until after Cami had returned from hers. "I won't need the full half-hour. I'm just going to grab a snack and a protein bar."

"No need to rush!" Ashley called from behind her as Cami made her way towards the staff locker rooms. "And you'll need more than a protein bar to make it 'til five. Take your time."

Cami nodded absentmindedly before turning the corner. In the locker room, she grabbed her purse and immediately checked her phone. As a single mother of a three-year-old, Cami was always worried about her daughter. If it wasn't against hospital policy, she'd keep her cell with her at all times in case of an emergency.

But for now, her mother knew the direct number for the ER nurses' station, where Cami spent most of her time. If something went wrong at home, or there was any issue with her daughter Madison, Cami had no doubt that her mother would be able to easily contact her. Still, like any mother, she worried.

She smiled as she looked at the picture on her phone's lock screen, a beautiful photo of Madison greeting her. The girl's strawberry blonde hair was quite a bit lighter than Cami's own fiery red, but the vibrant green eyes of her daughter matched her own, as did the mischievous smile of the three-year-old staring back at her. Every time Cami picked up her phone and looked at the picture, her heart lurched a little, swelling with pride and love. Before Madison, Cami hadn't known that it was possible to love someone this much.

After smiling down at the picture for a moment,

Cami swiped to unlock her phone. She couldn't help but groan a little in frustration. Instead of any calls or texts from her mother—who often sent her picture messages of Madison throughout the day, even if Cami could only see them on her breaks—there were two missed calls and a text from her ex-husband, Ken.

Call me! was all the text read. Cami rolled her eyes, really not wanting to deal with whatever the irresponsible bastard had to say during her short break. It was Ken's turn to take Madison this Friday, and he was probably trying to get out of it. He only had her every other weekend, but he still ended up canceling half the time. As much as she didn't want to talk to him now, Cami knew that if she waited until after her shift, she'd definitely be too tired to deal with his crap.

Instead of calling him back immediately, Cami made her way towards the cafeteria. Once she was armed with strong coffee and a protein bar, she found a secluded area outside to make the call. Steeling herself, and aided by a much-needed caffeine and sugar boost, she dialed the number of her ex.

"Hey, Cam," Ken said instead of hello.

His voice was a little too chipper, and Cami immediately knew something was up. She also hated the intimate way he still referred to her, despite the hostile divorce. It was like the last two years had never happened.

"What's so important, Ken?" Cami asked, not

bothering to keep the exasperation out of her voice. "You need to make this quick. I'm on my break."

"Do you have a moment to talk? If not, I can call back later. There are a few things I need to talk to you about."

"I won't have time after my shift," Cami replied flatly. "I'll be tired and I'll have Madison. Just tell me whatever it is that you need to talk to me about so badly."

"Okay, yeah," Ken replied, but then said nothing else.

"Just spit it out, Ken," Cami demanded, growing even more frustrated. Her break was dwindling, and she didn't have time to waste on yet another bout of her ex's shit.

"I just wanted to let you know—before you saw it on Facebook or something—that I asked Natalie to marry me last weekend. And she said yes."

"Oh," was all Cami could think of to say.

Ken had begun dating Natalie almost immediately after their split. In fact, Cami had a sneaking suspicion that he'd begun seeing the blonde even before Cami had finally left him.

Natalie was everything Cami was not. She was tall and thin, where Cami was short and voluptuous. While Cami had always been proud of her curves, Ken had often made comments about her needing to lose weight—especially after the birth of Madison. That was only one of many reasons why she'd eventually decided to divorce him. There had also been the drinking, the partying, and—if her suspicions were true—the cheating.

Still, Cami couldn't help the small pang of jealousy creeping up her spine. It's not like she wanted Ken back or anything. She was definitely happy to be rid of him. But he had so easily found someone new to warm his bed, while Cami hadn't even been on a date in over a year. She loved Madison, and being a mother was her number-one priority. Yet she still yearned for someone to share her life with.

"So yeah," Ken began after an awkward moment of silence. "I just thought you should know, since she'll be a part of the family officially now. She'll be Madison's stepmom."

That statement made Cami cringe. She didn't want to imagine that woman having anything to do with Madison, much less being considered a parental figure.

"Well," Cami replied curtly. "Congratulations. I wish you every happiness. Now, if you don't mind, I need to get back to my break."

"Actually," Ken replied. "There's something else I want to talk to you about."

"What?" Cami couldn't keep the added level of annoyance out of her voice, but she really didn't care.

"Natalie has put in a notice at her job," Ken replied. "She wants to be a housewife."

She just wants to live off your money, Cami

thought, but she didn't say this aloud. If he wanted to marry a gold-digger, so be it. He was smart enough to make sure she wouldn't get anything in the divorce—same as he had done to Cami. Four years of marriage, and Cami had walked away with a menial monthly child support payment and no spousal support. That's what happens when your husband comes from a family full of lawyers and has unlimited funds, all while you can barely afford the cheapest lawyer in the phone book.

"Good for her," is all Cami said in reply.

"So we were thinking," Ken continued, "since you work so much, and Natalie is going to be a homemaker, Madison could spend more time with us. In fact, I was thinking that it would make more sense if we took over primary custody."

It took a moment for his words to sink in. Ken had never really seemed to be all that interested in more custody than he already had. In fact, it was often difficult to get him to keep Madison on the weekends he was already scheduled to have her. And now, he was expecting to take over primary custody.

Cami couldn't help but laugh: it had to be a joke.

"It's not funny," Ken replied. "I'm serious."

"Ken, there is no way you could handle any more custody than you already have. And there is absolutely no way I am giving up primary custody of Madison."

"You don't get to decide that on your own," Ken replied. His friendly tone was gone, and he was beginning to sound angry.

"No, Ken, the lawyers decided that during the divorce. And you agreed upon it."

"Yeah, well that was then. This is now. Natalie will be a stay-at-home mom. That's what Madison needs. It's more than you can provide for her."

"You have no idea what Madison needs!" Cami was nearly shouting now and she saw a few heads turn towards her in the courtyard. She swallowed and continued in a calmer, quieter tone. "Ken, where is this even coming from? I can't even get you to keep your scheduled time with Madison. Why are you asking for more now?"

"Things are different now. Natalie and I are getting married. We're going to be a family."

"That's awesome," Cami replied sarcastically. "Start your own family."

"We can't," he said quietly. "Natalie can't have kids."

Cami knew that she probably should have felt bad at hearing such a revelation, but instead she was incensed.

"So what?" she asked, voice rising again. "You think you can just take *my* daughter away from me to play house with? That's not going to happen."

"Yes, it will," Ken voice was forceful and confident. It made Cami cringe. "I was hoping we could work this out like adults, but obviously you're being too immature."

"*I'm* being immature?" Cami gasped. "You're the

one that thinks he can just decide to take my daughter away from me."

"Think about this rationally," Ken said. "Natalie and I can give her things you can't. You work ten-hour shifts at the hospital. You barely ever see her as it is."

"That's not true," Cami snapped. "I only work those long shifts so I have three days off a week to spend with Madison. You have no idea what you're talking about. You don't have the slightest clue what Madison needs."

"I know she needs security. I can provide that for her. Natalie and I can. We can provide for her."

"I'm providing for her just fine, no thanks to you!"

"Like I said, Cam, I was hoping to do this like civilized adults, but it is obvious that it's not going to happen, so I'll have my lawyer contact your lawyer. We'll have a sit-down sometime next week. If it has to go before a judge, so be it. I *will* be getting custody of my daughter."

Cami felt nauseated. Angry tears were sliding down her face, and she extended her hand to hold the phone away from her, so that Ken wouldn't be able to hear her distress. She knew that if Ken insisted on taking this to court, he would most likely win. He had money. He had fancy lawyers. Cami didn't even have a lawyer of her own. She could look up the lawyer she'd used during the divorce, but that idiot hadn't been much help then and she couldn't risk losing now.

Absentmindedly, Cami realized that Ken was still talking. She gently pushed the phone back against her ear.

"...that would be easiest. Just give me the name of your lawyer. I can have Gil get in touch with him directly, since you obviously can't handle this yourself." Cami cringed, both at the thought as well as the mention of Gil Dubois, Ken's lawyer and an old friend of the family. He had been the one to make sure that Cami walked away from the divorce with absolutely nothing.

"I don't have that information on me," Cami replied, making sure her voice sounded even and calm, though she felt anything but. "I'll have to get back to you with that."

"That's fine. I'll get it from you when I pick up Madison this weekend."

With that, Ken hung up. Cami appreciated that he hadn't tried to say goodbye or feign any sort of niceties. He'd made his intentions clear. He wasn't going to give up without a fight.

Cami stared down at her phone until the lock screen reappeared, along with the green-eyed, freckled face of Madison. No matter what, she couldn't lose her daughter. She didn't know how yet, but she would find a way to fight.

Also by Alexa Wilder

Don't Miss Out on New Releases, Free Stories and More!!

Join Alexa's Readers Group!

AlexaWilder.com/readers-group/

Visit Alexa on Facebook:

Facebook.com/AuthorAlexaWilder

The Wedding Rescue

The Courtship Maneuver

The Stubborn Suitor

The Reckless Secret

The Temptation Trap

The Surprising Catch

Made in the USA
San Bernardino, CA
18 August 2016